BLADES & BALLET

Enemy of the Wind

By Nathan Reese Maher

BLADES & BALLET
Enemy of the Wind

1st Edition, December 2023

Written by: Nathan Reese Maher
Cover Art by: Emrys Dailey
Photographer: Harley Maher
Map Illustration: Nathan Reese Maher

Printed in the United States.

ISBN – 978-0-9903201-6-6

Dedication

To Harley for his unwavering love and support; to Keagan for sharing my enthusiasm for ballet; and to them both for giving me the family I never felt I deserved. I am so lucky to have you.

To dancers everywhere:

I see your dedication, your devotion, your passion and your tears. No matter where you are right now, in this world, you are valid and your talents are an inspiration to us all. I see you. I applaud you. I am proud of you.

The Unknown
Serishone
Cornelis
Ithuway
Adalace
Anesian Coast
Tandermundt
Arcadia
Niece
Mycelian
Peninsula
The Moon-World of
ORABELLE

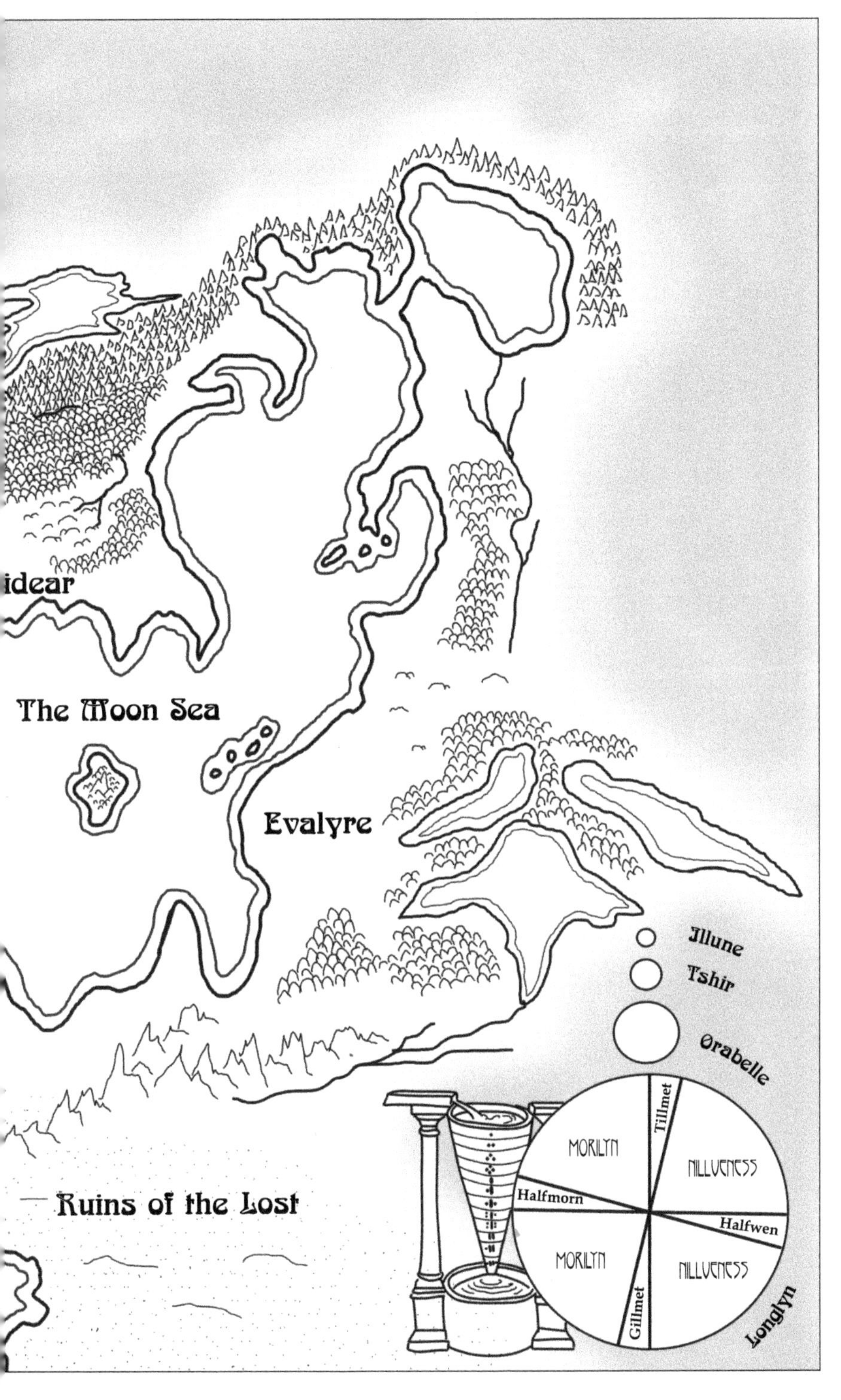
idear
The Moon Sea
Evalyre
Jllune
Tshir
Orabelle
Ruins of the Lost
Tillmet
MORILYN
NILLVENESS
Halfmorn
Halfwen
MORILYN
NILLVENESS
Gillmet
Longlyn

Prologue

"The Caetins are a western tribe, originating from the Emerald Hills and snuggled close against the Ilyfren Mountains, in the southern tip of the Arcadian Peninsula. They can be identified throughout all of Orabelle by their curved three-to-four inch horns protruding from their foreheads. Warmhearted, hospitable and overwhelmingly polite, these humble people treat everyone as if part of their own family; a true boon in their influence of the Rushinay for building closer family ties among all our people. One will find no better friends."

– *Wanderings*, Viliph Drosselmeyer

The villagers danced to the call of the drums, the enchantment of the lutes and the flirtations of the flutes. The fires of the lanterns and well-tended pyres threw tiny embers into the air, which swirled about like butterflies. It was the dawning of gilmet, two days of twilight that marked the end of the fourteen Longlyn days of night which nillveness brought, a celebration that the Caetin eagerly enjoyed in anticipation of the warmer sunlit days ahead.

Ayren was dressed in his tribe's ceremonial garb, made from swylnn and peppenach feathers coloring him with a variety of blues, greens and reds. He, along with all the other sixteen-year-old children, had practiced their dance for months for the upcoming festival. It was their time to announce their adulthood to the rest of the village. Some of them were nervous, not for the performance, but because many of them were betrothed, whose partners were already ahead of them in age, and it would only be a matter of a few cycles before they would complete their handfast. Intended at a young age, handfasted once sixteen, apprenticeship, then perhaps a family by age twenty. That was the tradition. The village, however, was small and Ayren's intended was nearly two years younger, so he would have to wait; not that he minded. The pressure of a new apprenticeship was more than enough.

He looked among the faces of all his joyous neighbors, hoping to catch Vera among them but was gravely disappointed when he could not locate them.

Nam noticed his friend overextending his neck to pierce through the crowds. He shook his head out of disapproval. A quick tap of his copper hand against Ayren's back, then flashed his friend a supportive smile, and said, "I'm sure they're around here somewhere."

"Who?" Ayren asked with a placid face in order to play off his neck craning as nothing more than stretching.

"Veeeeeerrrrrrrrra." Nam stretched out the pronunciation. "You know, finni, freckled." He placed a single finger up by each of his ears and pointed them down. "Faun blessed."

"And why would I be looking for Vera, huh?" Ayren pointed out as he smoothed a few feathers from off his shoulder guards. "Besides, they are probably with Thora."

Nam placed his hands on his hips. "You may have down-to-soil Caetin horns sprouting from your brow, but your head is in the sky."

"Whoa." Ayren spread his arms wide as if to welcome Nam into an embrace. "It's me." He gestured to himself. "I've got no worries."

"Uh-huh." Nam shifted his top knot and was about to stretch, but then nodded to someone behind him. "Hey, Vera."

Ayren spun around to where he had gestured, but instead of seeing his betrothed, he instead found a vacant spot tainted by the laughter of his friend and surrounding dancers.

A finni jumped behind him, who slung her arm around his neck, then pulled Ayren down into a headlock. "Look at how quickly he looked!" Felicity shouted to the rest of the troupe eager to embarrass him.

With a roll, Ayren broke free of her grip and shot back up to his feet. He dismissed the chuckles that grew around him like weeds through a field. "Excuse me for trusting my *friend*," he thumbed to himself. "I'm not the one getting his hand bound next season, unlike some people I know." He coughed out his friend's name, "*Nam!*"

Nam shook his head. "Oh, you may want to get a tincture for that. Can't have you getting sick now that you're all grown up." He shook his finger at Ayren playfully. "You're an adult now, with adult responsibilities. Couple of years, and you get to be a shepherd. Better get practicing those pantomimes."

His hand went up to his chin in dramatic pondering. "Mm-hmm, mm-hmm, I see what you are saying but…" Quickly his hands flew in front of him, where they spun down into a series of motions, interlocking of fingers, and rolling of his wrists. Once the last of his motions were locked in place, tiny sparkles skittered across his form, appearing to be absorbed by his skin. He disappeared entirely before their eyes!

Felicity's mouth gaped open in both awe and shock. The rest of the dancers' gasped and even Nam, who was used to Ayren's shenanigans, was taken by aback.

"Malfinae!" Nam's eyes were the size of khaydish eggs. "Witch!"

Ayren reappeared as quickly as he had vanished. "Relax, will ya? Did you forget I was born under the Bat constellation?" He shook his head in jest as he pointed to the stars. "What is it with you and crying malfinae? It's within my stars' influence, settle down."

Nam appeared cross, but Ayren knew he'd forget about it before too long.

"You're not supposed to use pantomimes that don't belong to your profession!" Felicity stuttered out as she took a step backwards. "It's bad luck."

"They trade pantomimes in Adalace all the time. Besides, give me two years – just like Nam said – and I'll be waist high in goats. Then no one would have to worry about luck," he cast Nam a teasing look, "and no one would think that I'm a malfinae."

The horns blew, signaling the end of the dance, then belted rapid notes to alert the children that it was soon their turn to perform.

Kom Arturo, aether to the Kom family and father to Vera, raised his hands above Caetin villagers – his people – who looked up to him as only second to his wife in leadership. All who saw him quieted themselves, while encouraging their neighbors to do the same. Soon a hush spread across them all and they listened.

Arturo shouted as loudly and clearly as he could, "Friends, family, tribe – NIИ's blessing to you all. Today marks the coming renewal of morilyn and its bright and sun-filled season and the end of nillveness, the long night. With it, it has blessed our youth which forever adds to their strength, wisdom and hearts to uplift us and lead us into an invigorated tomorrow."

A finni walked up beside him, an individual who all knew as Kom Illify, the matron of the Kom family. Her hair was long, dark auburn in color, and set with bands of cowrie shells, complemented with beads made from yellow and orange agates. Her dress was of fine cloth, the only dress she owned, with a wool hooded cloak lined with gray wrothlyn fur. Her right shoulder and arm was adorned with chevalières-styled leather armor with long red feathers tipped with a hint of black and white spots.

"On behalf of the shepherds, the tribal council and with the glowing grace of Queen Nowem, we present to you the Danse de L'arrivée."

The drums beat out their count before the other musicians

joined in.

The finnis of the dance troupe, headed by Felicity, called out to the sky in unison, whooping as they leapt high into the air and landed gracefully on their knees before drawing back onto their feet, pivoting on a single foot, drawing their left leg behind them in attitude, raising their bodies into the air while leading with their heads, then performed a double pirouetted before ending with their hands pressing downwards in front of their exposed stomachs.

A tour jeté ushered by Nam, where one leg launched the dancers high into the air and the other swept up behind them, launched them into the center of the space. While still skyborn, the once standing leg switched positions with the other, before they landed. Joining the rest of the dancers, they all quickly kicked forward, threw their torsos backwards until their heads were in direct alignment with the sky and yelled, "Hah!" in defiance of the growing clouds that were slowly devouring the stars one by one.

An unexpected breeze pushed Ayren and the other finnae forward. As they sprung higher into the air, spreading their arms and legs as if they were a sail, then rolled into a somersault as they jumped back up to their feet and shot a battement upwards, nearly striking themselves in the chest, before slamming their foot down to pommel the ground.

All in unison and in perfect spacing between one another, the dancers pliéd, then performed three turns in the air, before landing with their feet in fifth position. They outstretched their arms to their fullest length to better display their wingspan then jabbed their right fist down, with their arm at a 90-degree angle, while they thrust their left fist upwards. With a twist, they contorted their bodies so that one foot left the ground, they unraveled, and faced the opposite direction with their feet now spread farther apart in second position.

Ayren saw everything darkening around them, as if

something was stealing the light of the new dawn, and devouring the familiar blues of their host planet Longlyn. Despite the change, he did what he could to stay in sync with his fellow dancers and to meet the challenging motions that would come.

The dancers partnered up with one another, where the standing performer pulled the other close, released them, and allowed them to fall – catching them moments before they struck the ground with their bodies in a perfect line, and swept their partner around them, then up to their feet and into the air by the crease of their partner's back.

Nam partnered with Ayren, and found himself hoisted into the air. He allowed his arms to jet behind him as he pushed his chest upwards to create a perfect arch between where Ayren's hand was supporting him and the base of his neck. He drew his right pointed foot up his left leg, just below the knee cap, to reach passé. His eyes were shut, as he always hated this technique, but knew the dismount by heart.

The flames in the lanterns and the pyres flickered wildly, fighting against a sudden uptake in wind. The sky was much like the void, cold, black and hungry. The gale was enough to unbalance the children and immediately they brought their partners back down to the ground for safety.

They all knew what motions were next, but the primordial force against their bodies gave them pause. A few tents were knocked over, and festive garlands ripped off their fastenings and blew into the crowd of villagers. Tables decorated with foods and wines toppled over and rolled across the street. Dirt vomited into the air, sending tiny rocks into everyone's faces. The lanterns and pyres were extinguished, leaving them all in darkness.

Ayren shielded his eyes with his hands, and he turned to where Nam was last standing. "What is happening?" He shouted as a low rumbling gathered around them. As his eyes adjusted to accommodate the loss of light, everything became blurry as his dusk sight focused more on identifying outlines than details.

A few cries were heard as a pot blew into the crowd and crashed into a nearby building. Then, as quickly as it had come, the winds stopped and all was silent.

Nam looked around, noting the startled motions that everyone was exhibiting. It wasn't the storm season, and the weather had been predicted to be clear. There was a heavy smell of cut grass and upturned soil.

Felicity brushed herself off, as she had been covered with a thin layer of dust that had seemingly sought her out more than the rest of the crowd. "Is it over?" She asked with raised eyebrows and spitting out what dirt had flown into her mouth.

Then, from beneath the curtain of quiet came an immediate roar so loud that their ears felt like they would collapse. The sky flashed with a green bolt of lightning that illuminated a swirling vortex that twisted above them.

Screams.

The wind returned, this time with the strength of a demonic god. Debris shot into the air; swept up into a churning wall of blackness. The ceramic roof tiles of surrounding homes ripped off their holdings and soon too came the rafters. Tables, chairs, tents, carts, barrels and all other sorts of materials were sucked into oblivion. The Caetins felt the air snuffed from inside their lungs, drawn out like some gigantic billow.

Ayren was swept off his feet, followed by Nam, Felicity and all the other children. Then fell Vera's parents and all the villagers, handfuls ripped from their place on the moon world of Orabelle and drawn up into the writhing howl which drowned out their screams – screams no one would hear – as the wind claimed them.

Chapter 1
Vera

"The Finni are a group of people distinguishable by their horns which grow in a variety of shapes and lengths from their brow. There are additional physical characteristics such as pointed ears, faun-ears (much similar to that of a goat), nose ridges called 'quasils' and, in rare cases, a tail. The term finni, also applies to the female sex, while finnae to the male. Between them are the finnyr, who may exhibit characteristics of both sexes or unique in of themselves. Gender can be static or in flux, and is always specific to one's interpretation of their Kaeleen or inner world."

– Observations of Orabelle, Doctor Niecen Coppelius.

Vera sat on a hill, overlooking their family's trip. They stared up at the sky above and pondered the same questions that they had since they first cast their gaze to the heavens. The planet Longlyn, a giant in the sky, dominated the horizon and ushered in the coming light. It was blue, with several landmasses, and swirls of white puffy clouds drifting across its surface. They wondered what animals lived there, and if there was anyone – much like Vera - staring back up at them and thinking the same.

Orabelle's sister moons, Tshir and Illune, were brilliantly shining, they were both waxing but provided enough illumination to see across the moor without slipping into their dusk sight. Yet, it wasn't just the glow from the moons, or the titan they orbited which pierced the darkness, but the dawning of gillmet. Finally, two days of twilight before they entered morilyn, a period of fourteen Longlyn days of light.

"Happy returns, Vera." Arturo offered as he approached them. His hair was short and dark brown, one that laid perfectly around his three-inch pair of horns that designated him part of the Caetin tribe. He wore a long coat that was made of wool and lined with fur. The chill of nillveness would not abate until midday.

Gander who, until now, was content sitting quietly next to Vera, barked once in excitement and wagged his foot-long bushy tail. With a smile, Vera rustled the large Kornig's brown and white spotted head-feathers which reached mid-way down his back. With a lick, the hound bathed the child's entire face in drool.

"Ew!" Vera wiped their face with the sleeve of their coat, then held out the same hand to their father to help them to their feet.

Arturo grabbed his offspring's hand, and with a powerful grip he hoisted them to standing with such speed, one would think that they were launched from a sling. He wiped his hand on his breeches to free himself of the hound's remaining moisture.

"Happy Arrivée!" Vera beamed once they landed on the ground and adjusted their hair.

"Is that today?" He teased as he looked over the trip of goats and habitually counted them. When he reached 73 he was content and returned a mischievous grin.

"Yes – that's today!" They blurted out with feigned shock. "And you know what that means?" Vera's eyes widened to drink in his response.

"I believe there was some kind of agreement where you'd be free from chores to spend time with your friends. But, who would make such a deal?" He inquired sarcastically.

"I *believe* that was mom." Their eyebrow raised enough to push into their horn.

Gander barked twice in confirmation before he licked his nose.

Arturo gave a long shrug before he finally relented in the

game he was playing. "Who am I to argue with that?"

"Yes!" Vera threw their hands into the air in triumph. With a leap, Vera wrapped their arms around their father and squeezed as hard as they could. "Thank you! Thank you! Thank you! Today is going to be the best day ever!"

"After…" He paused to allow the sudden condition to sink into their head. "…you practice your pantomimes."

"Ugh!" Vera slackened in their stance and allowed a sneer to curl up the corner of their lip. "That sounds like a chore."

"They're not chores. They are lessons. If you don't practice every day, there's a big chance you will forget it. Always remember that pantomimes require perfection otherwise they won't work when you need them the most."

Vera sighed heavily but relented. They had been watching the goats for the past six hours and they were ready to get back home. "Fine…" they begrudged. "Which one should I practice first?"

Their father shifted a leg forward and leaned in, as he tended to do whenever he was about to instruct them on some matter or another. "First, tell me what the seven rules of pantomimes are."

They pulled in breath and held it as they searched their brain for the exact wording that he had used countless times before. With large exhalation, Vera tried to expel them all in a single breath. "Of beast and material—"

"—and their meanings." Arturo calmly added in order to avoid Vera from rushing through the names and later claiming he wasn't clear enough.

Drat. They thought as they resumed their normal breathing. "Pantomimes only affect things and beings of lower order. Fauni, Finni and those above are of higher orders and any attempt to affect them will always fail."

"Very good." He nodded with sincere satisfaction. "What else?"

"No larger than oneself. Pantomimes cannot affect things greater than one's height or weight."

"So far, so good."

"No farther than one's wings." Vera extended their arms out and looked down the length of their fingers. "Pantomimes only work on people or things no farther than the length of both of one's arms."

Their father nodded. "Correct."

They snickered at a thought. "But if you stretch really far…"

"Vera."

Trying their hardest to suppress a giggle, Vera continued onto the next rule. "In alignment of one's stars. All pantomimes are aligned to star constellations. For those pantomimes associated with one's constellation, one can affect themselves and those who consent."

Arturo pointed towards the sky. "And which constellation were you born under?"

This was one Vera knew by heart. "Gleisne! The people behind the Glass."

"And what are the other constellations?"

Vera slumped their shoulders and tilted their head. In absolute protest they expelled, "Are you kidding me?!"

Their answer came as a fit of laughter, one that was deep and spawned from his gut. After a few moments of gathering himself he said, "Your face… perfection! Yes, I'm joking. You have three more rules to go."

Their eyes narrowed with irritation. "Here I am, *trying* to recite these rules and there you go *trying* to sidetrack me with constellations."

"I'm sorry, I'm sorry, I'm sorry." He waved his hand at them before wiping a joyful tear from his eye. "You're right. Let's keep going."

Veran grumbled their displeasure before continuing, "What is done may be undone. All pantomimes have an opposite, which is the same motions but in reverse."

Again he nodded.

"Permanence in all things. All pantomimes are permanent unless undone by its reverse."

"And finally?" Arturo attempted to usher the response out of them by pulling his fingers towards himself.

"True love's kiss. A kiss given to you from a true love may break any or all pantomimes affecting someone so long as the pantomimes are unwanted. So—does it have to be a kiss? Can't we just, I don't know, hug it out instead or maybe give each other a kind handshake or something?"

"I'm not sure. Maybe it has something to do with spit."

"Gross!" Vera laughed briefly. "I hate spit!" They thumbed in the direction of their home. "So, I can take off now?"

Arturo shook his head. "Are you trying to pull the wool over my eyes? You haven't even practiced yet."

Double drat. "Okay then, what should I practice on?"

He thought for a moment and swept his gaze from several rocks, sparse trees and grass before settling on Gander. The feathered hound looked from Arturo to Vera, then whined and smooshed himself against the ground as much as possible. He covered his muzzle with his front paws and closed his eyes.

"I don't think that Gander is too happy about that." Vera

joked. They leaned down and started scratching the dog's back.

Quickly, the hound rolled over to expose his belly and Vera continued with their scratches. His tail wagged, his back left leg started kicking, and a gleeful rumble issued low in his throat.

"It'll be okay Gander." They reassured as they stepped away from him and positioned themselves about five feet away.

They thought that, perhaps, the best thing to start with was to calm Gander. The very first pantomime they had learned was one that was meant to sooth animals, especially those who were afraid or threatening. Vera bent their middle fingers so they were slightly dipped below the rest of their fingers and straightened the rest. They pulled their hands toward their chest and rotated their wrists so that their left hand's palm faced them, while the right hand's palm faced Gander. Then their right hand rolled, as if the fingers were caressing someone's face. Vera could feel the energies of the world flood into their heart like a warm glass of milk, and they exhaled, pushing the energy towards Gander.

A soft pallid glow sprung from their fingertips and floated like a lantern out between them before it enveloped the kornig like a splash of water before being absorbed into his yellowish-fur. Gander's disposition changed almost immediately, his tail was no longer wagging from the prior belly scratches, and his head eased down onto the ground as if he was enjoying some inaudible lullaby.

"Well done, but that's an easy one. Try reversing it." Arturo suggested as he tilted his head one way, then the other, in order to properly observe Gander's reactions.

Vera nodded, and just as quickly as they had spun the sooth pantomime, they reversed their motions and the light pulled back out from his fur and dissipated into the chilly air.

Gander sat up and began wagging his tail once more. He barked his congratulations to Vera excitedly.

"Now, show me the command pantomime."

Vera took in a large breath, as their body was filled with doubt. They had been practicing this very pantomime for months. It wasn't the gestures that were the problem, it was when they tried to redirect the energy. Every time it seemed like there was something blocking them from inside.

Biting their lip, Vera drew their hands towards themself, flayed out their fingers like a peppanach and touched their thumbs and pointer fingers together. As many times in the past, they could feel the energy flowing through them, roll up into their chest and settle into their heart. They pushed the energy outwards, feeling a slight crackle as it surged across their skin. They expelled it towards Gander, but instead of manifesting into some brilliant display, the energy sparked then quickly dissipated. Just like before, it failed.

They rubbed their hands on their coat to dull the tingling sensation the pantomime left behind before they tried it again. It too, had failed in the form of tiny jolts of static electricity.

Their head tightened then burned with aggravation. "I just—I just can't. I don't understand why."

"Don't worry about it, you'll figure it out one day. As you know, pantomimes can take a long time to learn and years to matron. If you keep at it, I'm sure you'll get it down."

Gander raised on all four of his legs and walked up to Vera, where he proceeded to nuzzle his head against their hand; inspiring a smile.

"I don't need to command you anyway, do I boy? You know exactly what I want." They scratched behind his ears and beneath his feathers.

"That's enough for today. I'm sure your mother is back at home making you breakfast."

Finally! Vera screamed in their head. It wasn't that they

didn't enjoy spending time with their father, but more that the desire to see their friends was bubbling over. Thora, their best friend in all of Orabelle, was on the top of Vera's list.

"Fan-tastic!" Vera pumped a fist in celebration. They rushed toward their father and embraced him in a powerful squeeze – enough to get him to gasp just slightly. "I love you, dad."

He chuckled at their enthusiasm and gave them a squeeze back. "I love you too. Have fun kid."

Quickly, Vera rushed off towards home. The wind was at their back now and it pushed them into longer strides as they ran. Gander sped barking after, knowing full well that there was food waiting for them at home.

Arturo kept a smile on his face as he watched his child bound off happily in the growing twilight. It reminded him of how he used to run through the moors in those bygone days when he was still young.

He turned back to face the goats to count them, as was his habit, but was stalled as he spied a tall figure dressed in crimson coat embroidered with gold flowers and vines, with a metallic epaulet on one shoulder and a full plate guard on the other. Peculiar, was the smiling Adalacian mask they wore which was finely painted with whites, gold, reds and silver. If the stranger was truly from Adalace, they certainly were a long way from home. Odder still, the figure was dancing alone across the moor like a jester in front of the court.

Chapter 2
Thora

"The Fauni share the world as one of the dominate species, though their exact influence is severely limited by those who prefer Finni in positions of power. Fauni are not known to have a homeland and instead are nomadic, moving their communities between Finni borders freely. They are distinguishable by their goat-like ears, and a pair of antlers which sprout from their brow that shed twice per year. Fauni suffer all manner of prejudices, mostly propagated by superstitions, and an unnatural ability to sense the coming of narghoulim."

- *Wanderings*, Viliph Drosselmeyer

Thora sat on a wall. It was made of stones gathered by the local Caetins and held tightly together by gray mortar. Though, based on how the nocturnalis covered the majority of it, one could argue that it was more the moss that bound it all. It had sprouted small flowers, with brilliant petals of blues and purples during nillveness, but now they were closing as the sun's rays slowly illuminated the sky with layers of orange before fading into various hues of blue and vanishing into a sea of darkness. She loved these periods, the transitions between night and light when things seemed the most still. She loved it even more when she was in Vera's birthplace of Tandermundt.

The worst she could ever expect from a Caetin was a suspicious glance, but she felt that the glimpses were more born of a shy curiosity that rarely was ever investigated, than the harsh cruelties that others harbored. Thora firmly believed that if a Mycili and a Caetin were to have a union, that they'd adopt every person into a beloved family; including the Fauni. Tandermundt was certainly far kinder to her than the rest of Finni villages she had visited.

She was happy for today. The excitement of the upcoming

festival, the food, the drinks, the dancing – it was something she looked forward to all year. While the pinions in her heart tingled across her chest in anxious revelry, she forced herself to focus and stay alert for Vera. There were still several lanterns lit across the village, allowing her eyes to keep themselves from shifting into her dusk vision.

Some barking caught Thora's attention and she turned her head to peek farther down the street with hopes of catching her friend's silhouette moving towards her. As far as she knew, Gander was the only kornig in Tandermundt; with Vera having chosen the pup from a town up north. It was quite the journey for Vera, who for the majority of their life had remained in their village as opposed to the long nomadic life of Thora's people.

As the barking grew, Thora's heart quaked with joyful anxiety, one that pounded into her limbs and encouraged her to fling herself off the stone wall and run towards her friend. To meet them in such a hurried fashion, for one reason or another, had been advised as unbecoming of a Fauni, especially when enthusiasm was easily mistaken in other villages as mischief.

As the shape got closer and closer, bounding in her direction like some wild beast after some delectable aroma, she heard the scraping of stone and the grinding of a shoe atop of dirt far closer than she felt comfortable. Thora shot herself to standing and cartwheeled on the top of the stone wall away from whatever intruder had intentionally crept up on her. Instinctively, her hands flashed into a fighting position, ready to strike should the perpetrator be a threat.

Instead of a brigand or hateful Finni, she was met by the freckled face of a familiar faun-blessed child. They had an androgynous face, short brown hair with bangs that occasionally fell into their sparkling withered-leaf brown eyes, angular-cut chin and curved Caetin horns jetting from their brow perhaps a quarter of an inch longer than the last season. Vera was tiptoeing their way closer to Thora, using their hound to distract her from seeing them coming. The sneaking, obviously didn't work.

Thora released a battle-cry whose effect was dampened by the tinge of gleeful excitement that boiled out any intimidation, as she charged off the top of the wall, leapt and crash-landed into the now wide-eyed Finni who braced for impact. Vera grabbed Thora around the waist, but couldn't hold her. Together, they collapsed onto the ground in a fit of laughter.

Vera's smile radiated across their face like a beam of starlight, while Thora giggled profusely as she shifted back to standing. Gander bounced around them and barked happily at their play and reunion. His tail thrashed the air with excitement.

"By the NIИ it seems like forever!" Thora professed through her grin. "Look at you, you're like a foot taller than last time I saw you!"

"A whole inch!" Vera raised their hand above their head to compare against Thora's estimate. "And while Vera could not discern if their friend had increased much in height, their antlers certainly had changed in formation and size, far dwarfing even the largest of Caetin horns, at nearly one and a half feet in height. "I'm loving your growth! It really came in gorgeous! Your best one yet!"

"Oh! These?" Thora poked her antlers as if they were some form of dress. "I spent so many hours concentrating on them, trying to get them to come in just the way I wanted. Our Shem caught me one evening and asked what I was so focused on and I lied and said I was thinking about the old stories and she became way too interested in which particular story. So I had to make something up and was stuck recounting what I remembered and it became *way* more than what I was prepared for – but I think all that wishing did them some good. I'll be sad when I shed them."

"I always wanted Nadin horns, you know, the big ones that

curl back. I'd even be okay with having a Leekyn or Gami horns. Caetin horns are so... tiny."

"But not insignificant!" Thora pointed out. "There's a lot of strength in those horns, and between you and me, I find Caetin horns to be the most delightful!" She beamed with sincerity, which reflected in the way she cupped her hands directly in front of her, the tilt of her head, the way her raven-colored hair pooled over her shoulders.

"Thank you!" Vera smiled. "You'd be surprised how a certain finnae I know gets when you make fun of his horns." They gave a wink.

Just then a thought came across Thora's face and she immediately twisted her body so that she could reach her satchel. "I just remembered! Your birthday is in two days and I made you something."

"You got me a birthday present? You really didn't have to—WHAT IS IT?!" Vera clapped their hands and shifted their weight between each foot in order to burn off the overflowing feeling of elation.

She pulled out an object wrapped in a hand-spun gifting cloth.

Vera's eyes marveled as they stood in anticipation.

Unwrapping it ceremoniously, Thora revealed a leather sheath where rested a knife with an antler handle. "I made this for you out of my old antlers and spent the last cycle chiseling the stone." She pulled the dagger from its recess, and revealed its black seven-inch blade. You see! It's made of obsidian, all the way from the Moon Sea."

"You traveled all the way from the Moon Sea to make me a knife for my birthday!" Vera carefully took hold of the sheath as Thora slipped the knife back inside. They stared at it with disbelief and wondered at how long it must have taken for her to make it.

Their friend simply chuckled and placed a hand on the back of her head. "Not exactly. I traded for the obsidian from a Mycili merchant in Cornelis. He said it was from the Moon Sea. So, I didn't exactly go to there to get it, but I might as well have!" She laughed again. "Do you like it?"

"Do I like it?! Are you kidding me?! I love it!" Vera pulled out the blade once again and turned it over and over again in their hands, to watch how the growing twilight danced across its surface. After a few moments trapped in admiration, they sheathed the blade with a delightful shhhhhrt sound, and hugged Thora tightly. Their head rested on their shoulder, and for a moment, Vera could feel Thora's heartbeat. "Thank you SO much!"

As Vera pulled away from their embrace, a low whine issued from Gander who sat a few feet away from their reunion. He was nearly twelve hands tall, with large broad shoulders and enough feathers to make him appear daunting whenever they were ruffled. Gander tilted his head so that he could better draw her attention towards him.

Once she shifted her gaze from her friend to the hound, Gander's feathers on the top of his head and the sides extended outwards and he barked excitedly. He stood up and twirled in place before rushing up to her.

Thora quickly grabbed hold of his cheek fur, then rustled his skin back and forth. "Oh, Gander! I've missed you so much! Who's a good, Gander? Huh? Who's a good, Gander!"

Gander sniffed her hands and arms, before moving towards her satchel. Something within was catching his attention, something he wanted to eat.

"I can't keep anything secret from you, can I? You always ruin the surprise with that nose of yours." Thora joked as she drowned her hand back inside the mysteries of her satchel's

21

main pocket. Before long, her hand produced a biscuit which was immediately snatched from her hand by the greedy kornig who horked it down in seconds.

His crunching was enough to send Vera into giggles. "That's Gander's way of saying thank you, I think!"

A radiant smile swept across Thora's face as she beamed with gratitude. "I'm glad he likes it."

Just like that, Gander's face drooped, his ears perked up and his eyes took on this faraway look as if he was listening to something that Vera or Thora couldn't detect. He pointed with his snoot towards the in-between of two houses, and erupted with a "errr-up, errr-up".

Vera ran her fingers playfully through his head feathers. "What is it, huh? What's over there that's causing you so much distress?"

In a few moments, they finally caught sight of what Gander was sensing. A finnae in his sixteenth-year strolled out into view, followed by two others similar in age. A couple of them laughed loudly, while a finni grabbed one around the neck and gave him a noogie. The noogie giver, was swatted away by their victim, a finnae with a top-knot who managed a smirk on his face while eagerly pointing Vera and Thora out.

"Well, well, looky what we have here." Came the finnae who kept a few strides ahead of the other teenagers. His hair was short, dark brown, and his eyes were amber in color. He wore a cloth tunic that had been dyed red at some point but had already faded to pink in some areas, while also blackened breaches with several tied strips of leather up the length of his out-seam. "Vera… Gander…" he paused while he took in the antlers on the fauni's head. "Wow, wow, wow… just look at the size of that rack. I could hang so many hats off those."

Both Vera and Thora cast a glance between them and a wicked smile possessed their lips.

Thora tilted her head calmly, stuck out a hip and placed a hand on it while gesturing towards his own caetin horns that were no larger than two and a half inches. "It's a pity you can't hang one off yours."

"Oooooo," came a chorus from his entourage including Vera who had crossed their arms over their chest in solidarity for their friend.

The comment may have stung his pride a little, but the response from his own friends seemed only to spurn him into a sneer.

"You know, in other villages, I've heard comments like that wouldn't end well for you."

Thora only smiled. "You're lucky you've grown up in a village where you only compare inches, instead of feet." She scrunched her pointer finger and thumb together in order to continue ridiculing him.

Laughter erupted from his group of friends.

The finnae became increasingly flustered. "Well you're—"

"Hey!" Vera stepped between their friend and the other Caetin. With narrowed eyes and a hardened face. Vera – only thirteen years of age and dwarfed by his size – bore into him with a disdainful stare. "Knock it off."

Gander barked to emphasize their command, then he produced a low growl as all the feathers on his body extended outwards to make him appear bigger.

"Or what?" The finnae shot back. "Are you going to do something about it?" His face was irritatingly smug.

Vera scraping dust off the ground with their feet and spitting it out into the air behind them, as they rushed towards him. They launched themself into the air, spun, and came down with a spin kick which would have connected with his torso, had he not swept his own leg forward to defend himself, connecting both of their ankles together and pressing it to the ground. Vera landed on both of their feet, bent their knees and drew up their hands in a defensive posture.

The finnae was taken aback that Vera would dare to challenge him. "You can't be serious."

"You insult my friend, you insult me. Bring it!" Vera spun again, this time their foot was aimed at his face!

Chapter 3
Kickfeet

"Governess belongs to the finni, with the finnyr beneath them, and the finnae at the bottom. One does not request the expertise of a finnae over the matrony of the finni. Profession, by right, must be adopted by the finnae after the handfast. The finnae will shed their horns to adopt those belonging to the tribe of their mate, and for all purposes their tribal identity shifts to match that of their finni partner. Finnyr may keep the horns of their originating tribe or later may choose to shed them, which is advantageous when elevating one's social strata. With the finnyr's versatility, one could argue that they are far superior than finni. Then again, when has society ever recognized those who would most benefit it."

– Caraboose, *Journal of a Malfinae*

A momentary look of shock froze upon Ayren's features, as the foot of his betrothed sped towards him! He leapt backwards just enough so that Vera's kick met empty air. Irritated at how hastily he was able to get out of the way, Vera slammed their foot down onto the ground for a quicker recovery.

Ayren cracked a smile. "You do realize that you're just going to lose." He crouched down into a fighting stance. "I'm older, stronger, faster…"

Vera launched themself at him once again, where they kicked out towards his torso with their right foot. Ayren saw his opportunity and kicked at their foot, only to have Vera retract their attack to perform a spin kick using their left – a feint – which left him completely open!

The finni's foot slapped against his, causing him to wobble in his balance slightly before he was able to recover.

"—Dumber!" Vera teased as they held up two fingers and scratched them down an invisible board. "Two points for me."

Ayren's friends cheered from the sidelines. "Go Vera! Teach him a lesson!" Then laughed.

"Hey!" He gave them an evil look. "Just whose side are you on anyhow?"

Nam, his best friend, and Felicity shared a wicked grin and in unison they replied, "Vera's."

"Less talking, more kicking!" Vera shouted as they shot a few rapid kicks at his feet.

He dodged as quickly as he could, throwing his feet to the side in a dance, then having to spin on his right heel to bring his left foot up behind him and around before spinning back to face Vera.

Vera knew this move all too well, it seemed to be his go-to, but like so many times before they weren't going to fall for it. They jumped back, creating a large space between the two of them, so that when Ayren kicked immediately down, waist-high, then at head length, Vera wasn't even in any danger of being tagged.

"—more predictable!" A grin flashed across Vera's face as they dropped slowly in their knees to become more grounded. Then, without warning, they threw themself into a baril leap, utilizing the momentum to send a kick down towards his feet at incredible speeds – only for Vera to tense their muscles to slow their foot's descent so as not to injury him, but to strike his foot enough where he could feel the impact.

Their foot connected and Ayren yelped out of surprise! He then jumped backwards to escape any further danger while positioning himself better for his next assault.

As the two of them recovered, they stared at one another for a brief pause. Attempting to read each other's body language in order to anticipate their next strategy.

Thora, caught up in the excitement, found herself drifting

over to where Nam and Felicity were cheering; taking an already aloof Gander with her. She crossed her arms over her chest and asked the duo, "So what's happening?"

Nam took an inhalation of breath to explain, even raised a finger, but Felicity beat him to it. "We have a game called kick-feet. The goal is to kick your opponent's foot without purposefully injuring them, in order to score points. The higher your opponent's foot, the more points you score. So, if you kick their foot at knee height, it's one point. Waist high? It's two points. Torso is three points and at the head it's four points. First one to ten wins, and if any point you fall over, you lose."

Thora pointed at the space between them. "Since Thora kicked his foot on the ground is that worth anything?"

"Just Ayren's pride." Nam explained with a laugh.

The two fighters continued to stare one another down, and it took Gander to bark at them to encourage a move. Vera darted towards Ayren then kicked towards his torso, but instead of connecting with their target, Ayren side stepped, wrapped his arm around their midsection, spun, and tossed them back onto the street.

Vera landed on their feet and skidded on the dirt, yet kept standing. With a smirk, Vera rushed towards the wall, leapt atop its surface, and retreated down its length away from their opponent.

"Running away I see!" Ayren teased as he gave pursuit.

Felicity grabbed Thora by the hand and pulled her after. "Come on! If we don't keep up, we're going to lose them."

Thora had little time to argue before she was yanked down the road. The fauni was able to find her footing quickly enough to keep up as the three of them ran after their friends with Gander not far behind them.

Ayren rushed along the top of the cobblestone wall and

knew that he could catch Vera in only a matter of seconds. However, when they stopped and stuck their foot out at torso height – he was not prepared at all, and rammed into their foot - and into his stomach, which caused him to stagger backwards from the blow. His foot almost slipped off the edge, but he barely managed to catch himself.

Vera laughed at their own cleverness before running away. It wasn't much farther before the stone wall made a 90 degree turn away from the road, and in its place was Finnae Havenricht's house which was built of cobblestones, wood, and a strong ceramic-tiled roof. Vera was not about to give up a perfectly good vantage point, so they boosted their speed enough so that when they reached the end of the wall, they leapt and grabbed hold of the first layer of roof tiles, then followed through with their momentum to hoist themself up onto the very top.

Finnae Havenricht worked at the mill and this morning he had already left to prepare for the festival. Had he been home, he would not have taken very kindly to a couple of adolescents messing about.

The tiles clinked as Vera found their balance. They moved swiftly across the roof in order to give Ayren enough room to get up there himself before preparing to charge him as soon as he planted his feet.

Ayren, on the other hand, after recovering from the previous blow, hurled himself off the wall and quickly pulled himself up. He knew the moment that he would get his footing, Vera would attempt another attack, however this time he was prepared.

Vera dropped their torso to the side as a counter weight, giving them the extra flexibility to jet their leg straight up into the air in an attempt to strike Ayren in the face, but Ayren was far too quick as he performed a roundhouse kick that struck the side of their foot. The force was enough that Vera had to continue through the spin and plant the foot far behind them and crouch in order to reduce the risk of falling.

"Four points for me!" Ayren boasted as he breathed on his fingernails and rubbed them against his shirt.

"Boo!" Nam shouted at him from the ground.

Vera narrowed their eyes and huffed, but instead of being goaded into an attack, they ran to the end of the roof and leapt across the spacing between and landed on Finnyr Gilshen's roof with ease.

Finnyr Gilshen was a tanner who Vera's family knew very well on account of their goats who either died by natural causes or in those instances where they were sent to slaughter. And when Vera's feet struck the top of the house, Finnyr Gilshen was roused from their chair – having been in the middle of some needlepoint – and opened a window to see what the clamor was about. It was just in that instance when Ayren had leapt across and landed on their roof, that Finnyr Gilshen spied the troublemaker and shouted up at him, "Naughtborrow Ayren, you get off my roof this instant!"

It was the kind of distraction that Vera took advantage of, as when Ayren shouted his apology to them, Vera kicked at his knees, enough where it caused him to stumble backwards towards the edge of the roof. As he frantically swung his arms to prevent himself from tumbling over, Vera rushed over and grabbed his shirt. "Hold on—"

With an evil grin, he grabbed Vera by the arm and with all his might pulled the both of them over the edge. Together, they plummeted to the ground and were only saved by a pile of carefully folded canvas meant for the pitching of canopies.

Vera was pummeled by Ayren's guffawing and in a fit of aggravation they scoffed as they pushed off his body that just so happened to be tangled with. "Get off, you cheater!"

Thora, Felicity and Nam had spied them as they had fallen,

and ran by the alley to see, what they believed, to be their friends' doom. They were quite relieved to see a very perturbed face on Vera, beset by Ayren's cackling.

Finnyr Gilshen's window faced the alleyway and they grimaced at the two children. "I don't know how many times I have to tell you kids, but stay off my roof. You could crack a tile and then I'd have to climb up there on my own and have to replace it. If you're going to hurt each other, do it somewhere else."

Vera found their legs and was able to brush themself off briefly before solemnly placing their hands behind their back and performed a short curtsy. "I'm really sorry. This is all my fault. I was bent on putting Ayren in his place, and it all went awry."

Fyr Gilshen's features softened and a touch of nostalgia seemingly overtook them and they said, "I see no mischief in teaching that finnae a lesson. Egotism is an unattractive feature, and it seems Ayren has more than his fair share." They turned to him with a glare. "You don't know how lucky you are to have someone as patient as Vera."

Ayren got to his feet and placed a hand on his head. "Many apologies, Fyr Gilshen. You're right, I am very lucky."

"Hmph – at least the boy admits it. Keep him out of trouble, Vera. We both know he isn't going to do it on his own." And with that, Fyr Gilshen disappeared inside, closing the shutters behind them.

Ayren stood there, hand still on his head, looking all sheepish, when Vera just rolled their eyes and grabbed his other hand. "Come on!" Vera tugged at his arm. "Let's get out of here."

Vera led him to where the rest of their friends were waiting at the mouth of the alley. Then pointed farther towards the west where they all went to get away from the village and the responsibilities of the day. Gander bounded off ahead of them, barking at whatever he felt needed barks. In their journey they passed the old water clock near the village square where it slowly dripped the passage of time into a bowl with clear markings.

With great anticipation and yet an uncanny calmness, Vera knew that in just a matter of hours, they would be celebrating the dawning of a new morilyn with the people they loved.

Chapter 4
Campfire on the Moor

"The moon world's past is seemingly timeless, where one after another, species and their civilizations both rose and fell. There are still ancients remaining, known only as the Lost, most having been driven to madness while others have become Eternals; the last of their kind who inherent immortality as either a blessing or as a curse. When all but one of the last Finni departs this world, they too will become an Eternal and will be forced to watch as the Fauni inherit all they worked for."

– The Forgotten Ones, Doctor Niecen Coppelius.

ou're right, Fyr Gilshen." Nam teased as they all walked up the western hillside.

"Shut up." Ayren retorted half-jokingly as Vera, Thora and Felicity giggled. "I was trying to be respectful."

Thora beamed at him with supple cheeks. "You two were on their roof! I think being respectful was the very least you could do. I'm glad you both apologized. I'm sure I'd be furious if someone was kicking around on my roof."

Vera grabbed hold of Ayren's hand, locking their fingers in with his. They puckered their lips. "But don't you remember? They saw no mischief in me putting you in your place. You're super lucky to have me!" They winked at him and their faun-like ears twitched with the gesture.

"Yes, yes, yes – I believe we just went through all that." Ayren sighed with a short smile. "I think you just like hearing it."

"Yup! That's why you have to say it again!" Vera decreed.

Gander barked his approval.

Felicity joined in. "You better say it, Ay. Otherwise we won't hear the end of it."

"I remember when Vera learned a Fauni dance in order to invoke a pantomime and they wouldn't stop asking me to show them for days until I gave in." Thora pointed out as she hopped over a couple of larger rocks that were in her path. "Not that the dance worked, mind you."

Vera grinned widely. "Ayren knows by now that I always get my way—eventually."

He relented. "Fine! Yes, I'm lucky to have you." He swung their hands back and forth like a pendulum to show he wasn't cross.

"See! I win."

"Hold up—Fauni have to dance in order to get their pantomimes to work?" Nam asked with wide eyes. He briefly looked at his hands then back at her. "That sounds tough."

"And it takes forever. You Finni don't know how easy you have it. Wiggle your fingers, hands and arms and poof – magic. It takes me over ten minutes just to light a candle. You do it in seconds. Well… some of you that is." Thora just remembered that Finnis tended to limit themselves in which pantomimes they learned as part of their cultural identity.

"You should show us some of your pantomime dancing, Thora!" Vera grabbed Thora's hand while maintaining their hold on Ayren's.

Nam's eyes got slightly bigger. "Yeeesss, I want to see that."

"Absolutely not!" Felicity chimed in with determination. "Fauni pantomimes attract narghoulim."

Vera and Thora, with a touch of aggravation, retorted at the same time. "They do NOT!"

"It's true!" Felicity's eyebrows shadowed their eyes. "I have cousins in Adalace and they have friends in the Rushinay who say that Fauni can summon narghoulim whenever they want and they tell the Old Gods what to destroy and who to kill."

Thora was dumbstruck, as she didn't think that Caetins were capable of saying such cruel things, especially not one whom she considered a semi-friend.

Felicity realized the mistake but tried to play it off as the best she could. "Not that you would do something like that, Thora, you're different than other Fauni."

It didn't help.

Vera was flabbergasted. Anger rose into their ears and all they wanted to do was demand an apology, but with Felicity, they knew that it was a lost cause as she would just match anger with anger. "Listen Felicity, your cousins or their friends, or whoever – they are just wrong. Fauni aren't like that, and if they had the ability to control narghoulim, why don't they ride them around like peppenach, huh? If I could control the Old Gods, I'd have them pick me up and put me on their shoulders and we'd go stomping around the Serishone Mountains just for fun where we couldn't hurt anyone. It's silly to think that Fauni would call them down just to hurt people. Fauni are no more malicious than you or me."

Thora was happy that her friend stuck up for her people, it wasn't every day that she encountered someone who was willing to do that. That was one of the big reasons that Vera was her friend.

Felicity thought about it for a moment.

"You know what I would do if I could control a narghoulim?" Thora offered as an olive branch. "I'd have one take me out to sea so that I could visit all the islands. I've been all across the mainland, but never out past the sea." She was soon possessed by a distant look in her eyes.

Felicity relented. "Maybe you're right. It does sound silly

that Fauni would only use them for bad. What I don't understand though, is why don't the narghoulim ever go after Fauni encampments?"

Thora shook her head. "Because no one cares what happens to Fauni tribes, so when one goes missing or gets eaten, everyone's so preoccupied with what's happening in the Finni world that it gets overlooked. We aren't immune to the narghoulim… but I will admit, they do seem to have a particular taste for your people over mine."

"Thank the NIИ we're here." Aryan declared as the current conversation was already putting his nerves on edge.

It was an ancient ruin, with half crumbled columns, perfectly cut moss-covered stone floors, partially erect stone walls, and weathered marble statues – much so that they were completely unrecognizable.

They all had been here before, but Thora less so than the others. She kept her eyes wandering from shadow to shadow, to ensure that there wasn't anything malicious hiding among the rocks. It was a Lost People ruin after all, and everything her tribe had told her of the Lost people are that they were dangerous.

Gander looked at Thora, sat alongside her and released a short whine out of concern.

Felicity approached a familiar spot where a few old lanterns had been left behind, nestled atop a few of the dilapidated walls and she set about working a pantomime, one she was very familiar with due to working the forge with her mother. In a combustion of flame, the lantern's wick ignited and she moved on to the next one.

While the night had slowly been peeled back like the skin of a roneshka fruit by the encroachment of a hungry dawn, the sun had only peeked out from the horizon and it was still difficult to see. Finni could see fairly well in the darkness using their dusk sight, closely akin to most animals, but it caused things to be blurry which made determining facial features extremely hard. Once the right amount of light was added though, things came into focus and no one would have to feel like they needed to strain themselves in order to see what was happening.

Thora tightened her grip on Vera's hand. "Do… do you all come up here a lot?" Her eyes locked onto one of the imposing statues, one who held a hammer and chisel, but also who appeared to stare directly at her.

"Sometimes." Vera replied as they squeezed Vera's hand three times in reassurance.

There was a small firepit with rocks surrounding the top edge in order to keep any wayward logs inside. Nam dropped a bunch of kindling in a pile while Felicity worked on another pantomime to ignite the flames. It was still chilly out and the wind carried the frigidity across the hills.

Vera lured both Thora and Ayren over towards the fire as it hungrily fed on the wood, causing it to snap and embers to dance into a plume of smoke. They all sat on a log, which so happened that Ayren and Nam, many seasons ago, had dragged up the hill for them to sit on. It didn't take long for their dusk sight to wane.

Thora carefully placed her hand into her lap, while Vera took hold of Ayren's arm and snuggled up against him for some additional warmth. Thora fidgeted as she continued to scan the ruins for anything that might wish them harm.

Gander found a spot slightly in front, where he laid down in anticipation of the fire warming his belly.

Ayren, who had been quiet most of the walk here, had noticed. "Hey, Thora, so… you okay? You seem nervous."

"My tribe avoids ruins belonging to the Lost People. Shem Zhalinya has warned us that trespassing in the old places angers the spirits. These… *creatures* fell from grace for a reason. I'm just..." She looked to an area on the hill where something seemed to have moved, but after careful examination she soon realized that it was just the wind rustling a bush. "...very uncomfortable."

Felicity plopped herself down on a rock, one she had claimed long ago because it gave her a few inches of a height over everyone else sitting around the fire. She straightened her back and placed her hands on her knees to stabilize herself. Despite feeling regal, keeping in this position was a lot of work. "Don't worry so much, we've been up here plenty of times. Besides, Old Shook is completely harmless. He lives in a cave not too far from here but rarely comes out."

"Yeah!" Nam exclaimed as he stood over the fire, hunched himself over, and extended his arms like claws over the fire and wiggled his fingers. "They say that those who look Old Shook in the eyes, are given a vision of their future. Most of the time, it's a vision of death!"

"Of death? Really, Nam?" Vera straightened themselves up in order to counter his claims. "I've never once heard that it was a vision of death. In fact, Turbit Gorm who helps with our flock, told me he saw Old Shook when he was younger and he saw the love of his life before he even met him."

Nam widened his arms in protest. "Why do you have to ruin my fun, huh?"

Vera narrowed their eyes. "It's not fun if you're scaring Thora. She said she was uncomfortable and here you are trying to make it worse."

"Geez, you're starting to sound like my mother." He rolled his eyes, crossed his arms but otherwise remained standing so he could lord over the fire.

Aryan interceded. "That's a compliment. His mother has a lot of sense."

Felicity ran her fingers through her raven hair. "You know… I've seen Old Shook before."

"What?!" Vera demanded in disbelief.

"No, you didn't!" Challenged Nam.

"I most certainly did!" Felicity shot back at the finnae. "I saw him last season when I was collecting wood. I turned around with my hands full of logs, when he was right there by a tree. He looked just like a statue. I could have thrown one of the logs at him, he was that close. "

"Were you scared?" Thora asked as she leaned closer, as if by proximity she would be transported to that very day.

"Of course, I was. I'm not stupid. I even turned away from him, so that I wouldn't look him in the eyes. But I still saw him at the edge of my vision, watching me. I just stood there, wishing for him to go away and after a few moments he did. He just walked off, as if he was on a stroll and we had never come across one another."

"I don't know what I would have done, probably screamed and ran!" Thora laughed out their nervousness. The very thought of coming face to face with Old Shook was terrifying to her.

Aryan crossed his arms over his chest and jumped into his pride. "I don't think I would run or scream. I think I would face him head on, look him directly in his eyes. I don't fear the future. Besides, what's the worst that I'm going to see? Me hip deep in goats?"

Vera scrunched their brow and their eyes turned sharply against their betrothed. "You see that as the worst?"

He dropped his arms and made a grab for the brisk air hoping that he could steady himself on what was coming next. "I—no, I didn't mean it that way! I'm saying that's where I see myself in the future, you know - with you. It's a good future."

Vera poked him in the chest playfully as they relaxed their face. "You better believe it's a good future – especially because I'm in it!"

Nam stood up. "Well, then what do you all say?"

"Say to what?" Felicity asked while warming her hands over the fire.

"Old Shook—let's go see our futures!"

Chapter 5
Old Shook

"Inside all of us is an infinitesimal world called the kaeleen. The kaeleen is who we are, defining our personalities, gender, and passions. Our bodies act as a vessel, like a ship in the sea, carrying us home to some distant destination. As our bodies – our ghosha – suffers, so too does our kaeleen, and when the ghosha dies, our kaeleen departs. The ocean in which the ghosha sails is the eshef, though distinct by the soil, water, air, sky, moons, planets and stars. Our vivitah, the last breath of who we are and all our spiritual energy impacts the world – no matter how insignificant one thinks we are. We are all connected together by the vivitah around us, and what we do to one another, will ultimately impact what our world does to us."

– The Musings of Divine Leekyn Tvay Anessa

I don't think this is a good idea..." Thora muttered beneath her breath as the children and Gander shifted among the rocks and brush of the moor.

They had all transitioned back into their dusk sight, able to see as well enough under the stars and illumination of the planet and moons, but with it came the all too familiar fuzziness of distant things and it put Thora on edge no matter how many times in the past her people had stealthily left an area in the cover of darkness.

Vera noted the worrisome expression she had on her face and nudged her friend with their shoulder as reassurance.

Nam and Aryan were at the front, leading everyone while also keeping an eye out for dangerous footing or otherwise. The moor in this part of the land reached up higher in elevation, which in turn left several cavities in the earth where wild creatures could have taken up roost.

Felicity hung back with Vera and Thora, and Gander just wandered as he tended to, sniffing plants and marking his territory whenever he encountered a bush or rock that he felt needed his presence.

"Thora, what do you know about the Lost People?" Felicity asked as they continued their way in hushed voices.

She thought for a few moments, pausing to consider the things that she's been told over the years. Some tales she knew weren't for Finni ears, as they were sacred stories, but there were a few things that she remembered that she could pass on. "Orabelle has seen many people of different culture and appearance live long enough to grow to prominence then fall to ruin. Some of those people are still out there, in small numbers, but they are feral and not like us. Our scholars believe that once a species reaches its end, they suffer a madness that cannot be cured until the culling, which will eventually leave only one of their species. The one remaining becomes an Eternal, cursed with immortality and with all the memories of their people's history."

"But why does that happen?" Felicity asked with protest. "It doesn't seem fair to me."

Thora shrugged her shoulders. "The NIⱮ wish it, and so it is. There must be reason for it, but such things are beyond our stories. Fauni try not to spend too much time questioning the way things are and instead flows with it. It is as natural to us as life and death. Things end, except the One. The One is to remember. Perhaps it's a way for stories to be told. What point is there to tragedy if no one is there to mourn it?"

"It sounds cruel." Vera added. "And lonely."

"I guess it depends on your point of view." Thora considered as she watched the finnae ahead of them. "If I were the last of my people, I'd find it an honor to tell our stories to anyone who would be willing to listen."

"What about Finni stories?" Felicity inquired.

"No, I would not tell Finni stories. Finni stories are for the Finni to tell. Just like Fauni stories are for the Fauni to tell. At times, our stories may overlap, however, it would be considered a grave injustice for a Fauni to tell a Finni's story – I think."

Vera wrapped their arm around Thora's waist and squeezed her close. "Unless the Finni and Fauni were best friends!"

A low whine caught the attention of Vera and they searched for Gander who, at one point, was a few strides ahead. Instead of finding him near their side, he was sitting on the ground a few paces back, seemingly unwilling to budge. He shifted on his paws and his head feathers flayed out. He bobbed his head, as if he were looking for the means to move forward but all he found was the same obstacle as before.

"Everyone hold up, there's something wrong with Gander." Vera released their friend and hustled to where Gander had rooted. They shifted their fingers so they would weave among the quills on his head in hopes of reassuring him. "What's the matter, boy?"

All Vera received was a whimper.

Aryan and Nam came up alongside Felicity while Thora moved behind and crouched next to Gander to inspect him. His eyes shifted from Vera to a spot in the darkness farther ahead.

"What's the matter with him?" Aryan asked as he shifted his weight onto one hip and cocked his head in concern.

"I'm not sure." Vera replied as they eased into petting the kornig. "He's never acted like this before."

Thora followed his eyes out into the twilight and towards a distant outcropping of rock. She pointed it out to the rest of them. "What's over there?"

They all turned to see whatever the fauni was pointing at.

"That might be the cave." Nam said with a hint of

uncertainty.

"Might be?" Ayran asked as he folded his arms over his chest.

"I don't know, okay?" Nam extended out his arms in surrender. "I've never been here before. It was just what I heard."

Thora recalled the cautionary stories her people had told about the Lost ones. *Dangerous.* She looked back at Gander for a few moments before shifting her gaze to her best friend. "I think Gander is afraid or maybe, afraid for us."

A sense of dread slowly seeped into Vera's chest as they stared at the outcropping, wondering what sort of creature dwelled within the cave and how it was influencing Gander. He was courageous, especially when defending the flock. They'd seen him attack a wyndeg who was trying to pick off one of the kids without fear.. "Maybe..." Vera felt the presence of the unknown growing into some invisible giant now towering over them. "...this isn't such a great idea."

"That's what I said earlier." Thora offered as she stood up and took a step back so she was alongside Gander.

"What, you're scared now?" Nam crossed his arms in protest. "It's just right over there. We go over, take a peek and leave. It's not like it's going to kill us. If it was, Felicity would be dead right now, but she's not."

Aryan jumped in. "I have to agree with Nam on this one. This is supposed to be scary. That's what makes it fun."

"Well, I'm not going to leave Gander here all by himself while the rest of us trek up to the cave." Vera protested.

"If you all want to go up there, you can go ahead." Felicity walked behind Gander. "I'll stay here until you get back. Besides, I've already seen Old Shook, I don't need to see him again."

43

"You see, problem solved." Nam pointed out impatiently.

"Come on, Vera. It'll be exciting. And, if I get in any trouble you can save me." Aryan flashed a smile and offered them a hand of encouragement.

"Fine, I'll go." They relented as they grabbed his hand and pulled closer to him. "If anything, to keep you out of trouble." Vera shot a glance back a Thora. "You don't have to come if you don't want to. We'll be quick."

Thora eyed Gander who was still firmly planted on his behind and shifting in his position as if preparing to move forward despite some invisible restraint. "It could be bad…" She muttered while feelings pulled her in multiple directions. But *"Perhaps"*, she thought, *"the Eternal was indeed harmless."* So with a heavy sigh she said, "…but who am I to stand in the way of fun." Thora skipped a few steps forward before landing her arm around Vera's waist.

The four of them aimed for the cave.

The mouth of it was wide, like the jaws of some terrifying creature, with extended stalactites that barred down like sharpened teeth. The chilling breeze curled inside of it, pulled deep into its hidden crevasses and returned with but a mild howl. It was dark, much like one would expect from a cave. Their dusk sight struggled to make out the shapes of rocks along the path, but it was enough not to trip as they inched along.

Vera wished they had a light of some kind, just something to bring enough features back from the blur that had swallowed the world. The light from morilyn was nowhere near its peak, but it did lend them some reprieve.

"How far in should we go?" Vera whispered so as not to draw the attention of Old Shook, even though that's exactly who they've come to see.

"Until we can't see anymore? There's no sense trying to see

someone if we cannot see." Nam replied, his voice slightly higher in whisper than Vera's.

Thora grabbed hold of Vera's hand to ensure that they wouldn't get separated. "Do you think he's in there?"

"I don't know, it's possible." Aryan observed. "Provided we found the right cave."

"Oh, this is the right cave all right. I can feel it in my bones." Nam took a few steps forward, testing his footing as he went.

Everyone else was right behind him.

They quietly made their way into the cave, the scraping of their footfalls against the rocks echoed into the chamber. They could hear the wind shifting along the ceiling, feeling its way through the darkness of the cave in search of some other way out.

Before long, they ran out of light and their dusk sight began to fail them.

"Is this where we turn back?" Thora asked in such a hushed tone that she worried no one had heard her.

There was a pause but eventually Nam replied, "Not yet… I think I see something ahead."

Vera gave Thora's hand a couple of squeezes to reassure her. They kept their other hand out in order to feel for anything such as a wall or a bit of stone that they otherwise wouldn't have seen. Each step felt as if it would careen into some unseen pit and pull them deep into the earth where'd they'd never be heard from again. But then, Vera saw it too, a glimmer of light caressing the walls of the cave from a side passage. It flickered like a flame's shadow causing their heart to quicken against the thought of coming face to face with an Eternal.

Their mind raced with depictions, trying to postulate out some form of expectation. A finni perhaps, or maybe a finnyr, like in appearance with frazzled hair, a long beard, and threadbare clothes. Perhaps Old Shook was lanky, tall, with really long arms and withered hands tipped with jagged claws. The more they thought about it, the more hideous the creature became; red glowing eyes, blood-stained teeth… Suddenly, as their mind invented horror after horror, they no longer wanted to be in the cave. Try as they might, their feet continued to press them further, following Aryan and Nam towards what seemed to be their end.

The company reached the passage and followed the light, granting them a stronger sense of their environment as the cave slowly revealed itself. There were torches tied to outcroppings of rocks, and beyond them leading towards the scent of a campfire. Nam slid up against the cavern wall, where it curved off to the right. He peered around it, then returned and pointed.

"He's over there." He mouthed without saying the words.

Aryan came up beside him, and peeped as well for what seemed an awfully long time. He came back, shook his head and shrugged his shoulders. Nam took another look and returned with disappointment. Aryan motioned for Vera and Thora to take their turn.

When Vera took a glance, they saw a ramshackle campsite. A low fire burned in a circle of rocks, where a spit hovered over top but had nothing cooking. There were barrels, presumably filled with water, a small hole laden tent that protected a patch of dried grass and blankets. There were baubles hanging from the ceiling affixed by pieces of string, some of them were made of glass and reflected the light from the fire. Yet, Vera could not see any sign of Old Shook. They stepped back, and gave Thora a look, who in turn shrugged their shoulders at the sight of it all.

"Where is he?" Nam asked as softly as he could.

Uncertainty breathed across all of their faces.

Thora looked back toward the way they had come, and her

heart stopped! Her entire body fell into trepidation as standing pressed against the cavern wall, mostly obscured by a hidden niche, was a towering figure. Its head was goat-like, with six arms and hands which pressed against the rocks, with a pair of long sharpened horns jetting from its brow. It stood upon satyr-like legs with hooves for feet.

A scream lurched its way into her throat, and the creature must have anticipated it, as it sprang from its place of hiding and met her gaze with its yellow-cast eyes. Thora reared her head back, her mouth tore agape in terror. It was a motion that roused Vera who gave the creature a swift kick to its torso, causing it to stagger backward.

"Run!" Vera yelled as they yanked Thora's arm and bolted back the way they had come.

Nam and Aryan released a yelp and they fled as quickly as they could. Thora was bewildered as she tried to make sense of her surroundings. She pulled her hand away from Vera's and stumbled from delirium. Vera stopped to grab her, but Nam and Aryan both tucked their arm beneath Thora's, plucked her up off the ground, and sped out of the cave with Vera close behind.

They ran as swiftly and as far as they could, and upon reaching Felicity and Gander, kept running. Without even asking, Felicity and the kornig followed after, taking flight as far from the cave as their legs and lungs could muster.

Chapter 6
Of Visions

"No matter how well planned, the future is never set. All we can ever do is our best, to aim for the planet below, the moons above, and the stars beyond and hope we catch the slightest glimpse of what could be and pray their guidance reflects well within us. The Rushinay was built to preserve our species from the never-ending assaults of the narghoulim. Families, bloodlines, entire ways of life lost in the jaws of oblivion. We must continue to stand together or we will fall."

– Aness Leekyn Shreeves Cali

"Thora! Thora!" Vera shook their friend who was stuck in a daze.

They had reached the safety of their campsite, far enough – it would seem – away from the accursed cave and Old Shook. Vera was trembling. Their childish sense of adventure had harmed their best friend. They blamed themselves. If Vera had heeded Thora's reservations none of this would have happened.

Vera cupped their hands against her cheeks to cradle their head. Vera looked deeply into her eyes. "Please snap out of it!"

Thora was distant, her eyes cloudy, like a swirl of murkiness which reached back to the deepest portions of her mind.

Gander whimpered his own vexations and worry.

"This is your fault, Nam!" Felicity jabbed her finger into the finnae's sternum. "If it wasn't for that kaedra-cursed idea of yours, Thora wouldn't be like this."

"How was I supposed to know that this is what would happen?!" He shouted back to defend himself both against Felicity and also the guilt which trying to well up his throat. "Besides, she didn't have to come along, she chose to come with us, which means it's just as much on her as the rest of us."

"Hey!" Vera barked over their shoulder at the feuding teens. "This isn't helping! *You're* not helping!"

Aryan was pacing back and forth, not knowing what to do until an idea jumped into his head. "Maybe she's cursed! How do we break curses?" His fingers drummed across his lips. He snapped his fingers. "True love's kiss! Is Thora dating anyone?"

"What? No! What's wrong with you!?" Vera angrily spat back.

Felicity retreated from her assault against Nam and slid forward, "No, he's right! True love's kiss can remove curses. You're best friends, right? Maybe that'll be enough."

"I'm not kissing Vera without her permission and she's practically comatose!"

"But you've kissed before, right?" Nam asked as he crowded around Felicity and Aryan who now hovered above Vera and Thora.

"Just on the cheek a couple times. As friends."

"Then kiss her on the cheek as friends!" Aryan encouraged with desperation settled deep into his voice.

"Geez, fine! I'll kiss her." Vera was now as uncomfortable as they were panicked. But, what other options did they have? They knew a pantomime to heal wounds and remove disease that they had used on animals before, and while likely that Thora would consent to having them used upon her to bring her back from whatever affliction she currently suffered from, it was very unlikely that the pantomime would have much effect since none of those fell beneath the influence of Vera's star constellation.

Vera leaned in and gave Thora a quick peck on the cheek, much in the same way as they had previously kissed in the past – as anything else would seem beyond what they've consented to. There seemed to be no change in her symptoms.

49

"You call that a kiss?" Nam asked, but was elbowed by Felicity.

"This isn't for your judgment or entertainment." Felicity shot him daggers and Nam shrunk down inside himself.

"I'm sorry." He muttered then remained silent.

"Thora! Come on. Don't make me have to get an adult, they'd be really mad." Vera half-joked as tears welled up in their eyes.

Gander's ears suddenly lifted as if he had smelled something on the wind. Then Thora seized Vera's wrist, and squeezed it tightly as she took a huge gulp of air as if she had been drowning.

The whiteness in her eyes cleared like the parting of mist. She violently pulled her arms and legs close to herself and scuttled backward a full stride, before recognizing her current surroundings. Everyone else reared back uncertain what was to happen next. However, Thora looked around, then landed on the familiar face of her best friend. Her fingers fell upon her cheek.

"Did you kiss me?" Thora asked all confused.

Vera lurched forward and wrapped her arms around the Fauni. "I'm so glad you're okay! I was so worried! Everyone thought you were cursed and so I kissed you to break the spell."

"No, I..." Thora took a big breath and wrapped her arms around her friend. She pressed her cheek against Vera's head. "I wasn't cursed, I—I had so many images, sounds and feelings inside my head it was so overwhelming, and I saw... Vera you..."

"What did you see?" Felicity pressed.

Aryan too was eager to know. "Yes! Tell us what you saw!"

There was a quiver in her voice, a sorrowful plunge into

some internal void as she remembered one scene in particular, one that had played in great detail over and over again. The cracks… her best friend. "I…" she shook her head and did her best to push it deep inside of herself. "I saw something… I just don't want to talk about it."

Felicity's eyes widened with realization. "You saw the future, didn't you?"

Vera interjected. "She said she doesn't want to talk about it. How about you all just lay off. What's important is that she's okay!"

Felicity sighed and relented. "You're right. I'm glad you're okay."

Aryan looked around at their campsite then tried to gauge the level of dim in the sky. "We should head back. We need to get dressed and ready for the Danse de L'arrivée. Vera, you'll be there, right?"

Vera examined Thora's olive face to double check that she was fine before responding, "And watch you all fall flat on your faces? I wouldn't miss it!"

"In that you're going to be greatly disappointed!" Nam threw his arm around Aryan's shoulder. "I'll have you know that we're the best dancers Tandermundt has ever seen or ever will see."

"You better hope so, I would hate for your handfasting to be darkened by a misstep."

"Yeah, yeah…" Nam waved the notion away as if it were unpalatable food at a royal setting.

"Are you going to be okay to walk?" Vera asked. "If not, we can just sit by the fire for a while and warm up."

Thora shook her head, her antlers carving through the breeze. "No, I can walk. I want to get out of here."

Vera nodded and helped their friend to her feet, and together they made their way back towards the village.

As they neared the edges of Tandermundt, Vera and Thora said their goodbyes to everyone before heading back towards Vera's home. Vera locked arms with Thora and they walked close together as Gander followed.

"I know you didn't want to talk about what you saw, but I'm not sure if you were just not feeling comfortable with them around. If you want to, I'd be happy to listen." Vera offered with sincerity.

Thora was hesitant, thinking of what or how exactly she was to put it all into words. She realized that she didn't have the capability to fully describe what she saw, or how even she felt. "It came so fast. And I'm afraid."

"Afraid of what?"

"That if I were to say it, that it would all become real. In my head, it's purely fiction. Like a thought that would pass in time or a dream."

"That makes perfect sense. It must be horrible for you." Vera placed their free hand over top of Thora's arm and rested it there for comfort.

"I saw… a lot of death. There were some good things, I think. Beautiful things. Yet it all ended with death."

"Whose death?" Vera asked as they continued their path through the tall grass belonging to the pasture that bordered Vera's family homestead.

Thora shook her head. "I won't let it be real."

The both of them continued to walk in silence until they reached Vera's home.

Gander shot ahead of them in the last leg, barking happily to announce their return. A light danced in the window from a pantomime that Vera's mother had placed there earlier today.

"We shouldn't be too long. I just need to get changed then we can head to the festival, if you're okay with that."

"Sounds fun." Thora shot back with a smile, hoping that the festival will help take her mind off of things. "I can go for something a little more normal."

The house was modest, with a wood exterior and a thatch roof. The outside was painted white, and had a variety of night flowers blooming in the window. As soon as they transitioned into morilyn, Vera would help their parents in transplanting day flowers. Despite the work, it was something that Vera looked forward to.

The oak door to the home opened, and out stepped their mother. She displayed her finest dress made of nyri silk which had come all the way from the Island of Niece. She had purchased it from traders just last season. Vera shared their mother's hair color, a dark auburn, which was down and set with cowrie shells and yellow and orange agate beads. She was in the process of clasping her wrothlyn fur cloak which would hang from her left shoulder in order to properly display the shoulder guard with red feathers. This was rarely the norm for their household, as most occasions they all dressed practically. Every cycle they worked alongside one another in care of the goats, keeping the animal pens, the fencing and the rest of the home maintained. They were the Kom family, and Vera's mother was the Shem of their village, a title of leadership.

Illify smiled at Vera and gave a slight bow to Thora, as was her custom when greeting anyone in order for them to feel welcome in her company. "Hello, Thora, it's so wonderful to see you. I know Vera has been looking forward to spending time with you. Have you three been catching up?" She raised an eyebrow to the kornig so he felt included.

Thora bowed slightly out of courtesy. "It's good to see you too! I'm always excited to return to Tandermundt, everyone here is very nice and hospitable. Vera, Gander and I have been having a fantastic time!"

"Look!" Vera displayed the knife that Thora had given them previously. "It's an early birthday gift. The handle is made out of one of Thora's antlers! Can you believe it? And the blade is obsidian!"

"Thora, you show amazing matrony in your craft. The dagger is exquisite! I'm sure that Vera will always treasure it."

Vera stowed the knife back into its sheath and placed it firmly on their belt. Their face softened with admiration. "You look beautiful mom."

"Thank you, but you forgot 'brilliant' as well." She winked at her child. "Your father and I are heading to the village now, there's a few things that I need to check on before things begin." She shifted her cloak. "I know I promised you free of chores today, but getting dressed took longer than what I anticipated and I didn't get a chance to check in with Gorn. He was kind enough to watch the goats for us this evening. There's a basket filled with food that I've prepared for him. Can you fetch it off the dining table and take it to him for me after you're done getting ready? I know he'd very much appreciate it, especially coming from you. You can take Thora with you and show her how much the trip has grown."

Thora gasped. "Do you have baby goats?!" She bounced with excitement.

"Of course, we have baby goats." Illify chuckled.

"VERA!?" Thora exclaimed before their friend had an opportunity to say anything. "WE HAVE TO SEE THE BABY GOATS!"

"Wow! Okay, I guess we'll bring the basket to Gorn and see

the baby goats." Vera's eyebrows raised with Thora's passionate outburst despite finding her excitement contagious.

Their mother teased, "Be sure to hurry though, you wouldn't want to miss Aryan dancing now, would you?"

"Aryan... Aryan... that name sounds familiar..." Vera feigned ignorance in order to reduce the chances of them blushing.

"Funny. Just like your father. Okay, give me a squeeze, I need to be off."

Vera walked up to their mother and wrapped their arms around her. They could feel the warmth and the familiar smell that reminded them of home and safety. Her mother's hands fell behind their back and the nap of their neck. She squeezed them tightly. Beautiful. Soft.

"I'll see you soon, mom."

Chapter 7
Baby Goat

"The narghoulim are revenants of old gods. They are primal and as uncaring as they are Eternal. These beings are possessed with the complete annihilation of the Finni species, spawned with an insatiable bloodlust that eradicates all life within their path. They are forces of destruction and elements of devastation. They have no need to eat, sleep or breathe. They are relentless in their killing, much so that even when felled, their taint inevitably resurrects them from beyond to feed once again."

– Lessons for a Chevalière, Coppélia

As Gander quenched his thirst from a bowl of water on the floor, the two of them visited Vera's room, which was small by most Finni's standard but far more spacious than the red-colored wagons that Thora was accustomed to.

While Thora sat upon Vera's bed, inspecting the contents of the room, Vera stripped off their clothes and changed into a blue undershirt, with a black corset-like top and a half-skirt, which was pleated in the back to appear like tail feathers. The skirt complimented the shoulders which were composed of pleated cotton that draped like a pair of folded wings. They slipped into tight nyri silk leggings which warmed with the body even in cold temperatures, and clasped a fur-lined cloak over their neck. There was a headpiece that their mother had insisted that they wear in order to reaffirm Vera's status among the villagers. They made it together, with curled pieces of copper twisted and shaped to look like vines and several black blade-like feathers, some a foot in length spread like a swan about to take flight.

Thora giggled at the adornment when Vera put it on their head. "That's very flashy." She said with as much support as she could muster.

Vera sighed and took it off. "I like it… just on other people."

The finni eased off the bed and rested her hands on one of Vera's shoulders. "You know, people in Adalace wear this kind of thing on a daily basis but often disguise themselves with masks. It's very enchanting, especially since people can display their vanity without it reflecting poorly upon themselves."

"I wish I could wear a mask, maybe then I wouldn't feel like everyone was staring at me."

"Well, if they are staring at you, it's because they admire you. And if it's Aryan who is staring at you, then it's because he admires you more." She smiled. "Now…" She cupped her friend's cheeks in the palms of her hands. "Show me baby goats!"

Vera laughed and pushed her gently away. "You are obsessed!"

Gander barked twice, then panted with eagerness before racing for the front door where Vera grabbed the basket on their way out.

Outside, the air was still brisk and carried the scent of dancer's trees across the moor, which was lightly sweet and mixed with the distant scent of the sea. Soon the trees would shed their bark, revealing a pristine white wood and the limbs would blossom with white star-shaped flowers which would remain until the end of morilyn, before being carried away by the tillmet winds.

They took the dirt path that Vera's family had worn into the ground from generations of shepherding. Their family had been here for over 80 years, from their mother's telling. Snuggled under a blanket and warming next to the hearth, their matron would tell them stories of all who had come before them and would recite them by heart, but Vera always struggled with remembering each of their names. It had all been written down in the family book, a token for them to hold onto if ever they wished to feel a connection to where they came from.

While the moor looked vacant in some areas, the ups and downs of the hills, and the gray stone outcroppings, smoothed by the wind, gave Vera a sense of wonder and magic about the place.

Their dusk sight helped them navigate through the dim. Vera returned to where they had been previously been keeping to find Gorn waist deep in goats, herding them close to him. Worms of warning crept across their chest, alerting them that something had to be wrong. Gander barked then his head feathers raised slightly to convey his own sense of caution.

"Something is wrong." The finni expelled as they hustled down the hillside.

"Why what's happened?" Thora hurried after.

Vera began to count as they rushed down the hillside to meet him. 72. They counted again as they got closer, doubting as to whether they had missed one in the huddle, but still the number had remained the same.

"Gorn!" Vera shouted. "What's wrong?"

"Vera, by the NIИ it's good to see you." He leaned on a wooden crook, clutching it tightly in his aged hands. His hair was disheveled, fluttering like pale wisps in the air. He was faun blessed, much as Vera was, which had served as a means for the two to bond as they had grown up. "Something spooked the trip. Sent them scattering in all directions. Took a lot of time to calm them all. I'm not as quick as I once was."

Thora eased onto one knee to pet the nearest goat. She rubbed her fingers between its horns, and gave some scratches to the winged-like feathers that sprouted from atop the beast's ears. The goat was incredibly calm, which only meant that it was beneath a pantomime for the time being.

"I only count 72. Is that right?" It had been a long time since a goat had gone missing and each time it was as if a heavy stone had lodged itself in their stomach, even worse when it was their fault.

"Aye, 72. A kid went over the western hill. Once I had gotten the majority under spell, I went to check but wasn't able to see it. You think Gander would be able to track it down?"

Vera glanced at their kornig then quickly shot their gaze off in the direction that Gorn had indicated and frowned. "I'm supposed to be at the festival. Aryan is performing in the Danse de L'arrivée this year. We could miss it."

Gorn remained quiet as he recognized their disappointment. He knew that they were working it out in their mind and that it was one of those pivotal moments in a child's life where they are met with managing responsibility.

"Hey… Thora bumped Vera's hip with her own. Gander can sniff out the kid, right? Maybe he'll find them quicker than you think."

Gander strolled over to Vera's side and sat on the ground. He looked up at them and started panting, with an optimistic look across his face – if ever a kornig could.

The finni placed their hand upon his head and scratched beneath his quills as a means to bolster their own confidence. "Okay boy…" Vera muttered with a sigh. "Let's sniff out that kid and bring them home."

Gander barked in compliance, sniffed the air, then the ground. He shifted his head back and forth, searching for the right scent, but then his eyebrow ridges pulled back then his legs kicked off as he raced after a distant odor with Vera and Thora in pursuit.

The kornig's nose kept to the ground, shifting through the varying smells wafting up from the earth. The capa grass was thick, with morilyn trumpets just starting to bloom, moor brush, and malfinae bushes. To one with a sensitive nose, they were prominent in scent, but nothing in comparison to the familiar essence of a goat. It was leading them further west and slightly north, a fair distance from Tandermundt.

Perhaps if they brought the goat with them to the festival… Vera wondered. *We could make it in time.*

They walked for perhaps ten minutes or more, until they reached the summit of a smaller hill. It was there at the top, that Gander barked toward a distant silhouette near the edge of their dusk sight, dimmed in clarity by the struggling light from the east. It appeared white, though small, standing at the mouth of Hagerd's Ravine. Not the normal place for a goat, let alone a kid, to wander to.

"If only I could reach the goat with a pantomime, I could lure them back towards us." Vera expelled as they quickened their step behind Gander. As it were, Vera would have to be within their wingspan, which was far closer than what they currently were.

"Let's hurry down. We might be able to catch them before they…" The kid bleated in protest to their presence and disappeared down into the gullet of the ravine. "Now why would you go and do a thing like that!" Thora protested. "We just want to return you to your family, and probably pet you and snuggle you!"

Vera smiled widely. "That sounds like a pretty great offer!" They shouted after the kid. "You're really going to miss out if you don't come back!"

There wasn't any response from the kid, now further between the steep-sided cliffs and likely shielded from hearing them.

Gander barked a few additional times as he bounded down the hill and towards the entrance to the ravine. His nose, from time to time, would dive towards the ground, sniffing in odd crescent patterns, before raising his head and continuing his pursuit.

The sky changed as they reached the last place the kid had previously been seen. A gathering of dark clouds choked back the rousing light, which stirred the wind into a harsher breeze, one which stung with the chill of dropping temperatures. The weather was supposed to be clear today, yet the sudden shift in the sky's demeanor left them feeling as if they were about to trespass on sacred ground.

The ravine itself was narrow, filled with rocks, and held a few sparse trees. Somewhere, they could hear water bubbling from farther within, though its origination came shrouded in shadows of handfuls of craigs.

Their dusk sight did not reveal where the goat had bounded off to. "Keep on them, Gander. The sooner we catch up to the kid, the sooner we can go to the festival."

Gander continued to sniff the ground, as well as the surrounding plants and boulders in search of the missing goat. Vera and Thora kept close behind, keeping their eyes darting from niche to cranny. The kid couldn't have gone far.

Above them, stalked a bulky shadow. It kept itself low, with its paws stepping lightly along a ledge overlooking the ravine wherein lay its prey. Its claws gripped the edge, as it craned its neck in order to assess the tasty morsels who wandered beneath it unaware of its presence. A voice, a ravenous command, nestled inside its brain urging it forward despite the presence of the other beast. It knew it would prevail. It *needed* to prevail. *Kill*, the voice commanded, *Kill!*

Following his nose, Gander lifted his head and barked in the direction of where the kid hid, behind a craig not a few paces away. Vera rushed to where the kornig had indicated, and it was there she found it, pacing back and forth as if confused by all that was around them. "Hey there…" Vera cradled the baby goat into their arms and pulled them close to their chest. "You little troublemaker."

Thora skipped up to them and rubbed the goat lightly beneath the chin. "You're so adorably cute!" She squeed.

Gander panted enthusiastically and wagged his tail. However, his nose, no longer buried in the scent of the missing, caught something sinister in the air. Gander raised his head. Following the invisible trail, his nose took his attention up the rocky hill face and to a ledge where a pair of blazing eyes and a bloodthirsty jaw belonged to a lupine shape against the cliff.

Thora and Vera's ears were accosted by two separate beasts bearing their teeth, growling at the other, where one was their beloved Gander, and the other a blackened nightmarish creature illuminated by a flash of green lightning.

Chapter 8
Stalked

"The ordinary animals of Orabelle are vast and varied. However, a particular characteristic that is shared by many are their feathers. It is surmised that these feathers originated during the epoch of the Kamar who dwelled long ago on the Island of Niece. It is uncertain as to why massive species evolved to include feathers, even ones whose past physiology showed no evidence in their lineage. Finni and Fauni have appropriated these feathers for use in their everyday clothing and accessories, even so much where feathers are utilized as currency atop the run of the mill cowrie shell."

-Observations of Fauna

The predator's pelt was the color of the void, with dark coal eyes and a pair of sharp horns which swept backwards from between its ears. Along its spine were serrated spikes that appeared as if it could impale a falling leaf, and extended all the way to the tip of its three-foot tail. It was as big as Gander, about five feet in length and four feet in height with massive muscles which tensed as it prepared to launch itself into an attack.

Vera knew it to be a wyndeg, an animal who would prey upon their goats, and if food was scarce enough, Finni children. The creature's claws dug into the stone outcropping as Gander snarled at his adversary. The feathers atop his head and back extended, causing him to appear like an agitated porcupine. Gander gnashed his teeth as a warning but the wyndeg could not be intimidated.

Thora pulled a knife from her belt and brandished it in front of her. Her knees bent, positioning her lower to the ground and she widened her stance so that she could dodge or stab at a second's need.

"Get behind me!" She yelled to Vera. "Keep back!"

Their aether had always warned, *never get close to a wyndeg, even if it meant losing a member of the flock.* Wyndeg's were dangerous and unpredictable, as wild as they came and twice as voracious. Vera held tightly to the kid in their hands, and the goat bleated.

"Don't hurt Gander!" Vera shouted at the beast, in hopes of spooking it.

Yet it wasn't enough to prevent the wyndeg from leaping down atop him with claws extended and maw agape!

Gander jumped backwards, which left the wyndeg to snap at empty air. As soon as he was clear, the kornig lunged forward with his teeth, growling and barking to assert his superiority and strength. The wyndeg turned enough that Gander's muzzle only skimmed off his flank, before it spun around to launch its next attack. Both brutes raised onto their hind legs, and dug their paws into the other's shoulders while tearing at the air with their baying. Each thrashed their heads about, knocking each other's muzzles to the side as the other attempted to latch onto the other's throat!

Vera's pantomimes flashed through their head like pages on a book, frantically looking for something that would help: *hide, heal, attract, command, sooth* and *vanish.* All but one did they claim matrony over..

As the hounds continued to do battle, and Thora stood ready with her knife, Vera placed the baby goat near a small niche in the rock face nearby and drew upon themself on the sooth pantomime. As they had done previously this day, Vera followed their teachings perfectly and caused a blue ball of light to manifest before them and it dissolved into the animal's white fur, preventing it from wanting to wander off or being scared away. Quickly, the kid's demeanor changed, causing it to lay down as if relaxing in the shade beneath the sun.

Their own words echoed in their mind from early, "*No*

Farther than One's Wing". Vera had to get close; too close. They could get caught in the tussle, injured, but what if Gander or even Thora got hurt – or worse, died. Without giving more moment's hesitation, Vera rushed towards the thrashing beasts. Their feet skidded against the rocks, kicking pebbles onto the battlefield as the dogs continued to gnash at one another, pushing each other one way, breaking apart, only to come back together again, face-to-face and tooth-to-tooth.

Thora came behind her friend, ready to pull them away at a moment's notice should she prove to be quick enough. She wanted to shout, to draw her friend away from the violence, but saying something could draw the predator's attention which could only make things worse.

Vera hastily drew their hands towards themselves, flayed out their fingers as before and touched their thumbs and pointer fingers together. They felt the energy as it flowed through them, rolled up into their chest and settled into their heart. They pushed the energy out demanding the wyndeg to run away! A surge of electrical pulses flooded from Vera's chest and arched between the space for which they inhabited and struck the wyndeg. The creature immediately dropped to its four paws and backed away, growling at the intrusion of yet another voice within them.

Gander planted himself on his own four paws and bared his fangs at his opponent. He barked, tossing spit from his mouth onto the ground.

The dark-hide creature tossed its head back and forth as it backed itself against the side of the ravine. *Kill! Flee! Kill! Flee!* Each word pounded against the inside of its skull, uncertain of which to follow. It snapped at the air in front of it, with its head downcast and eyes staring into the ground as if it would somehow release it from its inner struggle. It fought through hunger, and safety, but still arrived at the same impasse.

Gander readied himself, positioning his muscles to allow

him one fierce launch that would allow him to seize the creature by the throat and to put down the threat for good, but he cut his snarl. Both animals did. Their ears perked and their tails lowered. They both sniffed the air.

The wyndeg bolted to the entrance of the ravine, it howled a short desperate cry before vanishing completely. Gander did not watch it go, instead his paws shifted weight, then drew up off the ground only to be replaced on the ground again. There was something wrong, something in the air that now threatened to overcome them. He whined a high-pitched song of sadness and worry that pierced their ears. Gander was afraid.

A bolt of green lightning cracked from overhead as a burst of wind carved its way through the ravine. The wind struck them in the chest, causing them to stagger, as a hellish roar ripped through the passage. Thora sheathed her dagger, grabbed the baby goat and together, the four of them took cover behind a large craig. The wind whipped through, screaming like the chorus of tortured souls, causing the ground to shake. A loud thumping sound bore into their bodies and reverberated in their bones.

"What is happening!?" Vera shouted, but their words were smothered by the shrieks and rumbling of the wind.

Dirt, rocks and vegetation flew past them, with some blasting against the very rock that shielded them. Vera slung an arm around Gander's neck while another gripped Thora's hand tightly. All huddled close, pressing themselves against the stone as if it were their only raft in an unforgiving ocean.

Complete darkness descended upon them, lit only by the now ever-present maleficence that tore the sky in flashing emerald claws. *Thump! Thump! Thump!*

As quickly as it had come, the wind ceased, the lightning vanished, and the roar abated. The thumping was gone. The sky cleared, allowing for their dusk sight to return.

Dazed and bewildered, Thora cautiously eased to standing with the kid in her arms. "What was that?" She asked without expecting much of an answer.

Gander began panting happily, and even wagged his tail; thankful that they all emerged unscathed.

Vera gazed about, looking for signs of what could have caused the strange phenomenon. They had never experienced anything like it before, nor ever heard any stories from her parents or village elders that would even come close to what just occurred. Almost anything... something did come to Vera's mind, but it wasn't something they wanted to consider, or speak aloud for that matter.

"If it were true..." Vera muttered uncertain as to what it all could mean.

Thora helped them to stand by offering a hand up. "If what were true?" Thora begged with pleading eyes.

"Nothing." A feeling of dread swept over them and it laid down on their chest, causing all their veins to feel as if wracked with poison. Something in them made them ache, a hidden fear that made everything feel wrong.

In fact, something was wrong. Something was very, very wrong.

"Come on." Vera encouraged, desperate to prove their feelings incorrect. "We should get back."

"We should hurry." Thora insisted.

And they did... slow at first, but their legs picked up and they rushed out of the ravine and broke into a run. They ran as quickly as they could, with Gander alongside them, as far as their legs would carry them. Vera's heart pounded in their chest, quickened by the horror that squatted at the edge of their waking mind.

They returned to where the goats grazed but did not find any goats. Gorn's wrinkled face was not in his usual place. The field was empty, rocks and other debris scattered about. There were a few planks of wood, and pieces of what appeared to be a broken dish. A chill descended down Vera's back as they looked in all directions, searching for signs of which direction they may have gone. Vera's breathing increased, became heavy and difficult.

Thora looked each way as well and clutched tightly to the goat. "Where are they?"

Gander smelled the ground, and sniffed himself in circles before coming up with nothing but a low whine that something was terribly amiss.

"I…" tears started to well in Vera's eyes. "I don't know. It's too early to shift them south. Maybe they went south? Gorn was supposed to wait. Where's Gorn?"

"We should find your parents. I'm sure they'd know what to do." Thora insisted.

"Yes… they're at the festival back in Tandermundt. They'll know…" The coming of the storm, its ferocity, the noise. All of it sounded hungry and malicious, and it gnawed at their insides. Vera felt sick, as something awful churned in their stomach and tied itself into a pretzel. Suddenly, they were afraid. Not afraid of any anger that their parents would have for all the missing goats. They knew they wouldn't blame them for that. No, they were afraid of Tandermundt and what they would discover there.

Vera swallowed hard and hurried in that direction. Each step felt like there were boulders tied to their feet. Each foot wishing it could root itself into the ground. The air smelled heavily of dirt and freshly reaped grass.

Thora was in pursuit, keeping as close to her friend as possible as Gander ran alongside. The hound stopped only momentarily from time to time as he thought he caught a whiff of something familiar but like the goats, it soon vanished.

It was frighteningly quiet. Not a light could be seen with the exception of Longlyn's haunting blues and the spectral glow of the sister moons, Tshir and Illune. They all hung in the sky, like disembodied eyes staring down at them as they made their way back to the village.

When they got there, they were not greeted by the sounds of the festival, the familiar faces of family, or the accustomed homes belonging to all of Vera's neighbors. Not a light, nor a sound, no face or horn could be spotted.

There was nothing save for rubble and desolation.

Chapter 9
Gone Over the Mountains

"The narghoulim comes! Snickity-snack — with jaws of steel and claws a'clack! Gnash — Gnaw — Bite — Thraw! Here it comes over the mountains, child. Here it comes over the mountains. The narghoulim comes! The narghoulim comes! Tumble down, scamper past. Find your love — enfold and clasp. Dripity-drop, the waterclock stops. There we go over the mountain, child. There we end over the mountains."

– Finni nursery rhyme.

Skeletal outlines of stone foundations laid bare where once there were houses. The ceramic tiled roofs were gone. Their wooden walls were missing. All which remained were the dirt roads, wooden floors, and the stone waist-high walls which lined a few streets.

Panic coursed through them, beating with such intensity, that it felt as if insects now burrowed through their veins. *Thump. Thump. Thump.* Vera's eyes widened to take in the nightmare, to comprehend that everything was gone, while at the same time their mind refused to accept what was.

"Mom! Dad!" Vera shouted as they ran down the dirt road and toward the center of the village. They flung themselves in every direction, casting their eyes among the wreckage; searching for anything or anyone familiar. "Ayren! You idiot! Where are you?!"

Thora couldn't move. Her grip remained solid around the kid, fearing that should she let go, that it too would be taken by the winds. Gander lowered himself to the earth, dropped his head and whined. For him, there were no familiar scents. No remnants of the people he once knew.

"Mom!" Vera shouted once more as they scrambled up a

short wall, knocking a few loose stones to the ground, and stood atop it, scanning everywhere their dusk sight revealed. "Dad!" Came their echo. "Aryan...?" Their voice descended into a whisper as water beaded in their eyes. "Felicity... Nam..." They almost lost their balance, staggered, then they lowered themselves down to perch. "Where are you...?"

The cool wind licked their face and for a moment, Vera thought they caught the scent of their father in the breeze, but it was faint and it was brief. "No!" Vera screamed to the sky. "NO!" They grabbed a few stones and threw them at the coming of morilyn. "WHERE ARE YOU!?" They wailed. "WHERE?!" More rocks came into their hands and were flung into the ruins, plinking off foundations or skipping off into the twilight. And when all the rocks were gone, Vera kicked the wall over and over again, kicking even when it hurt in order to get more. "COME BACK! COME BACK! COME BACK!"

Thora couldn't watch anymore. She ran to where her best friend was emotionally dissolving and wrapped an arm around their front from behind and drew them close.

Vera continued to kick at the wall, their toenails pushing into cuticles and now bled through their shoes. "NO!" They fought to kick at it some more. "NO-NO-NO-No-No..." A couple additional kicks missed their target and instead passed helplessly through the wind. Thora pulled them back, towards the ground, where Vera collapsed in a fit of tears. Their breathing was labored as they struggled to catch the fleeting air.

Thora tried to shush them, to calm them down. "I'm here. I'm here, okay? I'm here."

Gander bounded over and laid down where Vera sprawled, nuzzled his nose beneath their hands, and pressed his face against their chest.

Vera stopped moving and stared into a void that only they could see. "Where are they, Gander... where did they go?" Their voice fell into a whisper. "Where did they go?"

Thora didn't want to say it aloud, but Thora knew where they went. She knew exactly what had happened. To speak it was both damning and a curse. *Narghoulim.* They were gone... *all taken over the mountain.*

Vera stopped speaking. They simply stared at the emptiness of their village, the quiet that was left behind on a day which should have been filled with joyous revelry. The village was supposed to smell like wild berry tarts, roasted peppifowl, roasted nuts and plumb pie. Thinking about it made them sick in the throat, this atop the stabbing of a thousand pins beneath their skin that seemed to bury themselves inside their veins.

Tears shed from Thora's eyes like two brooks, which cascaded off her cheeks and drizzled overtop her friend. This wasn't the first time that Thora had experienced the aftermath of a village victimized by a narghoulim, and as much as she could hope she knew it probably wouldn't be the last.

Something caught at the edge of Thora's peripheral and she looked up to see three figures standing at the entrance of the village, their heads adorn with antlers and long red hooded cloaks enveloping them down to the ankles. They bore spears upon their backs and caution on their faces.

The fire crackled like the splitting of bones as Vera sat upon a pillow graciously provided by Thora's tribe. Thora sat alongside them, staring into the flames as if it were a gateway into the future, one no longer filled with the cruelties of death clinging to her insides just grasping at her throat - screaming to be released. A sickness crept along her organs and forced her insides to trepidation.

Vera clung to Gander tightly, while slowly petting the still enchanted goat in their arms. Thora hoped that it would be a comfort to them, something familiar and homely, but comforts only went so far in these circumstances.

Vera stared blankly, their emotions swirling within them like a squall, one built on green lightning and a harrowing howl. A red cloak was draped around Vera's shoulders, a desire to keep them as warm as possible – anything to keep back the chill that was still slowly melting away with the rising of the sun.

Gone... Vera blinked and there was an older fauni folded into a sitting position across from them. The rest of Thora's tribe kept within the firelight, some standing, others leaning against their red-covered caravans. Listening. Waiting.

The older individual had antlers at least three feet in length, with several fine golden chains dangling between the points and connecting to others. Their hair was tied back into a bun, which was silver in color, and their eyes were a brilliant violet which seemingly glowed in the firelight. They wore a loose shirt over their thin graceful frame, with a wool vest, and darkly colored breeches and boots.

"I'm Shem Zhalinya Faunis. In this moment, I am he. I knew your parents. They were warm-hearted welcoming people who did everything in their power to make us feel like we belonged. The Caetins have always been friends of the Zhalinya. That's why we kept returning. Because of them, Thora was able to make a brave and honorable friend in you. Believe me when I say, I am sorry for their loss and the loss of your village. They will always hold a place in our heart." He paused for a few moments, as if the heat from the fire was needed in order to embolden his words. "The narghoulim who has trespassed here is known to us. I'm sorry to say, as you've been through so much already, but it will return to find you."

Those words burrowed deep into Vera's crumbling psyche. Vera quivered inside as dread reawakened inside their lungs. "What—" the words fainted in their throat, and they had to begin again, "What do you mean?"

"Most narghoulim, they travel in a single path and they devastate everything they come across. This particular one is especially meticulous. Once it has a taste of a people, it will continue to seek them until there are no more. It will hunt you, Vera. It will not stop, unless you are destroyed. I say this, not to frighten you, but to arm you. You must go where it will be too afraid to follow. You must go quickly." The Shem explained as calmly as he could manage.

"—Where?" Vera coughed out as they drew the red cloak tighter around them and embosomed the kid closer to their chest, resting their own chin on the goat's head, in desperation of quieting the quickening of their heart and to dispel the shakes.

"Adalace. Home of the chevalières, the narghoulim slayers. It is ground that those abominations will not tread. You will be safe there. Speak to Leekyn Shreeves Cali – the Aness – and invoke my name. She will help you find your place."

Vera tore their gaze from the fire and gazed hopeful towards the person across from them. "The Aness? You know the Aness of the Rushinay?"

"We've had conversations. If there is anyone in this world who can help you, it is her."

Their hands rolled over the goat's soft hide. "But, how will I get there? I can't get there on my own. And—" tears welled back within their eyes, "I don't have anything…"

"My dear sweet friend… the Zhalinya will provide. We will accompany you to the north. Take you as far as Cornelis, where the Serishone meets the Anesian Coast. From there, you'll need to book passage to Adalace. Now, listen…" He leaned in, allowing the flames to highlight his face as clearly as possible. "No matter what, you must never stop moving. To stop, is to invite death. Should you need to stop, you must seek shelter underground. Now, repeat to me what I just said."

Vera's heart continued to tremble, but they forced themselves to comply. "Book passage to Adalace in Cornelis. Never stop. If I have to stop, do so underground. But... what if I get lost?"

"You won't get lost." Thora interjected with steadfast determination. "Because I'm going with you."

The Zhalinya had camped east of Tandermundt. They slept and carried their belongings in red covered wagons which were drawn by large two-horned beasts called the gorm. The creatures snorted in minor protest as they were hitched to the front of the wagons, bowing their heads then goring the air with their curled horns, while stabbing with their straightened set. They were at least six feet in height, with the largest of them being around seven-foot tall, from head to bottom of their hooves. They had four legs, a short tail ending in a hairy tuft, and wide faces. Their charcoal eyes shifted back and forth, betraying a nervousness that Vera had recognized from how goats would respond to a hidden predator.

Thora had given Vera some of her clothes, which fit snuggly yet made them appear as if they were a Fauni who had recently shed their antlers. The clothes that they had worn for the festival were rolled up and placed in a separate pack, with their head piece carefully wrapped to prevent damage. In addition, Vera was given a satchel to carry some salted meats, honey buns and goats cheese; a water flask, as well as a pouch with 25 cowrie shells to afford them passage and purchase additional rations if needed. Everything was happening so fast it was making them feel like they were watching it all unfold from a safe distance.

As soon as all the animals were properly hitched, the Fauni all climbed into their respective wagons, while their teamsters clicked at their gorm to signal it was time to start moving. Gander kept alongside the wagon which both Vera and Thora sat within, where Thora kicked their legs out the back. It was as if cobwebs adhered Vera in place, lost in time, as they watched as the familiar landscape slowly faded into the distance. It had been a long time since they had left Tandermundt – a place they knew they would likely never see again. The kid still in their lap.

Everything was a bad dream, that any moment Vera would wake and their mother would be cooking alongside their father. That they'd all have breakfast together. Their father would give them pantomime lessons and their mother would later discuss family history from a book that was forever gone.

Vera knew that their village, friends and family were dead. Yet, they felt as if they had all decided to pick up and move somewhere, or that they were hiding from them and at any moment they would pop out from behind a rock or a neighboring wagon and they'd say, "*Surprise! We've been here the entire time!*" and, "*We moved the village to the west, it gets better sun there.*" This feeling, where everything was simply displaced, couldn't be shaken. Maybe that's why they say, "*They've gone over the mountain.*" An invisible pile of corpses carried off in the belly of a narghoulim, over the mountains – leaving nothing to bury.

Chapter 10
Road to Cornelis

"It is still a mystery as to why the Fauni escape the fangs of the narghoulim. Perhaps it is due to how quiet they are as a species? Perhaps their smell, or even their taste? Fauni unfortunates caught within the path of an old god's rampage has oftentimes left them unscathed as they stand in the center of ruination. This would seem to be why so many Finni think the Fauni are in league with the narghoulim. Mayhap it is in the pattern of their migrations, the food they eat, or the shape of their antlers? What is true, is that Fauni will not remain in the company of Finni else risk their people beneath the narghoulim's hunger, and Finni will always hold anger towards the Fauni for surviving."

– Coppélia's Observations, Vol. XV

Vera woke from a deep slumber. Somehow they had fallen asleep among the jostling of the wagon, the clinking of glassware, and the occasional protest of the gorm as it drew them northward. The chill of the air had given way to the growing warmth that radiated from the sun which now rose in the eastern sky. Morilyn had come.

Rubbing the sleep from their eyes, Vera sat up and gazed about them. Alongside, Thora had too fallen asleep. The baby goat snuggled up close to her for warmth, with the pantomime still keeping the animal calm. Once they stopped, Vera would need to reverse the effects to allow the kid to romp, play and eat its share of wild grass before they'd need to continue along their way. Gander had kept behind the wagon the entire time. Kornigs were built for long distances, animals who could trek all across Orabelle if they so chose. There was room for him, Vera made sure of that, should he ever desired to leap into the back of the wagon and rest. He seemed content.

A breeze shifted through the caravan and Vera remembered the wind. Forceful, harsh, violent. They swore they could hear a distant howl but their mind was playing tricks on them. Vera stared into the distance, back towards where their home was — used to be.

Thora stirred and her eyes fluttered open. She took a few moments to realize where she was before saying, "I dreamed we were at a lake, you and I. We were swans, I think." She sat up and draped her arms around her friend. "It was a far kinder feeling than where we are now. How are you doing?"

Vera took a labored breath, as if a part of it caught halfway inside them. They felt twisted inside, solidified, numb. Things felt distant, as if looking out from behind a mirror. "It sounds like you dreamed under the Swan constellation. My aether told me stories of Finni who were transformed into beautiful swans by a malfinae and confined them to a lake where they never saw their families again."

"It felt nice to be a swan." Thora paused for a moment. "At least, in my dream it did."

"I feel like a swan." A knot welled up inside them. "I'll never get to see my family again."

Thora held onto their friend as tightly as they could, hoping that she provided some sliver of comfort to someone who had lost everything. It was the silence between them that she feared the most, an empty silence where Vera was suffering on their own – overcome with pain and grief. "Tell me about what your aether taught you about the constellations."

"What about them?" Their voice sullen and cast to the

earth.

"What did he tell you about the stars you were born under?"

"The Gleisne? It's the people in the Glass. It tells a story about how a young finni was betrayed in love and ended up dying of a broken heart. She rose from the dead as a vengeful spirit, but instead of killing her ex-lover she forgave him and spared his life. She then was allowed to pass through the Glass, and lived happy and forever on the other side."

"What happened to her ex-lover?"

Tears welled in Vera's eyes and they quickly wiped them away. "I don't know. Probably fell down a well or something."

The fauni wanted to laugh; wanted to joke, but she kept it all inside to give Vera room to feel their feelings and to mourn. Above all else, Thora hoped that Vera would mourn. But Vera didn't mourn, instead they continued to stare into the distance.

"Did you know that some people believe that depending on the stars that you were born under that it dictates a part of your personality?"

Vera didn't say anything.

"For example, since you were born under the Gleisne constellation that means you are in-tuned, spiritual, reserved and well-adjusted. And me? I was born under—"

"The Rose constellation." They whispered between sighing breaths. "I remember."

"That's right! Which means I never forget, are

79

sentimental, doting and somewhat materialistic. I don't know how much that is true, but I certainly am sentimental and doting. So maybe some of it is accurate."

Many thoughts blew through Vera's mind, matching stars to the people they knew. As soon as they could remember who was born under what constellation, their faces and bodies were swept away into the sky by an unseen hand. They stopped on someone in particular, one who caused thistles to sprout around their heart.

"What about the Bat?"

"The Bat?" Thora thought for a while and as Vera's eyes searched through a catacomb of memories, she realized exactly who they were asking about. "Dark, mysterious, haunting and deep thinkers."

"Definitely haunting." Vera replied. The feelings rose within them, but they pushed them down. Pushed them deep. A place where they would sit, and a place where they would rot.

The last of the Kom family and only survivor of Tandermundt, did not, could not mourn.

The wagons slowed to a halt just a half mile from Cornelis. Thora stepped off the back of the wagon, and took the kid into her hands. She helped Vera step down onto the dirt road. They both took the opportunity to stretch before having to take up their packs upon their backs which were moderately heavy. After being fitted, Vera kneeled down and gave Gander a much-needed hug. They then gave him some water and some salted meat from their rations before scratching beneath the quills on his head.

Shem Zhalinya Faunis approached them, this time dressed with a tight fitted cross strap red shirt in the front, which accentuated their chest, revealing their belly button and well-toned stomach. A grey skirt hung loosely at their hips. They wore their silvery hair down which caressed the top of their shoulders. Several red, black and brown feathers fanned on each side of their head, appearing as if they had wings.

"Many happy returns of morilyn, dear children. In this moment, I am she. We've arrived just outside of Cornelis. It's here where we part ways." Her voice was soothing, yet unbending. "If circumstances were different, we would escort you all the way to Adalace, but as indebted to your parents' hospitality, we cannot put all of us at risk."

Vera nodded. "I understand."

"There is the matter of your animals. The kornig is bonded to you, but the kid is not. I'm afraid that you'll find caring for it far more difficult in Adalace than it was back home. The Rushinay will provide for you, but I'm afraid it would be difficult for you to provide for a kornig, nevermind a baby goat as well. Might I offer you a solution? Leave the kid with us. We will tend to it, care for it while you're away. When you are ready, you may come for it."

Vera swallowed hard. They didn't want to have to say goodbye to the last remnant of their family's trip. The kid reminded them of the hills, how they stood vigilant in the fields with their father and mother. It reminded them of the lessons they were taught and the conversations that they had. Vera hesitated, but in the end knew that it was something that they had to do in order to keep the herd safe.

With an unbridled heaviness, Vera took the goat from Thora's arms and snuggled it close. They took a deep breath, to remember the softness of its hide and the familiarity of the smell. As soon as they were ready, Vera placed the kid softly upon the ground and reversed the pantomime they had cast back in the ravine. Instantly, the kid stood up on its legs and danced around, jumping and leaping as it played – completely unaware of the devastation that had befallen its own family.

Vera felt something from her stomach lodge into their throat, as if a piece of themselves was completely out of place, knowing that one of the last surviving remnants of her home was going away. Who knows when they would see each other again, or even whether or not the goat would recognize them whenever they choose to reunite? They had to remind themselves, as the tears swelled in their eyes, that at least they have Gander and above all, how lucky they were to have Thora.

A few fingers intertwined with Vera's, and a quick glance reassured them that they belonged to Thora, who now carefully pulled them away and towards the final distance that separated them from Cornelis.

"We have to move." Thora encouraged with a softness to her voice.

The kid came up to Vera, perhaps recognizing some form of familiarity in them, and bleated a joyful sound. They knelt down, patted the goat on the head, and said, "I'll come back for you."

Their father's voice echoed in their mind, *"Don't name*

them unless you plan to keep them." It was a warning about getting too attached to the animals they planned to slaughter for food. Vera felt there had already been too much slaughter. "I'm going to call you Lemon Grass from now on, okay? I'll see you again, Lemon Grass."

Vera eased themself back up to standing before following the gentle tug of Thora's arm, said their goodbyes to the rest of Thora's tribe and they made their way on foot along the dirt road which led to the largest city Vera had ever been.

Cornelis was a small city composed of a single main street where merchants from all over Orabelle have gathered. There they had set up tents and makeshift booths to house their wares. The street was wide enough to accompany three Fauni wagons going separate directions with still plenty of room to spare. The stone road was cambered, flanked by walking paths, with sprinkles of wild flowers slowly blossoming in patches along the sides.

"Keep close to me, okay?" Thora encouraged as she drew her pouch close. "A Fauni would never travel alone in any city, as surely some disaster would befall them. But keeping you close will cause tragedy to think twice."

Vera nodded their head. Tragedy and disaster. Thora was referring to people. People would happen. They wondered exactly how much trouble they had encountered in their travels outside of Tandermundt. Vera quickened their pace to keep alongside.

The two of them were dwarfed in a sea of adults, as they all wisped between the stalls filling their sacks with goods and paying with salt, feathers and cowrie shells. They moved through them, doing their best from getting underfoot. They even had to shift to the other side of the road when an orselon, one nearly the size of a house, lumbered their direction hitched to a heavy wagon of goods. The creature's thick white outer plates glistened in the sunlight, and its black stripes were handsome despite their odd flat feet and short tail with a spiked ball at the end. Its flat face huffed as it labored, and seemed very ill-disposed towards moving out of the way for a pair of children.

Vera had never seen this many people being so busy at any given time. They estimated perhaps a few hundred, maybe even more, at least for what they could presently see. Yet the mood quickly shifted as a Gami, a finni with wavy horns that towered two and a half feet from their brow, ran to the middle of the street and placed a sounding horn to their lips. They were dressed in tight fitting nyri silk mixed with white leather armor plating. When they blew, the sound exploded into the market and everyone grew eerily silent.

Chapter 11
The Skullwalker

"Every chevalière is gifted with a resonance. A power that is fueled by the essence of the divine and one that builds during an allegro. This gift is bestowed upon a Finni when they are born and determined by the constellation of stars for which guides them. While facing the many foes of the Finni, a chevalière may summon this power in order to defeat their enemies. Without it, a chevalière may fall to the claws of the narghoulim and in doing so, doom the rest of us to a similar fate."

- Zhah Ississ Belle, Professor of Dance, The Regal Ballet Academy.

The silence was simply a pause for the panic that would ensue. All Finni looked to the hornblower, who pointed prominently in the direction that everyone needed to escape to. Screams and cries wailed out into the market, as people ran in a frenzy in desperation to escape whatever invisible threat was brought to their attention. There came a rumbling, heavy footsteps that shook the ground, one after another. It was far louder than a rampaging orselon, though not as loud as one would attribute to a thunderclap. The hornblower made a few additional blows of warning before joining in with the rest of the fleeing mob.

Vera and Thora dodged a group of Finni who rushed by, nearly running them over, as they all fled. It was mere moments, before it happen yet again, until someone grabbed them and pulled them behind a wagon. The individual wore a lavender colored cat mask, with gold vines that stretched across its surface and nestled at the edges. It was a Mycili, denoted by a seven-inch single horn curved upwards and another curved downwards originating from their brow, wearing a lone shoulder strap dress which was yellow with white lace and lavender embellishments.

"I have saved you, yes?" The Mycili purred as they placed their hands atop both Vera and Thora's head. "We should hide here. Watch the fun."

Neither of them said a word, but instead observed the soon emptied street, where now stood the vacant merchant stalls, abandoned goods, and coffers. However, it was not long before a troupe of finni, finnae, and finnyr wearing white nygri silk and leather armor – adorn with brown, red and white feathers – raced into the street in front of them. They were followed by three others, one Rowsch with luscious blonde hair that spilled down her back with horns that swept from her brow towards the back of her head before curling up at the tips; another with short raven hair, a Woubar whose horns extended over a foot from their brow directly to their sides and whose tips angled towards the ground; then a Halkis, whose horns were straight, jetted from the brow slightly to their sides, no more than four inches at best, with sandy brown hair that was tied back in a bun. All with exception to the Woubar, wore a scintillating tutu which shimmered as the light struck it, elegantly detailed with embroidery and lace trim. The tutu-adorn finni wore pointe shoes for which they relevéd upon and crisscrossed their feet, rising then lowering, to warm up their ankles. Each of them carried an enormous weapon in their hands, which were thick, highly sharpened, and otherwise so weighted in appearance that it seemed that no single Finni would be able to lift it. A spear, axe and sword – all ready to do battle with whatever was coming up over the horizon.

"Those are Geist weapons." The Mycili marveled. "Forged in the fires of Erishtoll by the Ashwyn. Narghoulim slayers. What I would give just to be able to touch one."

"Wait, does that mean there's a narghoulim coming?" Thora asked with terror bouncing off her words.

The Mycili nodded.

"Why aren't we running?!" Vera coughed out but still in

hushed tones as to not draw attention to them.

"There's no safer place than behind the chevalières. Besides, front row seats to the best show in all of Orabelle, no? Now, shush, the corps de ballet is preparing."

As if on cue, several Finni lined up, a total of eight who then staggered like a zigzag behind the three chevalières. They all closed their thighs tightly together and placed their feet in fifth position, with each foot pressed tightly against the other and toes pointing in opposite directions to their sides. Their hands gracefully lowered below their waist, with elbows bent and their fingers readied so that the index finger and thumb formed a U, and the middle and ring finger slightly bent inwards as if holding a pencil between the index and pinkie.

One counted, "Five..." They raised their arms, keeping a tight bowl shape in front of their chests, "six..." they parted their hands out towards the side, "seven..." they pulled their hands back together in the previous position, "eight..." their right hand rose above their head, their eyes following their fingers upwards, as the left hand extended outwards, and their right foot reached out in a tendu with their toes pointed sharply. They each fell into a tombè on their right foot, then extended their back leg high into the air behind them, and extended their upraised arm out in front of them to form an arabesque. Then, after holding the position for a few moments, they returned to where their hand was raised and foot was extended, yet this time had switched sides to do the motions again.

"This is the adagio." The cat-masked Mycili pointed out. "A sequence of slow movements which serve to channel the powers of divinity into the chevalières, infusing them with the power to defeat the narghoulim." The Mycili stopped, then pointed cautiously as if its simple reveal was enough to potentially curse them forever. "There, on the horizon. You can see it emerging."

It came with quakes and heavy foot falls. A creature over a hundred feet in height. It descended upon them from the north, a being much like a Finni with the exception of having no horns. Its skin was pale, stretched tightly across its skull, revealing empty sockets where eyes should be. Its shoulders were broad, and hunched over, burdened by the giant sword which jetted from behind its back and pierced out of its stomach. An enormous red crystal, perhaps the size of a small cottage, gleamed from the hilt. Its mouth hung slack, as if breathing in the scent of a potential meal.

"Skull Walker." The Mycili cursed. They raised their mask only slightly to spit, as if the word stung in their mouth.

The chevalières remained still, calm, and imposing. Their outlines began to shimmer, like the sun cast across water. The adagio, as the cat-masked stranger had said, was luring the powers of the divine out from behind the Glass, causing them to pour into the ballet-knights, readying them to do battle against the giant.

Several minutes passed, as the corps de ballet continued through the movements, enough time for the Skull Walker to lumber nearer to the city, drawn by the smells of Finni meat. The creature roared, throwing spit out of its disgusting mouth like strings of melted goat cheese. The air turned foul, reeking of a pungent musk that hung about it like a shroud of flies. As it grew dangerously close, the corps de ballet ended their dance, and quickly removed themselves from the battlefield for fear of being caught in the center of it.

The chevalières readied their weapons, crouched low to the ground, then leapt high into the sky, hundreds of feet off the ground, far surpassing the height of the narghoulim – higher and higher they soared, completely transcending the bindings that the ground held for Finni and other creatures of Orabelle. Then, as they descended, having breached the gap between the city and the Skull Walker, they brought their weapons to bear against the abomination.

Vera eased closer, leaning towards the battle as the ballet

knights danced, weaved and struck at the creature's legs –
attempting to slow it before it could cause damage to the city. Its
blood poured out like an overflowing bucket, revealing a dark
liquid that one would more closely attribute towards rot, than
that of a life-giving red. The crystal in the hilt of the sword grew
bright, and it seemed to have an effect upon the chevalières, as
if weight were added onto their shoulders, yet still they
maneuvered as gracefully as they had started.

As the one with a spear leapt atop the narghoulim's arm, she
raced en pointe towards its shoulders, utilizing a pas de bourree
then a cabriole, a leap where the ballet-knight's legs clapped
together before returning en pointe. Then, in one powerful
thrust, the finni with the long blonde hair pierced the horror in
the neck where she twisted and yanked, causing the flesh to rip
along the neckline like a crescent moon. Its blood spilled down
like a waterfall, drenching the front of its chest and the ground
beneath with its taint.

Unphased by pain or the wounds it now suffered, the Skull
Walker swatted at the chevalière, who leapt atop the creature's
head in order to escape the blow, while the other two knights
laid siege against the creature's ankles. It punched the ground,
where moments before there was a finni. Grass, dirt, and rock
flew into the air, as the force of the blow sent pieces of the earth
flying in every direction. The short raven-haired Woubar and
their Halkis partner leapt out of the way, escaping between the
monster's legs. As they landed, the Woubar took hold of the tutu
adorn Halkis's waist, and together they too leapt, and in their
descent brought their legs together in an assemble, before
melting towards the ground in a plie, then launched high into
the air onto the creature's head, meeting with the Rowsch.

Then, a flash of golden light erupted from the Halkis dancer,
as a ring of sunshine extended out from their heart. The ring
blazed with blinding luminescence while the ring expanded
around the chevalières' entire frame. The brilliance pulsed, then
vanished, only to reappear encircled around the Skull Walker's

89

neck.

"You see there!" The stranger excitedly pointed out. "That is the chevalières resonance! A power determined by their stars and the height of their presence!"

The Rowsch stabbed their spear deeply into the Skull Walker's head; leaving it in place. They then ran in a half circle, hooked one of their legs around the shaft of the spear and extended out their arms. On cue, the Halkis darted off the side of the monster's skull, leapt into a scissor leap, and their back foot was caught by the Rowsch spinning on the spear who drew them too into a twirl.

With their massive sword, a blade almost as thick as their body and just as long, was thrust into the narghoulim's neck. Both the finni and their blade spun around it, completing the half crescent, and decapitating the monster! As the head plummeted like a giant boulder and spilled a waterfall of blood onto the landscape, the spear-wielding chevalière released their partner, pulled out their spear with a squelching sound, and together the two of them dropped safely to the ground.

The beast fell to its knees, causing a minor rumble across the countryside. It tipped over, however, the blade from the sword jetting from its stomach jabbed into the soil and kept it aloft. Despite the satisfying blow against the dark god, the Skull Walker's gaping wound slowly began to mend as the gem in the hilt pulsed with a dreadful glow.

Without pause, the chevalières all leap their way back up the narghoulim's body, finding whatever foothold they could find, with two of them remaining on the tips of their pointe shoes in a dazzling display of beauty and fluency.

Just as the Wouber with the short raven hair, reached the guard of the gigantic sword - just beneath the crimson glow of the ominous gemstone - they expelled their own resonance. Two spectral figures, one composed of purple while the other a bluish light, manifested above the chevalières' form and kissed one another – becoming a single starburst of light and power. The light spread to the other chevalières in a brilliant burst, and encased them in an aura of blue and purple radiant rays.

Weapons raised, with the divine power swelling within them all, they concentrated a single coordinated attack. Their joint strike slammed onto the surface of the gemstone which then exploded into thousands of tiny shards. Those fragments glittered like a swarm of fireflies before dissipating into the day.

The sword crumbled, the narghoulim slumped then fell into a lifeless pile of metal and flesh.

Chapter 12
The Road to Adalace

"While one would think that a crisis large enough to erase Finni from the face of Orabelle would be enough to unite them, sadly, it seems when one lives long enough with it, the people return to their self-serving ways. Regardless of how hard the Rushnay aims to bring Finni together, tribes still war, neighbors continue to steal, and power is still worth killing for. As for the narghoulim? That's the chevalières' problem."

– The Musings of Von Rothbart Viktesh

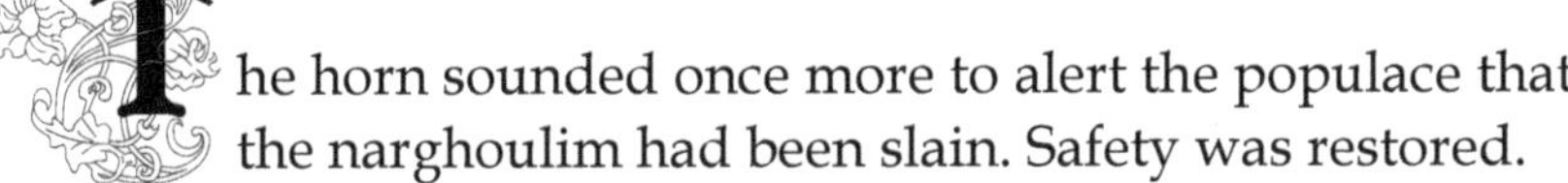

The horn sounded once more to alert the populace that the narghoulim had been slain. Safety was restored.

"Sadly, a short presentation." The cat-masked merchant lamented before coming out from hiding.

Thora brushed herself off, as during the commotion she had somehow been the target of dust clouds. Vera was far luckier, but had difficulties removing their gaze from the giant mound that was once the cause of so much terror. Their eyes flowed between the monstrosity and its missing head, to the three ballet knights who – as if in tribute to an invisible audience – performed a brief reverence, a curtsy and bow before being approached by the corps de ballet with a cart in tow in order to relieve them of their weapons.

Gander emerged from behind a group of crates, while Vera marveled at what they had just witnessed. To think, a Finni capable of such ability to stand against the giant monsters, perhaps as powerful enough to kill the one who had taken their village. All their life they had been told stories of the ballet-knights and how they faced down monstrosities that threatened all Finnis. They remembered their mother reading to them about the life of chevalières; trained from a young age in ballet in order to break the Glass that separated their world from the divine, and using that power to protect people. If only they themself had been taken at a young age to learn, maybe they could have stopped the…

Vera turned to Thora, a pain danced in their chest, "We should find passage to Adalace." There was urgency, as the blood of the narghoulim gave flashes in Vera's mind of friends and family, suffering in agony, blood pooling in some nefarious abomination's gullet.

"I agree. The sooner the better." Thora looked to all sides of them, attempting to capture one of the returning Finnis' expressions who may be as desperate to escape the area as they were.

However, those returning to the streets chased cheers and applause, all aimed at the chevalières who had slain the evil being that was the Skull Walker. A crowd gathered around the heroes of Cornelis and many wanted to touch the Geist weapons that fell the beast.

The cat-masked stranger tilted their head where their horn curled down and asked, "Adalace? A perfect idea! No one will buy anything for a while, not with celebrations coming to bear. A good time to leave, I think. You come with me. I would not mind the company. I would need a few hands to help load my wagon. This is agreeable, yes?"

Thora looked between each other and nodded. "That would be lovely, thank you." Thora offered in response.

"Before we begin, I just need a touch. The Geist weapons are being prepared as we speak."

Loading the merchant's cart was no small matter, there were heavy rugs, crates of spices, bottles of perfume, books and other trinkets. It was all rather eclectic and the cat-masked individual didn't seem to have any organization. It felt like several hours, and every so often Vera would look up into the sky to watch for any nefarious shift in the clouds, but was relieved each time when the sky remained blessed with morilyn's light.

There was a weight deep within their chest, something that gnawed at them and sent shivers through their veins like water from a frigid spring. In their own sense, they were a water clock, like the one that had existed in the center of Tandermundt, slowly dripping the moments away until the narghoulim would return to finish its recent meal. The work did help to keep Vera's mind occupied, but when all was done, Vera could not help their thoughts from drowning in the faces of all who were gone.

Gander sensed their shift and nuzzled up against them. Vera was too preoccupied to pet him. Everything felt distant and hopeless. Thora came alongside Vera and placed her hand in theirs.

"We should climb on board. The merchant is hitching the ruffeloven to the wagon and we'll soon be on our way."

Vera squeezed their friend's hand. "What will we do, then, Thora? How will Adalace replace what I have lost?"

Without a moment's thought, Thora pulled Vera into a hug and leaned her head against theirs. "Nothing in the world can replace what you have lost. But we will find something, someway for you to continue on. Shem Zhalinya said that the Rushinay could help us, maybe you have family somewhere. They will know. Then maybe, in time, you'll know."

Their voice was lost and in despair. "And what if I don't want to continue on? What if I was meant to be taken over the mountain with my family?"

"By the NIИ, you were spared and I am grateful that you were. There is no meaning in being taken over the mountain, it's needless and horrific. You are meant to be where you are, and continue to be. I know it's hard, but you aren't alone. Gander and I are here for you, every step of the way."

Thora's eyes teared up, and she fought to keep them at bay so that she could be strong for her friend. She too had suffered loss as well, as Tandermundt was like a home to her. Her people roamed, never staying in the same place for more than a week before picking up and moving again. Vera's family had been especially kind to her, something she rarely experienced outside of Arcadia. Her heart had broken seeing Vera in the ruins of their village surrounded by nothing familiar. She didn't have time to mourn, she wasn't in a place for tears. Right now, she had to get her friend to safety.

When their embrace ended, Thora turned slightly to dry their tears so that Vera would not be burdened by them. With a hand, Thora assisted them into the wagon, and Gander leapt up into the back and curled around them in order to provide comfort.

Once the ruffeloven was properly secured, the Myceli signaled to the beast it was time to go, and the creature pushed itself eastward down the stone road towards Adalace. As the wagon passed varying Finni and merchants stalls, a single individual took notice. A finnae wearing a black wide-brimmed shade hat and carrying an eight-foot-long bundle wrapped in black cloth on his back. A deep set eyes and a haunting gaze all cut beneath his bushy eyebrows. His original destination was west, but he felt a tinge in the air, and it followed the children like a funeral shroud. He continued to watch them as they passed, turned, then proceeded after them at a steady walking pace.

Both of the children spied him, and his very presence caused a touch of nervousness, enough to raise the hairs on the backs of their necks.

The Myceli hummed a tune to themselves as they continued to drive them eastward. For several hours they traveled through parts of the country decorated with the skeletal frames of vineyards, as well as recently tilled soil in preparation for planting of wheat which would grow to full height by the first day of tillmet. In the distance, Vera and Thora could spot finni topless beneath the sun, working the fields and preparing for the next day's planting. They only had 13 Longlyn days left before harvest then nillveness would return. It was always a treat, come halftmorn when the crops would reach knee high.

Gander rested his head on the wagon's rails, and panted his body on the ground, as the sunlight brushed across his fur and feathers. Vera was ready for the warmer weather.

The ruffeloven kept at a steady pace as its hooves struck the new stone road with a slight clack. Its hide was brown, which covered all nine feet of its length. The creature stood at six feet, yet its head was about four times the size of Vera's and they swore the creature could fit their entire foot in its mouth. It had two rolled horns that jetted from its brow and a single horn that extended about one and a half feet from its forehead. At one point in the beast's ancestry, it was temperamental and would charge those it thought were a threat. Given that most ruffelovens weighed up to two-thousand pounds, it was just as likely to trample you to death, rather than gore you. However, hundreds of years of domestication have made the creature docile and willing to perform labor for those who were able to feed them.

The merchant stopped humming.

"Very strange to see two Faunis traveling alone together, especially so young. Did you get separated from your tribe?" The Myceli asked in order to fill the silence of the trip with something more entertaining than watching the ruffeloven swat flies with its tail.

Thora answered on behalf of them, finding that having conversations with others might be more than what Vera was willing to manage right now. "No, my friend is a Caetin. I'm helping them to get to Adalace to see the Rushinay. We hope to discover some family of theirs to stay with."

"Caetin? Good people from Arcadia. They buy rugs mostly. Sell cheese, wool. I've traded all the way to the southern peninsula. What village?"

"Tandermundt."

Vera winced at hearing the name but otherwise remained silent.

"Yes. Very nice place. I'd like to go back soon. You think they'd buy rugs there too?"

Thora shook her head despite the fact that the merchant was too focused on keeping the ruffeloven walking in a straight path than to notice. "I'm afraid not. It's gone now. Vera is the last of their village."

"Narghoulim?" The merchant spat on the ground by the mention. "By the NIИ, many apologies and condolences to those who were taken over the mountain. If it is not too painful to answer, by what manner of cursed creature took them?"

"I'm not sure…" Thora reflected on their conversation they had around the fire outside of the desolation that was Vera's village. "It was known to my Shem. There was a horrid wind, dark clouds, green lightning, and there was this…" Vera felt like they were back behind the rock, hearing the howling of the wind, the ground shaking beating that resounded all around them. "…thumping."

"You speak of the velocitrix. A cyclone of terror. My greatest condolences to you my young Caetin for you are double cursed with the loss of your village, and now it follows you."

The merchant's words rolled over them like the chilling breath of a malfinae. *Cursed. Is that what I am now?* Vera thought as they rubbed their hands together in order to keep the realization from seeping in too deep.

"That's why we are going to Adalace. You said so yourself, that there are no safer places than behind the chevalières." Thora offered as a beacon of hope.

A chuckle came from behind their cat mask. "I did so indeed! Apologies, as I cannot take you as far as I believed. The ruffeloven will need rest, yes? But the narghoulim affords you none. Halfway to Ithuway and I must stop, and you both must continue on. For all our sakes."

Thora's brow scrunched out of aggravation. "You can't take us any fur—"

"—that's fine." Vera interrupted, downcast and sorrowful. "We understand. For all our sakes."

The Myceli was true to their word, and brought them halfway to Ithuway, as the ruffeloven needed a break to rest and eat. The merchant pointed down the path of the stone highway. "Straight to Adalace. If you're lucky, you'll make it by halfmorn. I wish you both speed of a peppenach and the luck of the NIИ."

Thora frowned. Haftmorn was a long way away and they would have to find shelter along to protect them. In a wagon they could rest and sleep, but on their own it would be hard to come by. The road to Adalace was separated from the coast with high cliffs, and rocky hills which would offer them some protection. Vera started their walk, knowing that to stop would only invite the narghoulim.

It would soon prove apparent that walking wasn't quick enough.

Chapter 13
Thump, Thump, Thump

"It was the Tintergeist, a narghoulim of winter, who had decimated the Leekyn's home in Tinterland which almost wiped out their entire tribe. It was as high as a mountain, over eight-thousand feet. When it stepped, there came an insufferable blizzard which froze all before being devoured. It was our Finni Anessa, who survived, rebuilt her tribe, and aided those they encountered along the way. It was she who founded the Rushinay, a spiritual organization dedicated to the preservation of the Finni and now refuge to the lost."

- Excerpt from, *Chronicles of the Rushinay*

The sky darkened behind them and erected a multi-layered wall whereupon its battlements glowed with the ghosts of green flashes. The distant rumble licked at their feet as Vera and Thora sprinted down the road, followed by Gander who wished that his companions were able to move as quickly as he could. Their eyes dashed from edifice to cranny, desperate to find something that would provide them greater shelter than hiding behind a rock and hoping for the best – would they be so lucky this time around.

Wind brushed against their hair, breathing in their delectable scent, whispering that the narghoulim was right behind them. Both Vera and Thora felt their own hearts beating in their ears, a taste of the soon deafening sound as it would inevitably fall upon them, sweep them off their feet, and take them forever over the mountain.

Vera's lungs grew tight and they burned as they continued to push themselves as far as the air would allow them. They had already been running for quite some time, the wind, it seemed, enjoyed watching them scramble. It was the killer with the raised knife, steadily walking behind, confident that his blade would taste blood yet savoring the chase. Despite their attempts to outrun the clouds, it descended upon them.

Thora looked over her shoulder as a funnel cloud formed behind them, swirling like a malicious vortex of her very nightmares, and far larger than anything she had ever seen. It exploded with green, as a streak of electricity cracked the sky. Then came the howling, the long scream of the winds as they took shape and slammed onto the ground behind them – still many miles away, yet only a few strides to a hungry god.

"It's coming!" Thora shrieked as she pushed herself, throwing her feet to the ground as rapidly as her body would allow.

Vera could feel their insides crying out from the strain of their racing, but knew that if they stopped, there would be nothing left of them to feel its sting. From rock, to cliff, to tree, to boulder, there had to be somewhere that they could take shelter, something that was strong enough to keep the winds at bay. Then they saw it, a mouth to a cave, a shadowed maw which led deep into the earth.

"There!" Vera shouted. "On the left, just up ahead!" The words were hard to expel, as they stole bits of the good air inside them.

"I see it!" Thora cried out with relief. The very savior to their situation was upon them.

The narghoulim must have sensed a change in their demeanor, no longer was their flight filled with terror and instead was replaced with a touch of hope. Its winds quickened around it, swirling like a corkscrew across the ground, ripping up stones, trees, dirt and grass. Its thumping increased, a heavy booming sound that resounded in the children's tiny little bodies. Hastily it would be upon them.

Thora ran off the road, up a small mound before reaching the entrance to the cave. She did not stop, and allowed herself to be swallowed inside its rocky gullet. Gander too had made it within, but would halt only momentarily to ensure that Vera was not far behind. Within a swallow's time, Vera passed through the mouth and continued until they reached the safety of their friend before feeling the ground quake, as the horrific wind of the narghoulim engulfed the cavern's entrance. Its howl intensified with rage, and the winds twisted ferociously blocking out the light which had barely filtered inside. The snapping teeth of green lightning assaulted the three of them as the narghoulim continued its onslaught. The cave would not relent its protection it provided them.

Vera and Thora huddled together against an outcropping, which shielded them from the continued breaths intent on sucking them back outside to be devoured. Gander stayed with them. They both closed their eyes tightly, keeping the monstrosity at bay, as they found darkness their only true friend against a rampaging, powerful and hungry god.

It seemed to go on forever, yet as all things do, it diminished. The dark clouds abated and the world returned to calm. The smell of upturned grass fell away to the scent of the sea, and not too distant lapping of the waves reassured them of safety. However, the dismal dread that resounded inside them refused to move on and instead settled into their very being. On foot, the velocitrix would return, and without a cave to take shelter in, they would become its next meal.

Despite it all, they could not linger.

Hand-in-hand, Thora and Vera eased out of the cavern's maw and into the sunlight. Gander too, was cautious, sniffing the air just in case there was some hint that the creature would return and they would have to scamper back inside.

Thora took a moment as she stood still, adjusted her face to meet the sun, closed her eyes and breathed in the warmth of the world. When she opened her eyes and turned to address her friend, she didn't see a moment of peace, instead she saw a finni transfixed on something a stone's throw from their location.

101

Vera was frozen in place, a pit of despair had grown deeper inside them, and the grasping vines of horror reached for them. Their eyes could not move from that which was displayed, a haunting image that would forever be embedded in their memories.

Following their gaze, Thora happened upon the very thing that had invoked such a ghastly expression. There, resting on a rock, displayed like an offering, was an adult finni hand severed at the wrist, fingers sprawled out and pointing towards them.

It wasn't just any hand, it was a hand that used to comfort, one that would cook, direct, and lead. It was a hand that would turn the pages of storybooks and family history, one that would stroke Vera's hair at night, and one that would embrace them as they returned from watching the goats. It was a mother's hand. Their mother's hand! A reminder left intentionally for Vera of the unspoken truth of their family's fate. Each one was dismembered and devoured, and some pieces were saved for later.

Vera fell to their knees without a word, pulled out the knife that Thora had gifted them. *"Look! It's an early birthday gift. The handle is made out of one of Thora's antlers! Can you believe it? And the blade is obsidian!"* That's what they said to their mom when they showed it to her. They plunged their dagger into the soil, and started digging.

"Is that..." Thora stopped with her question, the face that Vera made was confirmation enough. She pulled out her own dagger, cut a piece of her cloak off and used the scrap piece of cloth to wrap the hand as delicately as she could. She carefully carried the bundle over and set it on the ground next to where Vera was digging, and – once Vera cleaned the blade and returned it to its sheath – the two of them continued to clear away the dirt and rocks until there was a hole deep enough that Vera was confident scavengers wouldn't find it. They buried the hand without a word.

As soon as the deed was done, Vera stood up and started walking back towards the road. Thora planted a stone at the spot, marked it with an X using her dagger, then raced to catch up to the finni who couldn't mourn.

The road was marred with an uncomfortable silence, one that hid away the grim present that had been left by the narghoulim. Thora wasn't sure whose hand it was, but by Vera's reaction, it was someone they had known.

She took a glance above them and noted that the sky was still clear, which was a good sign, but it left a knot of anxiety in her stomach that it could change at any moment. The desire that she should be comforting her friend as much as possible was almost just as great as that of the fear of being devoured by the velocitrix.

"Vera? Do you want to talk about the hand?"

Vera shook their head and remained quiet. Talking about it would make it any better, and they still had such a long way to go. Their lip quivered with the memory as it edged towards the front of their mind, like some daydream trying to hop the wall of their focus; what little of it they had.

Gander kept ahead of them, smelling the bushes, the road, the trees, and whatever else was new and exciting – which to him was everything. Yet, during one of his sniffs his ears perked up and honed in on a sound that came from behind them. He turned to face the cause of the noise, panted, then stared, panted, then stared. It was something farther down the road, but it was set to a good pace.

"I am here for you." Thora reminded them. "If you feel up to talking about how you feel, about… well, everything." She thought for a moment. "Or anyone."

"How far until the next town?" The question was something

at least, something to help keep their mind off the rising emotion inside of them that swirled about like a vortex ready to swallow them whole.

"Tethshone is the next largest settlement between here and Adalace. Though, you might see a few villages here and there. They grow in greater numbers the closer we get to a chevalières outpost. Though, at our rate, we won't get there until halftmorn." With how the narghoulim seems to be following them, Thora worried if they would even make it at all.

However, her thoughts did not fixate on their possible doom for long as Gander barked at something behind them. It was the exact kind of bark that he would use to alert Vera of danger to their trip. Vera stopped and turned to see what could be the cause for warning.

Descending upon them was a sole rider astride a brightly blue colored bird, set with a long neck, a delicate beak, and legs nearly as tall as they were. Behind it, and only suspended a mere few inches off the ground, was a long train of brown and green feathers fixed with several eye-patterns of emeralds, citrines and sapphires. Its wings were tucked safely beneath a wide saddle, where a rider clutched tightly to the fowl's reins. It was a peppenach, a creature used to carrying light-weight riders long distances. And this one bore a finnae wearing a black wide-brimmed shade hat.

With the sun at their back, Vera was able to recognize him as the man who had taken interest in them back in Cornelis. The very one who had changed his direction and started following them.

"I think we have trouble." Vera mentioned as their hand went to the handle of their dagger.

"Only if we let it." Thora replied with caution. "Turn around, keep your head down, don't acknowledge him. Keep your dagger ready and if he tarries, then we know he has malintent and we'll have to strike. Otherwise, he might just pass us by."

"Gander, come." Vera commanded, which summoned the kornig to their side. Better to have him at the ready in the event that they would need to defend themselves.

Vera did as Thora had instructed, they turned back towards the road, head down, yet their hand gripped the antler handle, ready to draw it at a moment's notice.

The peppenach approached quickly, the sound of its talons striking the road created a resounding and rapid thudding noise the closer it appeared. Thora repeated a thought in their head, *"Please ride on by. Please ride on by."* Hoping that what occurred in Cornelis was simply a matter of coincidence and that the individual held no interest in the two of them. Yet, when the peppenach's pace slowed rather than be steered around them, the prayer in their head converted to a tighter grip on their blade.

Gander growled as he continued in step with Vera and Thora. Thora could tell that the kornig was getting agitated and that one word from Vera would be all he needed to do battle with whatever threat the rider and his peppenach posed towards his charges.

The peppenach soon kept pace, following no more than ten feet behind them. Still the rider said nothing, and dedicated himself to their harassment. Several minutes passed, and still nothing was uttered, and as Gander's growling intensified, and their own nerves had fallen to the knife's edge, Vera spun around, flashed their knife into the sunlight and dropped into a crouch ready to strike!

Chapter 14
Astride a Peppenach

"There is a world beyond ours known as the Faydren; home to the gleasne- the people in the mirrors - fairies and other beings. It is a place where trees speak and statues move, where water flows upwards, where stones sing and the wind whispers intimate things. The spirits of our ancestors may only pass from the Eshef, our world, into the Faydren with permission from their loved ones. It is the duty of the mourner, a sacred role, to encourage the bereaved to lament their loss and aid in their passage into the eternal dream. Spirits who have no one to cry for them, find their passage barred, then are doomed to stagnant and grow violent."

– Sacred Writings of Leekyn Tvay Anessa

ho are you and what do you want?!" Vera demanded as they gritted their teeth with ferocity.

Thora pulled her own weapon from its sheath and prepared to meet the new threat against them, while Gander spun around and barked viciously at the rider.

The peppenach evoked an ear-piercing screech to ward off its attackers, but the finnae pulled back at the reins enough to end it.

"Many apologies to you three." His voice was smooth and calming like a placid lake. "I mean you no harm. My name is Kyph Ravoysn Tage." He raised his head enough for them to better see his features. As before when they noticed him in Cornelis, he had sunken eyes which were blue, yet still maintained a haunting gaze. He raised his bushy eyebrows and offered a labored smile. He appeared to be eighteen years of age, yet his countenance showed a lifetime of hardship. "I sensed a myriad of spirits following you, however, I'm uncertain as to which of you suffered the loss. I'll attest that I've never felt so many at a single time and it is overwhelming." He took a long breath of air. "They still are. I'm here to offer you my services."

While his words appeared sincere, Vera was not willing to put away their dagger quite yet. "What services, exactly?"

"To mourn." He answered with a melted heart. "To help you shed your tears for your loved ones so they may cross into the Faydren. To help you heal."

Thora lowered her weapon. She knew of the mourners, an entire profession dedicated to the passing of spirits. Even the Fauni had their own mourners, who were held in high spiritual esteem by everyone in her tribe. From her understanding, they held similar respect in Finni culture.

Vera pulled back the tip of their blade to knick the sky only to thrust it forward again. "No." From that single word, they turned back around and continued their way eastward.

Gander, no longer sensing danger, dropped his defensive pose, lulled his tongue out of his mouth and resumed walking alongside Vera towards their destination.

Tage eased his peppenach into a slow stride, and while anyone else would be seething with rejection, he maintained his composure and empathically asked, "Why?"

Thora followed along keeping an eye on both Tage and Vera, and eagerly listened.

"I don't owe an answer to a complete stranger." Vera spat out as they focused on the path ahead.

"I see…" Tage pondered on their words, mulling it over and over again for a few moments. "Then I suppose the best thing for us to do is get acquainted."

"With you?" Vera kept walking. "We don't have the time. We have to get to Adalace."

"What a coincidence." Tage offered with a hint of enthusiasm. "That's exactly where I'm going."

107

Vera rolled their eyes.

With a flick of the reins, he spurred the peppenach ahead of them just a few feet then stopped with the animal's flank exposed. "You seem to be in a hurry and you say you don't have the time. Let's make the time, shall we? Hop on. I promise to deliver you all, safe and sound, to wherever it is you are needing to go."

The Caetin stopped and examined him. *Is he sincere? Trustworthy? Dangerous?* So many thoughts stumbled through their mind, yet one was far more pressing than the others, that the narghoulim was not far behind.

"Thora?" Vera asked as they turned their head towards their friend. "You want to ride?"

Thora nodded her silent approval.

The peppenach was swift, carrying them farther in a single hour than they would have been able to accomplish in a single Longlyn day.

Back in Tandermundt, the water clock at the center of the town held a large basin of water for which to capture the drips from its water supply. As the floater in the reservoir raised, so too did its rod which had teeth at its highest point which fed the wheel, causing the needle to move along the dial indicating at what hour they were in, per each of the fourteen Longlyn days that made each season. Tillmet is the period between dusk and night, where the last beams of sunlight would disappear beneath the horizon and shroud the world in darkness, called nillveness. Between day seven and eight in nillveness, would be halfwen when the connection between the living and the dead are at its strongest. Then came gillmet, the last season where the sun would slowly rise in the east, before committing to morilyn, a new fourteen days of daylight, halfmorn arrives much like halfwen, during the seventh and eigth day of morilyn, which is usually the hottest of seasons.

They had already spent a good day by cart, their walking pace would have placed them in Adalace by tillmet. As quickly as a peppenach can move, they would be able to reach Adalace halfway to halfmorn. Lucky for them, Tage was focused on his task and didn't speak until it was time to allow the peppenach to rest, and in turn, rest themselves.

Thora directed them to another cave, this one farther off the road. It was one that her people had used several times in the past in order to avoid the harsh rain storms that the Anesian Coast was known for. And like all Fauni stops, there was no evidence they had ever been there.

The cave was damp from the moisture carried off the ocean, but they were able to find some dry spots to set up a campfire. While the peppenach was tied to a grouping of stalagmites and provided a bag of feed, Gander laid next to Vera who snuggled him close to alleviate some of the mental anguish they suffered from. Thora broke out some food and shared it only between the three of them, while Tage had his own, which were delicately wrapped in cloth. His food consisted of dried fruit, nuts, bread and cheese.

Next to him he had set his long bundle, an item wrapped in cloth and tied in order to keep it from unraveling. It was eight feet in length and no more than four inches in width on all sides.

Vera found themself staring at the package, wondering what was inside. Whatever it was, it seemed as though it would remain a secret as they were not comfortable enough to inquire about it.

"We haven't much farther to go. A day or so, and we'll be at the gates to Adalace. Have you decided where your destination is, once you get there? It is a large city, and I would hate for you to have made it this far and get lost." Tage calmly asked between bites of his food.

"The Rushinay." Thora confirmed. "We're hoping to find out if Vera has any family there."

"A very noble pursuit, to be sure." He nodded. "Have either of you been to Adalace before?"

They looked at one another, but shook their heads in confirmation not only to him, but to themselves.

"I've never gone very far from home before." Vera admitted with a pain in their heart.

"And Fauni do their best to avoid highly populated areas." Thora added.

"The Rushinay have built their citadel, Adaris'a Monti, into the side of Cajourin Mountains. The Aness, Aponae, and the Sisaness all reside there. I hear they have records dating all the way back to Leekyn Tvay Anessa. I'm sure if anyone can find your family, they would be able to." He cocked his head to the side. "Do you plan to stay with them, your family, that is?"

Thora looked to Vera, who seemed very focused on the conversation at hand. They appeared more lively than before, no longer as distant or existing in the pain that they've carried with them since the loss of their village. Vera had leaned in, hands tucked into their lap, and eyes locked with Tage's with only the crackling of the flames from the campfire between them. Their freckles seemed to dance in the firelight.

"No."

"No?" Thora had thought that was the plan, to find Vera their family, so that they wouldn't be alone. She pushed her raven-colored hair behind her, hoping that whatever decision that Vera was about to make wouldn't be lost in the flames before reaching her ears.

Vera diverted their gaze to their best friend to show their

commitment. They had been thinking about it since they had seen the chevalières fell that narghoulim in Cornelis, but what made up her mind was their mother's hand. While the hand was intended as an instrument of terror, Vera saw it as something more.

"I'm going to become a chevalière."

"What!?" The news struck Thora like a rock. "Are you serious?"

"I've never been more serious!" There was fire dancing in their eyes, and not the flames from the campfire. This new passion had straightened their spine, lifted their chest, and extinguished the weight they had been carrying this entire journey.

Thora saw a hint of their old friend again, one who was determined, confident, capable of handling anything that got thrown their way. Despite the huge amounts of concern that sounded in their mind, in their heart, Thora was happy to see their return to some semblance of their former self.

"One does not simply become a chevalière. There is training. You would be giving up many years of your youth, left with but a chance at breaching the Glass and reaching apotheosis - becoming infused with divinity. Even if you were successful, it would put you on a path to facing the narghoulim. Is this something you're prepared for?" Tage asked, but not in a manner in which to discourage them from their declaration, but instead as a means to solidify their commitment.

Vera returned their gaze to the man with the fuzzy eyebrows and nodded. "I've never been more certain. The signs are clear. I will train to become a ballet knight, I will breach the Glass, and I will fight to destroy the narghoulim – starting with the one who took my family from me."

Thora placed her hand on her friend's leg. "If this is what

you want, then I'm with you Vera. All the way."

Gander barked his approval.

"This is your path then. I know the admissions for Nisnafell, the Regal Ballet Academy, have already closed for the season. However, special exceptions can be made only by appointment by the Aponae."

Thora interjected before Vera could. "Then that's who we'll see."

The peppenach carried them swiftly along the Anesian Coast, beyond the hills and rolling farmland. They passed through villages and towns, not stopping unless needing to rest. It took several more Longlyn days, but in time they were able to reach the magnificent stone gates, nearly 100 feet in height, and half as much in thickness. Two gigantic statues of finni chevalières, raised en pointe, adorn in armor, pancake tutus and bearing spears, flanked either side of the doors which were forty-feet in height, made of thick steel and gold plated with elaborate floral designs.

There was a regiment of guards, equipped with plate armor and swan embellished helmets and shields minding the flow of incoming and outgoing traffic which led deeper into the city. Beyond those opened gates, were close multi-storied houses, fixed with red shingled roofs, white-washed walls, and artistically designed windows set in a natural style.

The streets were wide, paved with tightly laid gray stones, with a white stone paved promenade on either side, before reaching elegant homes, shops with glass windows and painted signs, all guarded with pantomime lit metal street lights that were forged to appear like tiny trees with vine adornments.

The city rose, and with each level was encircled by another set of walls, each as tall and awe inspiring as the last, reaching all the way to the base of the mountain where ivory towers, beautiful garden laced balconies, and majestic waterfalls flowed down from its rocky walls.

Vera's mouth slacked open as they expelled an exhalation of awe at the sheer beauty and the overwhelming number of people who walked the promenade and traversed the main thoroughfare astride a variety of birds, creatures, or even settled in carriages, carts or wagons.

They strode through the main gates, navigating the traffic, and headed straight for the Hall of the Aponae.

Chapter 15
The Aponae

"The chevalière must be fierce. They must be dedicated and devoted. There is no room for failure and there is no place for fear. In order to breach the Glass, one must put aside all things that anchor you to this world and, with talent and luck, you will touch the soul of the divine. Your instructors can help you find your talent. The rest is up to you."

– Zhah Ississ Belle, Professor of Dance, The Regal Ballet Academy.

At the end of the wide street, flanked by ten marble pedestals on either side where upon enormous statues of chevalières stood tall and glorious, was where the all-embracing staircase that led up the base of the mountain and to the entrance hall to the Rushinay, and seat of government over the city of Arabelle resided. The steps appeared to have been carved directly out of the rock of the hill, with the first fifty steps reaching up towards a landing, perhaps thirty feet in width and twenty in length before returning to an ascent.

Four Finni, adorn in detailed armor depicting various birds, and flowers were etched into its metal along the edges of its breastplate, shoulder guards, vambraces and shin guards stood at the base of the stairs. The helmets they wore gave them the appearance of birds, with decorative feathers fanning behind their head, with red and white plumage, which appeared far more intimidating than the partisans they held firmly outstretched from their person.

The air was filled with the scent of burning bergamot and sandalwood, and there was a crispness to the air. Vera felt lighter, as if someone had removed a pile of rocks off their back for which they had no realization it had been there before.

Thora slipped off the back of the peppanach and landed

with both of her feet on the road alongside Gander who was still excited by the bustle of the city. He sniffed the ground, followed a scent for a few paces, lifted his head, and reveled in the sensation before following a new scent. Vera was not far behind. They looked up the flight of stairs, a laborious journey in its own right, for what they could determine to be at least three-hundred steps before reaching the top.

One of the guards approached and with a calm yet authoritative voice asked, "What business do you have?"

Tage was quick to respond. "I am Kyph Ravoysn Tage, bearing escort. They wish to speak with the Aponae in regards to late entry into Nisnafell. They also bear grave news from Arcadia."

Thora straightened her back, pressed her shoulders down and raised her head to better meet the guard. "Tell the Aponae, we bear tidings from Shem Zhalinya Faunis. And we would be honored by an audience with his Grace."

Vera felt rather out of place in regards to exerting any form of demands or requests. They were from a small village, and even though they were the offspring of the Shem, there was little authority or matrony over others. However, the guard seemed to find the information newsworthy, and took a few steps back.

They jetted out their fist, then extended all of their fingers downward, then drove their left elbow up and directly in line with their other arm, before extending out their fingers and brushed their way towards their wrist. Their right hand rotated upwards, swiveling their extended fingers until they pointed upwards, creating a cup in their palm. Trails of scintillating azure magic flowed into the guard's hand forming a glowing sphere of light about the size of an apple. They then leaned in and whispered into the ball. As soon as the finni was finished, the orb whisked away, up the stairs, then disappeared entirely as it searched for its recipient.

Vera recognized it as a *send* pantomime, something they had seen their mother use but not something that was ever taught to them. They remembered her saying, "Once you become the Shem, then you'll learn, but until then you must learn to be a shepherd and the pantomimes inherent to your profession." Growing up, they had known that one day they would be asked to step into the role that their mother had filled, but it was a distant happening – something they had been reassured time and time again that it would not be anytime soon. Now… it would never happen. It's hard being Shem of your people when you have no people.

After a few moments, the ball returned, however this time it had a message for the guard, one that only they could hear. Briefly, it relayed its message then vanished into a trickle of dying magical embers which never reached the ground.

"I've been ordered to escort you to the audience chambers. The Aponae will see you." The guard turned toward the base of the stairs. "Follow me."

While Tage's demeanor didn't waver, Thora's was quite the opposite. Outside of her culture, the Aponae was the second highest member of the Rushinay in power. He is known to the fauni, and gaining an audience with him directly was like being granted a chest full of cowrie shells from a complete stranger on the street.

"We're seeing the Aponae?" She swallowed hard, and suddenly started brushing off any imagined dust from her clothes, adjusted her hair, and straightened her garments as best as she could.

Vera, on the other hand, took no attempts to correct how they looked. They were focused on meeting with the Aponae and making a request that could determine their very future. It felt as if they had swallowed a swarm of insects, all skittering about inside of them. It was very clear, at least to them, on what they needed to do. *But what if he says no?* Vera worried, because in the event he did say no, they would have no plan, no future, and would be stuck inside this city for the rest of their life in fear for what happens should they leave. Vera took a deep breath in, focused on the sounds of the city around them, and stood in the aroma cast from the burning incense. With that, they started after the guard, with Thora, Gander and Tage not far behind.

The stairs up to the main doors were difficult, but once inside the entry hall acted as a reward for those who made the trek. There were stained glass windows stretching all the way to the ceiling depicting chevalières in majestic tutus, pointe shoes, and wielding powerful Geist weapons. There were also mirrors, set between each window, with elegantly engraved frames depicting woodland scenes, that were twice the height of Vera, which reflected the hall. The ceiling was at least thirty or more feet tall, with arching wooden beams and clear glass ceilings with iron cast leaves set across it to create the appearance and shadows of a forested canopy.

As they walked through the lengthy hall towards the larger set of doors at the end, Vera noticed movement among the reflective glass. Alongside their own images, were ethereal beings flying side-by-side. There were at least seven of them, each exhibiting a youthful playfulness as one floated overhead pretending to stroke Vera's hair, while another silently counted the tips of Thora's antlers. A few of them danced, twirling in pirouettes, while another performed a tour en l'air, spinning multiple times and descending slowly as if they were a feather. They wore white translucent clothing, which trailed from their shapely physiques like waves in the sea. Some of them bared Vera's face, with each smiling in joyous celebration – as if seeing an old friend from a long parting. Others shifted their guise, taking on Thora's features, or Tage's, and occasionally the guard who paid them little mind.

"Gleasne." Thora whispered to Vera in hopes of not scaring them away. "People of the Glass."

"I've never seen one before." Vera returned while captivated by their graceful motions and effortless steps.

Tage's voice arose with his usual volume. "They more frequent cities, where there is an abundance of mirrors for them to dance between. They love to be seen."

"Why are they so quiet?" Vera asked as one bearing their face pressed their hands against the glass and mouthed the word, *Hello.*

"They just don't make noise. One can lip read, guess at charades, or mind anything they write on the mirrors, but otherwise their world is silent to us." Tage offered.

Both Thora and Vera were enamored with them, returning waves, offering a *hello* back or even stopping briefly to offer a bow and receiving a few in return. However, their journey soon took them to the end of the hall, where the mirrors no longer continued into the next chamber.

The room was far larger than Vera had ever even imagined. It was dome shaped, cut directly out of the mountain and hollowed. It was held aloft by numerous pillars which would take at least three or four Vera's to hug in order to touch one another's hand in the process; each holding its own post where a guard stood dutifully. At least twice the height of the hallway in height, the room offered a paper-doll-like set of windows strung forty feet high and angled inward to cast as much light into the audience chamber as possible. Several glowing motes of light twinkled high above them and slowly circled, allowing the room to be fully illuminated in order for those on the ground to see the murals painted on the ceiling which depicted the exploits of Anessa, helping her people and those she would later meet on her path to founding the Rushnay.

At the end of the audience chamber, centered on a half-a-flight of stairs, was a high throne made of gold and red tufted pillows. A mural was painted above the chair, one of seven tall figures in long white robes and the blackest of skin under white watchful eyes, with two figures in long black robes, white skin and black eyes. They each carried a golden ring which levitated above their cradled hands, while the two dark robed individuals carried a tarnished ring. The beings were the NIИ, painted to give guidance to the finnae who presently occupied the seat below them.

"Enter and approach!" His voice commanded, bold, loud and eager. His horns jetted from his brow nearly a foot-and-a-half and curled upwards slightly at their tips, identifying him as part of the Leekyn tribe. Despite sitting down, his height was imposing at nearly six-foot-six, with broad shoulders and tight muscles on his exposed chest with nothing more than a purple cloak draped over one shoulder and spilling over an arm of the chair and down onto the ground. His hair was dark, fluffed and it flowed down his body and ended at his bulging abs. His skin was bronze and his eyes popped with a black eyeliner.

Tage stayed behind, yet ushered silently with his hand for both Vera and Thora to follow the finnae's instruction. The two of them swallowed, almost at the same time, in order to rally their courage and did as they were asked. However, once they reached halfway, they halted to the motion of his raised hand.

"I am Gorvo, the Aponae, and the voice of the Aness Leekyn Shreeves Cali. I am told that Shem Zhalinya Faunis sends you to me, that you wish entry into the school of ballet," he straightened his back and leaned forward in his seat, "and you bring me terrible news. So… what is this news you bring with you, hmm? What is so important that you have need to invoke the Shem of the Faunis?"

Vera felt a giant pressure from above sweep down upon them, like a crushing invisible hand cementing them to the floor. Their heart started pounding loudly in their chest, a sensation that caused centipedes of anxiety crawling throughout their body. Vera exhaled, in order to find their voice amongst the tempest that was brewing inside them, a storm filled with winds and green lightning.

119

With a curtsy, they did their best to pull back a flood of tears that threatened to break past their eyes. "My village, Tandermundt of Arcadia, is gone. Everything… everyone was taken over the mountain by a velocitrix." Vera looked down and a horrendous thought entered their mind, *You should have died with them.* They did everything they could to push the thought away and bury it deep inside. "The narghoulim hunts me and will continue to do so until one of us is dead."

The Aponae folded his massive hands and rested them mid-chest. With ease, he pulled himself forward, leaning into the severity of the news. "Many condolences for the dead, and for your loss. I am relieved that you were able to make it within the protection of our city. Worry not, the velocitrix will not dare to seek you here. Not unless it has a death wish." He stood up, his muscles stretching themselves as the light cascaded off of him, building shadows in places that only made him look bigger and more intimidating. "And it's your wish to train to become a chevalière, is that correct? To seek revenge?"

The word *revenge* sent pinpricks across their skin and their heart flashed with a fire which steadied her resolve. "To seek vengeance for my neighbors, friends and family! But also to make sure that this never has to happen again!"

"I am sad to inform you that this will happen again, even if you manage to defeat all odds and break the Glass. Narghoulims, no matter how many times they are slain, eventually return – and they return hungry."

"Then so long as I live, I'll slay every narghoulim that dares to return!" Vera clenched their fists tightly, fear that they would be denied entry to the Regal Ballet Academy, which quickly turned to anger.

Thora watched her friend, concerned that all of this was too much. Perhaps asking for something like this was too rash, too soon, by not giving them the opportunity to grieve. But Vera was their own person, no family to steer them back from a turbulent sea of pain. Yet, Vera wanted to fight, much like they have in the past for the people they loved. Who was she to deny them that?

Gorvo nodded, "I respect your dedication." He pulled his arms behind his back and wrapped his hands around his forearms as he descended the stairs of the throne and moved towards them. "However, becoming a chevalière takes more than that. Most students train at the age of seven and work their entire lives. You are already miles behind in training. You'd only have until your sixteenth year to break the Glass, and should you fail, you would have lost that time from an apprenticeship." He stopped no more than ten feet away. "Are you sure this is what you want?"

Vera stood in their resolve. "Yes, this is what I want."

He paused, looked the two of them over, examined their limbs, legs, estimated their stride and muscles. "Very well..." he returned towards the stairs. "Consider this your audition, Caetin. Show me how you can move. You only have one opportunity to convince me." He returned to his throne and sat. "You may start whenever you're ready."

Chapter 16
The Audition

"The star constellation Gleisne represents the people behind the glass, the passing of ancestors into their realm and the tale of those spirits who are trapped in-between. For the ballet-knight who is born beneath it, may resonate the dance of the dead, a ghostly corps de ballet, who appear at the dancer's side and restore the chevalière's power."

– Almanac of Stars and Constellations.

Vera glanced at Thora, who nodded and ushered them forward while she backed away to provide them additional room. With a strong inhalation of breath, and a fortifying of their nerves, Vera stood in preparation for what would come next.

They remembered Ayren, Felicity and Nam, as the three of them practiced together for the Danse de L'arrivée. The very dance that would have marked them as adults, the same dance that Vera would have performed as soon as they had turned sixteen as well. There was an order to it, one that Vera couldn't quite remember, as well as motions that were excluded from the original performance. It all didn't matter now, all that mattered was that they were there fighting for their friends, family and neighbors.

Without any music, partners or ceremonial dress, Vera launched themself forward, hands outstretched, and shifted into a baril tour. A flash of wind trespassed in Vera's mind, a harsh roar which twisted as they spun. Anger brewed inside them, like a serpent coiled around their heart, they lashed out, thrusting their left fist upwards to strike at the sky, then – as if blasted by a bolt of green lightning – Vera's chest fell backward, shoulders popping forwards, as they leaned backward, fallen down, as their knees buckled.

Upon their knees, they spread them wide, then twisted so one leg would jet outwards and rotate on their heel. With a push, as if fighting against an onslaught, they rotated upwards, onto their foot, while swinging their back leg in attitude. Vera imagined that moment, tents pitched, laughter and music, the smell of meats roasting, of sweet cakes and salted nuts. They twirled in reverie, leading with their raised leg like a spinning top, their arms over their head as if attempting to capture the sun within their hands.

They kicked high, they kicked low – Ayren was challenging them again. They ran, leaping rooftop to rooftop in their mind, ducking, dodging, facing their intended. At the fire now, reaching out for his hand, wanting to bring it close to their chest to feel his warmth on their sternum so he could feel their heartbeat. Vera threw themself to the ground, as the phantom of him vanished leaving them in desolation. The village… empty as it was without sign of structure. A broken wall.

Vera raised themself back up, and leapt high into the air, they spun, and spun, and crashed down once more. Vera spread themself across the floor, hands reaching to all who had been taken over the mountain, until they pounded their fist onto the ground. Not defeated, not destroyed, not desolate. They drew themself up to their feet, thrust both fists down and rolled them outwards, feet striking the ground like spears into the flesh of a narghoulim. Right hand up, palm extended, rotating into the sky, then back again meeting with the left, and repeat on the opposite side. Forward step, back step, twist in the hips, and turn – hands extended, reaching for a partner, for a friend, for a neighbor.

Left step, right step, jump. Hands released, fingers closed, and Vera slashed the air and crisscrossed their arms in front of them. Right step, left step, jump.

The Aponae leaned forward, eyes squinting as if seeing something that was lying hidden from the rest of the world. Tage raised his head, and set his eyes on the empty spaces beside and behind the child. Both finnae sensed something there, a presence of spirits who followed Vera's motions, who danced alongside them invisible and with purpose.

Gorvo raised his hand from his throne. "Enough." His voice echoed through the hall like a damning proclamation one which startled Vera, ripping them out of their emotions that continued to crash inside of them.

He stood, causing his muscles to bulge, and he stepped down from his higher floor and came down the stairs with his hands crossed behind his back. He stopped in front of Vera, towering over them like an orselon.

Vera's heart trembled at the thought of being told to leave, at being denied and sent on their way without the opportunity of being able to at least try.

Gorvo smiled, his voice deep and mysterious. "Follow me."

Vera felt nervousness pirouette inside them, an unending chain of worry of whether or not they had managed to pass the Aponae's test. Thora and Gander followed alongside Vera, while Tage was not far behind. The Aponae kept a firm stride, one that took them through several rooms, hallways, and passages that moved deep into the mountain.

Where is he taking us? Why isn't he saying anything? Wherever they were headed Vera knew it would be their fate. *Is he taking me to the Rushinay to help me find other family members to take care of me? Will I forever be trapped within the walls of Adalace?*

Thora sensed Vera's growing anxiety and placed her hand in theirs, gripping them tightly. Their travels were met with beautiful architecture, marble statues, elegant mirrors, hand-crafted furniture, beautiful tapestries and galleries. In what would seem like a funeral march, they eventually broke through the exterior of the mountain and stepped back into sunlight.

From the high platform from which they stepped upon, which led down several flights of steps, and into the city, Vera was able to behold a sight which lit a bonfire in their heart; dispelling all the fear they had experienced along the way.

Nestled in a leg of the mountain, shining like a beacon of hope, and protected by numerous statues of chevalières of the past, was Nisnafell – the Regal Ballet Academy.

Vera could not contain themself. "Am I being enrolled? Are you letting me train to be a chevalière?"

"If that is what you wish, I believe you may have a chance." The Aponae offered as he took his first steps down the flight of stairs.

"He thinks I have a chance, Thora!" Vera squealed with delight, joy bursting at their cheeks, and excitement threatening to cause them to burst. With incredible speed, the Caetin grabbed hold of their best friend and squeezed them in both relief and elation.

Gander barked his own excitement and jumped up into the air in celebration.

Vera rushed to him as well, seized him around the mane and wrapped their arms around his neck. Tears of happiness poured from the Caetin's eyes as they imagined the possibilities, the chance at fighting back.

The Aponae stalled at the top steps. "Your journey has been hard, and now it will become even harder. Training to become a chevalière will be intensive, grueling, and you'll have little time to do anything else."

Vera released their kornig, and returned to where they previously stood. With a nod they affirmed their commitment. "I'll do whatever it takes."

"Good." He turned back towards the stairs and motioned for them to follow. "Because you have only a few years to matron ballet. All the training in the world may not be enough for you to break through the Glass. Should you fail, like so many do, your options are quite limited. Usually, you'd be invited to join the corps de ballet, but with the velocitrix hunting you, you would become a danger to those around you. You could be out on a mission, your chevalière fighting another narghoulim. Defenseless, that is when it would strike."

Vera swallowed hard as they followed him. "So… if I can't break through the Glass, does that mean I will have to leave?" The wind rustled their hair as a stark reminder of what waited for them outside the walls of the city.

"You'd have to continue with your apprenticeship outside of the Nisnafell and you'd never be able to leave Adalace, not unless the velocitrix is slain." Gorvo replied sternly.

"When was the last time a velocitrix was slain?" Thora asked with peaked curiosity.

"Only once before." He paused as he conquered a few more stairs. "While devastating as it is, the world is lucky that the velocitrix does not appear very often."

Despite their grim conversation, it held no bearing over the excitement which continued to pump through Vera's veins. Despite the fatigue from having traveled so far, Vera continued to move through each stride with purpose. In time, they reached the front doors of the Regal Ballet Academy.

The exterior of the building, like the rest of the city, was inspired by the natural world. It held several organic shapes, budding arches, with many different styles of flowers, vines and leaves. The doors themselves were carved to appear like dancer's trees, with nude silhouttes of finni, faunae and finnyr wrapped together in some graceful pas de trois with other branches carrying spade-shaped leaves and star-shaped blossoms.

Without even an introduction, the Aponae pulled one of the

giant rings, drawing the doors open as if they were a mere inconvenience. He revealed a grand hall, one marked with several statues of dancers, some wielding giant Geist weapons, while others performing a variety of dance techniques. Three stories in height, the hall was adorned with a grand staircase leading up to the higher floors. Around them, they could hear the echoes of music, all disjointed from one another playing completely different melodies and by varying instruments such as a piano or a violin. The air had a tinge of sweat mixed with the scent of resin. Throughout, the place adhered to a similar style as to the exterior of the building, with elements of nature incorporated into nearly every feature of the room. The wooden stairs had flowers engraved into their fronts, the railings extended upwards like a growing vine, and even the walls had smooth statues chiseled directly out of the stone.

There was more beauty here than Vera had seen in an entire lifetime.

The hall was empty, as it seemed everyone was in attendance of classes. Gorvo strolled inside, across the marble flooring with a mosaic of intricate golden branch-like designs, and up the stairs towards a higher floor. They each kept in pace with him, until they reached the third floor, where he turned down a hallway and continued until he reached a pair of double doors with red handles. An instructor's voice could be heard counting out the beats as a piano played within.

Without care to interruption, the Aponae flung the doors wide open, revealing a massive twenty-foot tall ballroom, with tall arched windows lining the back wall which drew in the rays of the sun like a host welcoming her guests. In the center of the floor were five wooden barres, where in each were decorated with four dancers in black nyri silk tights – staggered two to each side – following a set of motions.

The music interrupted as soon as the pianist recognized the individual who trespassed into the classroom. The instructor was an aged finni with silver hair which was meticulously tied

127

up in a bun and held in place with a gold ribbon. She too was dressed in nyri silk, the fabric pressing firmly against her body which complimented her toned physique and was coupled with a translucent skirt. She turned in aggravation towards the sudden interruption. Her horns were large, which curled downwards from her brow and ended with its tips pointing towards the outer edges of her cheeks; denoting her part of the Zhah tribe. They appeared as if they were helping to bring the finni to smile, but the finni was not smiling, she grimaced.

"You're interrupting." The ballet matron scoffed.

His back straight, his shoulders pressed, the Aponae returned a sly smile. "So I am. I'm enrolling these two students. I expect them to receive the same level of dedication that you provide all your other students."

She tilted her head to see past the muscular man, then crossed her arms over her chest in defiance. "They are both too old to start instruction now, the beginning age is seven. As you know."

The students, all appearing around the same age as Vera and Thora, giggled amongst themselves in witness to the exchange.

Vera could feel heat pouring into their cheeks. They weren't expecting to be drawn into the center of a feud, but it was already apparent that they were, and have always been, at odds with one another.

"All the same, you will train them." Gorvo stood his ground and as first finnae to the Aness, he was within his rights.

"I will be registering a complaint with the Aness. You can be certain of that."

He chuckled and placed his arms firmly behind his back. "As you do." He turned his head and nodded to both Vera and Thora before he left the room and exited through the hallway.

However, the ballet matron was not finished. She shouted

after him, "Fauni cannot become chevalière!"

The students giggled more while some whispered to their barre mates, and while Vera couldn't hear exactly what was being said, they knew that it was about the two of them.

The matron turned back around to address her students. "I take it you all remember the combination? Opeena, please lead everyone through the motions until I return."

A thin finni with long legs, and horns similar to those of Gorvo, moved to the center floor and began counting… "And five, six, seven, eight—"

The music began again.

The rest of the students scrambled to get into first position, one hand on the barre, the other lowered to mid-thigh, raised it to chest level with their hand partially turned at the wrist inwardly, their outer fingers raised as if holding a pencil between them, and arm extended outwards to the side before they struck the ground with their foot opposite the barre in frappe.

"Now," the finni approached them gracefully, yet held them in place with a stern glare. "You two."

Vera and Thora both swallowed hard. Barely a minute in, and already they were in trouble.

Chapter 17
Shoes and Placement

"The nyri is a tiny rodent characterized by a smashed face, long ears - for which they are known to step on - four dexterous feet and a lengthy tail. Capable of extreme feats of flexibility, the nyri can bend backwards and touch their nose to their rump. From their bellies, they are able to produce a strand of silk, which they use for their nests and for trapping bugs. Nyri silk is harvested then woven into clothing which has enormous elasticity and breathability. Students of ballet are frequent wearers of nyri silk tights which provide a level of modesty while showing off their forms for precise instruction."

– Zoology of Orabelle

The ballet matron harshly called for them to follow. Her strides were long, and her motions quick, causing both Vera and Thora to rush to keep up. Already Vera felt as if they had done something wrong. Despite their hussle, Tage and Gander kept up and remained silent.

They arrived at a hallway which led to three other classrooms, each filled with students of different ages either working from the barre to the sound of accompaniment, stretching or in the center floor working on foot and body placement. The door she halted at appeared heavy, wooden but otherwise ordinary which was unusual due to the artistry of the rest of the academy.

She placed her hand on the door knob, and strictly announced, "This is a staff only supply closet. If you need to requisition anything, you'll submit your request with Coppelia." With a loud creak, the door opened in her direction and she briefly went inside, only to return with two pair of tights and leotards for each of them.

Quickly, she shoved the garments towards Thora, who struggled at first with understanding that she was meant to carry them.

After closing the door, the finni honed her hawkish gaze upon Tage as if for the first time. "And your purpose is?"

"Apologies, auguri. I was here only to deliver them to their destination." Tage kept calm, and was very soft spoken.

"Job well done." She professed in agitation. "No guests allowed, so you'll need to leave."

"Of course, auguri." Tage tipped the brim of his hat and without further word or goodbyes, he left.

The ballet matron called after. "And don't forget your pet."

"Um, excuse me, auguri." Vera offered in hopes of appeasing her. "Gander belongs to me."

The finni straightened her back and looked down on Vera with condemnation. "You will refer to me as Fin Ississ. I will take you to Fyr Drussel who will have you fitted for shoes, then you will immediately report to Fin Benopal who will sort out your lodgings, schedule and placement for your…" she stressed the word with disdain, "pet."

Gander sat on the floor, stared up at the finni, panted a few times, then licked the side of his mouth before returning to his stare.

"This way." She insisted.

She lured them down towards the ground floor and to another corridor, beyond where the music from other classrooms could reach. Fin Ississ stopped at the foot of the hallway and pointed down its stretches. "Third door on your right. Tell him you're both here for a fitting." She gave Vera a distasteful look, scoffed, then she hastily walked away.

Thora turned to Vera. "I get the feeling that we're not exactly welcome here."

131

Vera nodded with a touch of nervousness, but then a smile crept back upon their face. "But we're in! I can become a chevalière and we get to be fitted for shoes. Free shoes!"

A gleam of joy raised in Thora's cheeks. "I like shoes."

The door was already opened, revealing a vast chamber filled with shelves who were bursting with different kinds of pointe shoes. Each shoe was made from a variety of colors, many for matching variances in skin color while others were simply for comfort of style. The shelves themselves were intricate with vines and flowers engraved upon their surfaces. In one corner of the room, there were ballet slippers arranged by color and by size. Further, there were knee-high and thigh-high versions of the shoes which were made of leather, but lacked the typical construction of most boots such as no heel and the soles of the feet were protected by a type of soft hide rather than hardened leather.

Light filtered in through a number of tiny windows set at the very top of the wall, which provided more than enough to see by. Towards the back of the room, huddled over a small worn wooden desk was an older finnyr, whose facial features were androgynous though sharp in the chin and cheekbones. A small set of horns, about three times longer than Vera's, were nestled atop their brow and grew outwards before curling inwards, denoting the finnyr as belonging to the Davonii tribe. Their white hair swept backwards, taught against their brow, and appeared slightly oiled to give it a slick look. All their hair was bound by a pink ribbon and tied into a perfect bow. Their clothes were fairly ordinary, but kept a green apron which was suspended around their neck and tied behind their back. Inside the pockets a few tools poked their heads out, as well as a single pointe shoe which seemed to be missing its mate.

"Excuse me." Vera offered meekly. "Are you Fyr Drussel?"

Fyr Drussel turned around and straightened their back, only

six inches higher than Thora, yet appeared in peak health. "Oh, my, new students. You're both so… well, much older than our usual enrollees."

"That seems to be a growing observation." Thora replied as she shifted her head, but was careful not to bump into anything with her antlers.

The Davonii gasped and briefly placed their hands over their heart. "And you have a kornig! I love kornigs so much." They hurried over so that they were only an arms-length away. "May I pet him? He looks like such a good little boy."

Vera and Thora cast a glance between themselves before Vera smiled. "I don't see why not."

Gander sat on his rump, while Fyr Drussel bent over and placed their hand on his head and stroked between his head feathers. The petting turned to scratching, and Gander hummed with contentedness.

"You're such a good boy, aren't you? Who's a good boy?" Fyr Drussel continued with being enraptured with the beast.

Soon there was a rapid thudding on the floor as Gander's tail wagged happily.

Vera giggled, which was perhaps the first time they had done so since they had left Tandermundt. It made Thora smilee.

After Fyr Drussel got their fill, they straightened back up and motioned with their hand to come farther into the room. "Looks like I'll need to get everyone fitted for some shoes, except this guy." They petted Gander once again. "We don't have any pointe shoes in your size, I'm afraid."

"How long have you been working here at the academy?" Vera asked as they were shown to a chair to sit.

"Forever, it seems, and before you ask – yes, I've been loving every minute of it. Also, yes to your previous question. I am Fyr

133

Drussel. I always pride myself on getting to know every student. And who might you two be?" The Davonii helped Vera out of their boots, placed their fingers on the Caetin's foot, felt for muscular patterns, then switched to the other one.

"I'm Caetin Kom Vera." Vera said as they winced from Fyr Drussel hitting a sore spot from all that walking.

"And I'm Thora of the Faunis, but I prefer just Thora."

"You may be surprised to learn this, but you aren't the first Faunis to grace these halls and I'm certain you won't be the last."

Thora nodded. "Metalli Faunis. I am familiar with his stories."

"That's right, it was Metalli. Such a pleasant faunae. It's too bad your people can't breach the Glass and become chevalières. However, if anyone could, he would have. I'm certain of it."

Fyr Drussel placed Vera's foot back on the ground. "Okay, next customer."

Thora took her turn in the chair with Vera, but she took her own boots off before Fyr Drussel started in on feeling her feet.

Thora looked grim. "Fauni can't become chevalières, how come?"

"That's a very hard question to answer." Fyr Drussel seemed to struggle with getting around the callouses that Thora had, evidence of her nomadic life. "It may have to do with the same reason as to why they are unable to perform pantomimes."

Thora nodded. "Our Shem tells us that the Fauni are tied to the soil which is why we cannot breach the Glass, nor would any Fauni want to. When it comes to pantomimes, we may not be able to create the motions with our hands, but we have dances which can be similar. It just takes us a little longer."

"Which explains why Fauni are so well suited for the corps

de ballet." The elder Davonii smiled warmly, and finished off their work with Thora's feet. "Perfect." Fyr Drussel eased Thora's foot to the floor after their prodding, then eased back up to standing.

With precise movements, the finnyr strolled up to a shelf containing ballet slippers of varying sizes, chose two black pairs, then shifted to an adjacent shelf and delicately selected a pair of tan colored pointe shoes. "For Thora, I recommend these Majester pointe shoes, since you have long slender feet. And for Vera…" They reached up and grabbed a pair that was slightly darker in coloration from the higher shelf. "These are Luchelian's, which will give you more comfort in the box."

Fyr Drussel handed the shoes over to the two of them, which Vera accepted with excitement and Thora took humbly. Then grabbed two pairs of ballet slippers and handed them to each of them respectively.

"Thank you so much!" Vera offered with swollen cheeks of joy.

The finnyr nodded. "I suppose the two of you will need to meet Fin Benopal. She can help you with classroom placement. I'll take you to her. This place can be impossible to navigate on your first day." With a flourish of the Fyr Drussel's arm, they pointed to the exit. "This way, my dears."

Fyr Drussel was correct, the Regal Ballet Academy was quite the labyrinth once they moved away from the grand foyer. There were hallways that lead deep into the side of the mountain, and some which curled around it like a snake. While impressive from the outside, it surely did not give them any indication as to how large the place truly was.

However, Fyr Drussel kept to a decent pace and delivered them to an office where a finni, an Alshep whose horns towered a foot from their brow and twisted in the center, sat comfortably

135

behind a desk covered in papers, books, and an assortment of writing quills. Her hair was long and brown, with several cowrie shells braided into her hair. She appeared close to Vera's mother's age, was plump and was faun-blessed in her ears. Her style was unique, as she wore a white dress, several beaded necklaces with dangling charms, bracelets, and sandals. As she smiled at their entry, her cheeks swelled and grew rosy as if she had been stung twice by a bee.

"And who are these fine individuals, Le'Shoon?" She swayed her shoulders back and forth with excitement for the potential of new students.

Fyr Drussel placed their hand briefly on both Thora's and Vera's shoulder as they called out their name, "This is Thora and this is Vera. We've just had their fitting and need placement."

"This is so wonderful. We usually don't see new students after the initial enrollment period. This is a delight! An absolute delight!" She placed a hand on her sternum. "I'm Fin Benopal, or you can just call me Mattie. I help students with classes, room assignments, complaints, accommodations, you name it, I'm there to help." Mattie released a quick high-pitched giggle that one would expect more from a child than an adult. She selected a quill with a peppenach feather and dipped it in ink. "Now, should we get to it? How much ballet experience have you had and which teacher did you train under?"

"I'm afraid," Vera spoke up with a drop of confidence, "That neither of us have had any ballet experience, exactly, but we do know how to dance that we learned from our families and communities."

Mattie's eyebrows sunk and her face contorted into shock. Perplexed, she turned to Fyr Drussel. "My goodness, does Fin Ississ know?" Her voice was filled with worry.

"That's who took us to see Fyr Drussel. She did not seem very happy about it. We wouldn't have been allowed in, I believe, if it wasn't for the Aponae's insistence." Thora pointed out in hopes of calming everyone's concerns.

"The Aponae!" Mattie gasped.

"Oh dear!" Fyr Drussel echoed in a similar tone.

"Well, I am certainly not one to question the Aponae or his methods." Mattie crossed her hands at the wrists and straightened her fingers in prayer. "May the NIИ protect, and the Aness guide us with her wisdom." She returned in preparation to write. "Now, I won't coat things with honey, you both have a lot of catch up to do. I'm afraid I'll need to double up your classes, which will not leave much time for other things. How old are you both?"

"Thora and I are 13—" but Vera wasn't 13, they had a birthday while they were on the run from the velocitrix. "I mean…" they swallowed hard at the realization that not only did they miss it entirely, but the party, the friends, the family, all of it was gone. "Thora is 13 and I'm 14. My birthday was a few days ago." They grew quiet and stared off into the distance that existed in the deepest grains of Mattie's desk.

"Happy belated Birthday!" Both Fyr Drussel and Mattie said in unison.

Thora stole a glance at her best friend and felt her heart drop into her stomach.

"Don't you two worry about a thing. I'll put you both into our beginning courses, as well as have you in some of the intermediate levels just so that you know what to aspire to. However, be sure in the intermediate courses to only observe floor work because your ankles aren't ready for what everyone else can do, okay? I'd hate for you to have to be rushed off to Rudy."

Mattie wrote out a slip and handed it to Vera. "And you'll need to take your pet to Silva's for boarding."

137

"Boarding?" Vera asked after taking the slip of paper and turning it over in their hands.

"No pets aloud in the academy, sweetheart. But don't worry, you can stop in at Silva's whenever you have a free moment." Mattie stood up and nodded to Fry Drussel. "I'll take you both to your room assignments, okay? You'll be able to get settled in there."

Vera missed their birthday, and now they'll have to give up Gander for boarding outside of the Academy… this was once a promising day. *"What more could go wrong?"* They pondered gloomily to themselves.

Chapter 18
Roommates

"There are those who are born beneath the Chevalière constellation, believed to be empowered by all the ballet knights who came before. Despite the namesake, those born beneath these stars are no more likely to become a ballet knight than any other student. However, because of their influence over healing pantomimes, they are highly valued members of society especially when lending a hand or two to student injuries."

- Zhah Ississ Belle, Professor of Dance, The Regal Ballet Academy.

After climbing many flights of stairs, Mattie led them to a long hallway, where several doors flanked them on either side. They had made their way to the residence hall, where numerous dancers of varying ages lived. It had been a long walk, and though it was far from the classrooms, Vera could still hear the music coming from ballet lessons. It was certainly something they would have to get used to.

Seven doors down on the left-hand side, Mattie stopped and knocked lightly. A monotone seeped through the cracks, "It's open" Without any hesitation, Mattie turned the knob and strolled inside.

"Lyro, how is the injury?" Mattie asked casually to the presence in the room.

When Vera and Thora entered behind her, they were confronted by an androgynous ebony face that inspected them from atop a bed near the center of the room. Their hair was long, dark and curled near its tips. Their eyes sparkled like brilliant emeralds and their lips were lush and full, which curved downards in a smile – as their head hung upside down off the foot of the bed, and aimed towards the door. A pair of thick horns curved back from their brow overtop their head a good

139

nine to ten inches in length, denoting them as a member of the Ishaya tribe.

"Coming along, I believe." Lyro offered without taking their eyes off the two new students. Their voice was very chant-like, offering no hint one way or the other of whether they appreciated guests, yet there was a calmness to it.

Vera shifted their eyes to Lyro's foot which was elevated atop a pillow, bare and wrapped with white tape to keep kindness to it.

"Not to worry, I'm sure Ruby will be along shortly to tend to your foot and you'll be back to the barre in no time." Mattie smiled, which puffed out her cheeks and brightened the rosiness of them.

She extended her hand out to Vera and Thora who still stood but a single step into the room, while Gander sniffed the exterior of the hallway. "These are new students, Vera and Thora. They'll be sharing the room with you. I hope you don't mind."

Lyro focused on Vera and stared at their eyes long enough that they wondered if they had taken an interest in them. "Not at all. This room is quite empty with just me inside." Their eyes shifted to where they would be staying which included a wardrobe, a nightstand, a small chest and a single bed for each of them. Lyro's side of the room was filled with clothes, a few books of poetry, some artists' brushes and pens, ink and paper.

"Vera and Thora, this is Lyro. Lyro knows the academy well, so if either of you have any questions, I'm sure they'll be happy to provide them to you. Now I've written you both a schedule starting tomorrow, please be early to classes if you wish to leave a good impression with your instructors." Mattie extended her hand, offering Vera two slips of paper.

Vera took them and thanked her with a nod.

"I'll leave you both to it then." Mattie exited the room, then briefly poked her head in. "And don't forget to take your pet to Silva's, okay? We can't have it roaming around the academy while you're in class. Ississ would have a fit."

Lyro continued to watch them unmoved from their upside down position on the bed. "I had thought that it would see another year without roommates." A grin turned downward on their face in a very sluggish manner. They looked straight ahead, "Things are just now becoming interesting." The last comment seemed more of a commentary to the room, rather than directed at them particularly.

A few moments passed, and it seemed that Lyro was content with staring at a spot on the wall, rather than engaging in further conversation. So the two of them nervously strolled across to the other side and chose their beds. Vera took the one towards the middle of the room while Thora took the farthest from the door.

They didn't have much to unpack.

Gander spent his time sniffing about the room, chasing down invisible scents in one corner to the other, under furniture and near the window. It was the scent of past feet, resin, perfumes and other ointments used to mask the scent of hours of painstaking dancing. As he was through the majority of his investigation, nose down to the wood, Lyro made an additional comment to the room.

"Such a shame." They sighed.

"I'm sorry?" Asked Vera as they stuffed their bag beneath the bed and stowed the dagger beneath their pillow that Thora had given to them for their birthday.

"It would have been lovely to have a kornig around to liven up everyone's spirits. So many days are spent dancing, studying and training, yet very little is dedicated to leisure. I imagine it would be difficult for either of you to get time away to visit Silva's. All that time spent in a kennel." Lyro sighed once more.

141

"Makes my heart ache just thinking about it."

"There won't be any time? None at all?" Vera asked now having fallen into a pit of desperation.

"We all don't have much time left, you know? Up to the hour of our sixteenth birthday, we must shatter the Glass or forever barred from becoming a chevalière." They turned their head to look at them both. "Years can go quickly here, but for those in Silva's care? Might seem like forever with no one to visit them."

"There has to be some time." Thora implored as she struggled to pull Vera away from the edge of panic.

"I can't send Gander away! He would get so lonely and he'd feel like I would abandon him! He's the only family left, Thora!" Vera quickly strolled over to Gander and wrapped their arms around him tightly. "What are we to do?"

Thora thought quickly. "What if we hide him up here in the room? That way he won't be by himself for very long."

"No, that won't work. He needs bathroom breaks, and can't be cooped up for long periods of time. He's used to the outside. He's used to being with me." Vera just hugged him tighter.

"If only there was a way for him to go undetected through the school. Perhaps no one would even notice that he was there." Lyro pondered as they rested their head back into its prior position as they now stared at the ceiling.

Vera's face brightened. "Wait… Lyro you're a genius!"

"Am I?" Lyro asked as a question towards themself.

"Thora! I could use a pantomime to make him invisible! That way he can be with us and no one will know that he is there."

Lyro smiled to themself, thinking of tall grass, vast fields, and a herd of beasts munching away for the daily meal while a Caetin watched over them vigilantly.

"Won't he move about during classes, or bump into students?" Thora asked with a touch of concern. "What if he's discovered?"

"Gander does everything that I ask him to! You'll see. He's very well behaved when he needs to be. There is no way that he'll get caught." Vera released him from their embrace and stood up in order to keep in proper distance for the pantomime.

"Lyro, what do you think?" Thora pleaded for a voice of reason. "Can a kornig go undetected like that?"

"Well..." Lyro paused in thought. "I think it's certainly worth a try. What other option do you have?"

Vera nodded. "You won't say anything will you, Lyro? Not to anyone?"

"Cross my heart and hope to die." Lyro chuckled to themself on that last part.

"Then that settles it!" Vera declared. "They pressed their thumbs together, curled their fingers into their palms and made their knuckles touch. Then, in a tiny dance of fingers, their pointer fingers extended, touched, then retreated back into their palms, followed by pinkie and ring fingers. They rolled their wrists, keeping their pointer fingers and thumbs touching and opened with palms facing away from them. Their hands closed, palms together, then tilted downwards to point at Gander.

With an intake of air, Vera blew across the top of their pointer fingers sending a sparkling cloud of dust out into the room. The cloud drifted down over top of Gander, who tried to lick it up while it gently settled atop him from head to tail. Quickly it absorbed into him and the kornig disappeared completely.

"I did it!" Vera clapped their hands together briefly in excitement, having a small sliver of doubt that the pantomime they had previously learned with their father would have left their memory.

"Let's hope that we don't accidentally trip over him." Thora mused with worry.

A low whine came from the spot where Gander had previously been.

A new knock came at the door and Lyro grinned. "Come in." A joyful tone seemed to have snuck into their words.

Both Vera and Thora snapped up. A touch of blush flooded into their cheeks due to having to put the invisible Gander to test so soon.

The door opened and in walked a young finnae with brown hair that was pulled up into a bun, which rested between a pair of two feet long horns that jetted straight from their brow. Their fashions were simple, with a cotton grey shirt, a pair of black shorts and was wrapped with a belt which held several pouches. Their voice was deep yet soft and reassuring. "Hello. I hear that you stumbled and injured your foot. How are you managing?"

"I'll survive for a little longer, I think." Lyro offered with a sense of calm. "Thank you for coming so quickly."

"I wouldn't want you to miss more class than you already have." The individual smiled as warmly as possible. They motioned with their hand towards their injured foot. "Do you mind if I take a look?"

"Feel free."

As the individual shifted to the bedside to tend to Lyro's foot, Lyro turned their head, causing their dark curls to shift on the bed. "Vera and Thora, this is Fan Erdo Pench Ruby. Ruby is one of the academy's Chevals."

"A pleasure." Ruby offered with kindness without shifting his attention from Lyro's foot.

Vera's eyebrows dropped and their forehead scrunched.

"What's a Cheval?"

"Someone born under the Chevalière constellation which grants influence over healing pantomimes." Lyro offered.

"Certainly a gift which comes in handy when ensuring the health of the students here, that's for sure." Ruby advised as he pushed on some points of Lyro's foot, with one such spot causing Lyro to flinch with pain and hiss through their teeth.

"Nothing needs to be set, so if you give me a few moments I'll have your foot as good as new." Ruby made himself comfortable on the bed, and started shifting his fingers into different positions in order to work out a pantomime; the exact motions Vera was unable to catch from their view in the room. A flash of sunlight brightened the head of the bed, where it descended in individual rays down atop Lyro's injury. The light quickly soaked into their foot and in a moment, the pantomime was over.

Lyro flexed their foot back and forth to ensure that all was well. They then shifted from lying down into a sitting position. "Thank you so much. It's back to feeling like normal. I can head back to class now."

Ruby nodded while he returned to standing. "If you experience any kind of discomfort, make sure you let your instructors know. I do not want you putting any kind of strain on your feet if they aren't ready. You understand?"

"Yes, Ruby, thank you."

"And that goes for the two of you as well. I'm sure I'll see you for your physicals later, but if you are ever injured do not continue to dance under any circumstance. You could make it worse, and in some cases recovery may be impossible. We can't endanger your chevalière futures over something we could have easily avoided."

Thora and Vera both nodded. "Yes, of course." They said in

unison.

An affirmative bark resounded in the room coming from an empty space on the ground. Gander had seemingly wanted to be part of the conversation as well.

With suspicious eyes, Ruby scanned about the room for its source. "Did you hear that? It sounded like a bark."

Vera bit their lower lip, while Thora looked off to the wall in order to act as if nothing had occurred.

"A bark? No… I didn't hear anything." Vera stumbled to keep their words from giving Gander away.

Thora shook her head but remained silent.

Ruby looked to Lyro who just shrugged their shoulders nonchalantly.

He pondered dubiously for a few moments but relented. "I'm glad that I was able to help. I have a few more appointments today so I should get to them as quickly as possible." He strolled towards the door. "It was good meeting you two." He gave a charming wave, exited the room and closed the door behind him.

Thora and Vera looked at each other and grinned with delight. It seemed that Gander would be able to stay after all. Besides, how much trouble could an invisible kornig get into?

Chapter 19
Gander the Invisible

"A chevalière must train from a young age. It takes years to matron muscular reflexes, flexibility, gain intricate precision and to build one's repertoire of technique. As a dancer progresses through childhood, they must display a memory that is reactive to a command, and only require it to be said once. A chevalière cannot doubt themself or give in to over-thinking, as a second could mean the difference between life and death."

-Coppelia, Professor of Dance, The Regal Ballet Academy, Adalace.

With luck, both Vera and Thora were placed together in their first class. Unfortunately, and most awkwardly, they were the oldest students in the room. Dressed in their black leotards, white tights and ballet slippers, they towered over the rest by a foot and a half in some cases. Filled with a variety of different tribes, skin tones, hair styles, and genders their classmates all seemed distracted by the two of them.

The room was exceptionally large, nearly four times Vera's height and at least forty feet on each wall. There were windows that stretched from ceiling to floor, facing south so as not to catch too much of the sunlight. A grand piano rested in a far corner, where a Phildhilyn finnae – a tribe known for piracy in the Moon Sea and identified by their thick horns jetting from the sides of their head before swooping downward and twisting outward about a good foot – was well-dressed and delicately shifting through his sheets of music.

Everyone was stretching. Some made use of one of the barres that were arranged evenly throughout the room, placing one foot on the highest rung then lending their torso over top of it, while others sat in the sideways splits and leaned over to one side then the other. Each individual's hands moved fluidly, as if they were part of some grand performance that was being marked by a hidden instructor.

Lyro was kind enough to show them stretches for their first class, how to breathe properly with each motion, and most importantly, how to warm up their muscles just before barre work began. Vera tried their best to follow what they had learned, but they were distracted knowing that not far away was Gander. He had come in with them and instead of walking through the thick of the room, they decided it was best to walk around the outskirts before finding an empty place for the two of them among the barres in the center floor at the back. And despite the size of the room, having a kornig around made the space around them seem very small. Giving him commands was, to say the least, difficult with so many curious minds about.

A small finni Viliph, with horns that grew out long and curled backwards towards the end, approached them and sweetly asked, "Are you two lost?"

Thora smiled her best smile and continued to stretch, leaving the question best answered for Vera who blinked a few times rather doubtfully and replied, "I don't believe so. We're new here and were told we needed to take lower-level classes."

Gander, of course, who was very excited to meet new people, had risen up from laying on the ground and began sniffing the air to determine whether he liked her scent.

"Really?" The finni seemed astonished, as if she had hadn't heard of anything like that before. She checked her bun on her head as it felt too tight before asking, "I've never seen a Fauni before either." She motioned towards Thora with her eyes, with them tracing the points of her antlers.

Thora continued to smile. "We don't come to Adalace very often. We prefer to travel around and stay out of large cities."

"Why do you move around so much?" Her eyes were lit

with wonder.

Not quite ready to discuss the finer points of Fauni culture, especially when the professor could walk in at any moment, she gave the easiest of answers, "Because we don't like sleeping in the same place. It's very uncomfortable, you know."

Gander positioned himself right in front of the finni, hoping that his presence would enact some form of interaction. Typically when he met new people they would reach out to pet him and talk to him in some way, but it seemed the finni wasn't interested in him at all, or perhaps she was just shy.

"But you're staying here now, right? How are you going to sleep, if you don't like sleeping in the same place?" Thora's response only seemed to solicit more questions, one's that she was not prepared to answer.

Vera quickly jumped in with a lie. "Well, I've been talking with a lot of other students and so far a few of them have agreed to switch beds with Vera, just so that she feels more comfortable. One night she'll be in my bed, then our roommate's bed, then the bed further down the hall and we all just rotate."

"That's really nice of them." She gave a trusting smile.

Just then, Gander – having lost patience to be recognized by the tiny finni – nuzzled his cold wet nose into the open palm of the girl and she yelped with surprise!

Quickly she pulled back her hand and took a few steps backwards in fright. "Something just touched me!"

"Gander, no!" Vera whispered harshly to the nothingness around them. "Go lay down."

Thora, not certain at first what had happened suddenly had the realization that the invisible kornig must have been involved and started moving her leg around in search of the beast and hoped that the action would be perceived as stretching.

Everyone in the classroom immediately halted what they were doing, and quickly turned their attention to the drama that was now unfolding in the classroom hoping to catch a piece of something to talk to their friends about after class.

A couple of the finni's friends came over and asked what had happened and she, quite loudly stated, "Something touched my hand! See!" She showed them her hand. "It's wet and gross!"

One of the finni's friends stared long and hard at Thora and asked rather accusingly, "What did you do?"

"Excuse me, Thora didn't do anything!" Vera snapped at her.

Just then, the doors to the classroom opened and in walked a lanky Tiff, whose horns curled down into half crescents and nearly poked her cheeks. She instantly noticed the commotion and clapped her hands together.

"Whatever it is that is happening, it's time to set it aside. Everyone at the barre please."

Everyone hastily complied without so much of a word, including the Villiph Gander had distressed though not without given the two of them a strange look.

The instructor glided near the piano and placed her hand at an empty place on a barre closest to her. "We'll start off in first position, two pliés, two grand pliés, relevé hold, tendu to second, repeat, place in third, repeat, forth, repeat, and fifth, repeat, then combré forward with circular port de bras, and combré back with circular port de bra, relevé and hold."

With each term, she showed the motion, with both hand and head position, even on the repeats, she went through each technique as thoroughly as the dancers themselves would.

"For those of us who are new, if you get lost, watch your neighbor. Follow as best as you can. Ed, if you please."

The pianist moved into an eight-count melody, striking the keys softly so that they could focus on the motions.

"And five, six, seven and eight…" and as she counted, her feet already in first position with each heel touching back-to-back, her fingers opposite of the barre raised slightly then pulled inward towards her navel, raised up her arm into a half bowl in front of her, and opened it wide to her side like opening a wing.

Both Vera and Thora did their best to follow after, though they were already making a mess of it. Everyone else showed a level of grace that was far outside of their reach, and at times felt very stop-go, as they watched the much younger students perform them with little difficulty. For Vera, it was maddening.

If this is how I dance, at this rate, I'm never going to be able to become a chevalière, they thought as they attempted the port de bras only to find themself two beats behind.

When the music ended, and the students returned to their starting position, Vera frowned with disappointment.

The lanky instructor addressed the entirety of the class. "Now remember," she placed her hand on her sternum. "We want to keep our chest pulled up, as if there is a beam of light pouring out of it and we don't want to blind anyone." She placed her hand atop her head and pulled at an invisible string which then pulled her body into alignment. "We must imagine that string through the center of our body, controlling us like a puppet would. Pull that string tight and your entire body will follow."

The Tiff smiled to everyone then walked over to Vera. "Do you mind if I use you for a demonstration?"

Vera, uncertain as to what that actually meant, just shook their head out of being agreeable and hoped that the instructor wouldn't otherwise call them out for their failings.

She squatted down and looked at Vera's outside foot, and

positioned herself so that the entire class could see, who it seemed, had their eyes glued to her every action.

"Can you perform a tendu please? So, push your foot forward."

Vera complied to the best of their ability, which was shaky especially since the instructor placed her hand on the top of their ankle to help guide it. "Now everyone, I saw that some of you over-crossed in first position, we want to ensure that we lead with the toes, keeping them connected to the floor." She pushed Vera's leg forward, then pressed down so that their big toe never left the floor. "Then as we reach the front, we lead with the ankle which will be lifted upwards and its side presented to the sky, with your toes never leaving contact with the floor." As Vera followed through with the directions, they began to see a few steps that they were missing to make routine better – at least more presentable.

The Tiff instructor nodded to Vera, then returned to standing. "Also, keep in mind we want to keep our hips square, and rotate in the thighs whenever we move our leg forward, or en devant." She showed the twisting movement at her own thigh, shifting her hands to present the motion clearly. "Now, do we all think we can do a little better? Do you want to go through the motions again? See what we learned?"

All the younger dancers nodded their heads, while some of them looked down at their feet, performed a few tendus in first position, as others straightened in their posture.

Thora leaned forward, over the barre to whisper to Vera. "Looks like we're all learning."

Vera smiled, and with a touch of their confidence restored, nodded in agreement.

Class proceeded, with Vera going through the motions again, then learning a few additional variations. Then, the instructor announced that the barre work was completed and everyone was to move to the center floor.

Without even being asked, the students picked up the barres together, and shifted them towards the back of the room. Vera and Thora followed after, being of course the last ones to put theirs in place alongside the others.

Gander, having been disturbed by all the movement, scampered off to the side, and on one occasion, brushed against a student who was returning to the center floor, who let out a yelp. With all the commotion that came from the transition from barre to center floor, very few students noticed – all except for Vera and Thora.

"Gander!" Vera whispered harshly. "Please go lay down."

Thora kept an eye about, first trying to locate where Gander had wandered off to in the room, as well as hoping that no one was paying any attention. However, there was one individual staring at Vera, the same finni Viliph from before who had gotten licked by Gander. She had the most suspicious of faces, and of course, Vera calling out to something was all the more peculiar.

With a quick tap and a motion of her head, Thora suggested, "I think someone is on to us."

Vera took a quick glance only to catch the child's gaze momentarily before she shifted it back to the front of the class where the instructor was about to speak.

"All right everyone, we're going to do some warm ups with some sautés." She presented herself in front of the class, arms down below her hips but positioned to appear like she's holding a bowl. "We start with feet in first position, get really deep in that demi-plie." She bent her knees to show how far down she wanted everyone to reach. "Then, spring upwards into a jump." She leapt into the air, and quickly returned back into position. "Notice how I rolled through my feet rather than push through my feet like with the tendus? Remember to keep your toes

153

pointed, and mind your turnout. With sautés it's really easy to drift out of each position, so you want to keep them tight with each jump. Okay? After first position, we'll move to second, third, fourth and ending in fifth position, four counts on each. I'll demonstrate, follow along during it, then we'll do it with music."

She put herself into first position, with her ankles touching the backs of each other, and her toes pointed to the sides. "And five, six, seven, eight..." she dropped into her demi-plie and leapt upwards, jumping on each count, "One, two, three and four. Switch on five. Six, seven, eight." At the end of each four count, the positioning of her feet changed while remaining in place despite pointing her feet after leaving the ground.

After she completed the exercise, all the students prepared themselves in first position waiting for the counts and music to begin. Vera and Thora both felt they had a strong hold over it, even managed to get through the motions without the need to look at their neighbor.

Maybe I can manage this afterall. Vera pondered happily to themself. Yet when class was over, the two of them would proceed into the advanced class, which is when everything went wrong.

Chapter 20
The Advanced Class

"Vivitah is a spiritual essence which pools behind the Glass, a mirror-like wall which separates the Eshef - our physical world - from the Ghosha - the vessel. Composed of the emotional experiences from the Ghosha, vivitah influences everything around us from the lowly flower to the most wicked of narghoulim. Vivitah can create, and vivitah can destroy. It is what allows us to perform pantomimes, and it is what infuses into the chevalières when they breach the Glass. And, if harnessed properly, can be used to bring life to the inanimate, or to cause death in the animate."

– Doctor Coppelius

Next on Vera and Thora's schedule was an advanced class with Zhah Ississ Belle, the cantankerous finni they had met when the Aponae had first brought them to the school. The room for which class was to take place, was just as glorious as it had been the first time they saw it. It was twenty-foot tall, and nearly twice that on all sides. There were arched windows that stretched across the back wall which allowed sunlight to pour into the room like a fountain. A grand piano rested off to one side, while a stretch of mirrors spanning two sides of the ballroom appeared built into the wall and were over twelve feet high themselves.

Already there were students who had arrived early to class who were shifting wooden barres towards the center of the room, while others were starting in on their stretches. The gleasne, the spirits in the glass, where already fluttering about, some making funny faces at a couple of the students who would also in turn make faces back, while others silently offered corrections to the posture of another.

Vera kept Gander on their left side, closest to the wall and Thora drew up behind him, ensuring that no one would accidentally bump into him. Most students moved around the

155

slow-moving newcomers, and thought nothing of them stalling at the pair of double doors which lead into their next class. All except for one student, who was at least six-foot in height, was broad in the shoulders and carried heavy muscles on all limbs. The finni had her blonde hair tied back into a bun, and had nearly two-feet of horns which sprouted from her head like a pair of insect antennae, denoting her from the Erdo tribe. If it weren't for her horns, her alabaster skin alone gave her away as being from the far north along the Serishone mountains. The massive student knocked Vera in the arm as the finni ducked slightly to avoid scraping the frame with her horns, which caused Vera to stumble and be caught by a powerful, yet thankfully quiet, kornig.

"Oh geez, I am so sorry." The student professed immediately. "I didn't hurt you, did I? I get so off balance sometimes whenever I'm stooping through doors. I really didn't mean to bonk ya there." Her hands were out in front of her, as if prepared to catch Vera should they themselves fall.

Vera rubbed their arm, not from any sort of pain, but to settle the nerves back into their usual sense of feeling. "No, I'm perfectly fine. Don't worry about it."

"Thank the NIИ on that one. I always worry that I'm going to one day hurt someone unintentionally and I'll never forgive myself." She paused for a moment, as if going through a thick catalog of faces inside her mind. "Hey, ah, are you two new? I don't think I have ever seen you before." She rubbed the back of her head, hoping that she hadn't simply forgotten their faces, rather than not recognizing them.

"That's right." Thora offered as a means to ease any confusion. "We were both enrolled several hours ago."

"Oh geez, and Fin Ississ already has you in this class? She can be really hard, and if you don't have the best memory, you could struggle a lot like I do."

A voice rang out from behind them that sounded awfully familiar. "Hey Saffie! Have you introduced yourself yet?"

The three of them glanced behind them and discovered, Lyro, whose beautiful hair was now pulled back tightly into a bun in preparation for class.

"Oh, I'm so sorry. I should have said my name already. I'm Erdo Penelope Saffie, but you can just call me Saffie, like Lyro does."

"I'm Caetin Kom Vera, and this is Thora of the Faunis. You can just call me Vera and her Thora." Vera offered in return, still overtaken by the finni's size.

"Wow, we're on a third-name basis already." Saffie smiled extensively.

"We can all get to know each other later on, but we should all start warming up before Fin Ississ drills us, otherwise we'll all be in a world of hurt. Come on, Saffie, let's find our way to the barre." Lyro turned to Vera and Thora and said, "And I'll be seeing you three later," then gave a wink.

As the two of them walked away, Vera could hear the perplexed Saffie ask, "Don't you mean the two of them, Lyro? Because, I don't think there was a third person, was there? I didn't miss someone, did I?"

Then came a light giggle from Lyro as they positioned themselves at a barre in the center of the floor.

Thora scanned the room as quickly as she could and was ecstatic to find an empty place at one of the barres which was at a distant corner of the room. It even had a good view of the mirrors which was helpful when trying to ensure their motions matched what the rest of the dancers were performing. She nudged Vera then nodded in that direction. Vera ran their hand over top Gander's feathers, then softly steered him towards it.

157

Several Gleasne drifted towards them as soon as they arrived at the barre. Some pointed at the vacant spot where Gander was and covered their mouths in surprise, while others pointed and laughed silently to themselves. There was one though who seemed more serious than the rest who floated down and occupied a vacant place on the barre in the reflection; eager to be part of their exercises. Vera smiled at them, placed a finger up to their mouth and quietly shushed them so that they wouldn't give Gander away.

"Okay boy, just lay down, okay? Stay here." Vera encouraged with a hint of worry.

Gander complied, and laid down on the floor.

Vera could hear the ruffling of Gander's feathers and knew that some sort of action had taken place. Hopeful that he had followed their orders. They approached the barre, giving space to the gleasne in the mirror, and began stretching as best as they knew how. Thora followed in turn, taking a place on the opposite side.

It was not but a few moments later when Fin Ississ entered the room. "Hello class." She announced. Her gray hair was as neat as the moment they first met her. Without even casting a gaze towards Vera and Thora, she declared to the whole class, "We have a couple new students joining us today. If you find yourself out of place in motions, do not watch them as their level in skill is not sufficient. They will be following along to the best of their ability, but they will not be participating during floor work."

Vera felt beside themself, especially when the majority of the class turned to look at the two of them, before returning their faces to Fin Ississ. *Of course we aren't sufficient*, Vera complained in their head, *we just started!* The sudden albeit brief attention seemed as a means to shame them rather than as a warning to other students not to watch their technique. *Any dolt could see…*

A finnae had snuck inside the room right after Fin Ississ, and quietly positioned himself at the piano. Vera thought it might be a Wyldfnn based on the curvature of his horns but it was rather difficult to tell since part of the piano obscured his head.

She continued to address the class, "We all know why we're here. So let's get started, shall we?" And without motion she rattled off a string of exercises, most of which Vera and Thora had never heard of before. "Starting in fifth position, petit développé to fondu devon away from the barre, drop to fifth demi pointe, up to retiré, two counts, extend to attitude devon then extend for two counts – tombé devon, rattata back to the barre, arms in fourth, fondu imposé – attitude derriere, extend to arabesque and close fifth. Combré front, combré back, raise to relevé; start on the new side." She then gestured to the piano. "Ivicti, if you please?"

The pianist took his cue and played a piece of music. It was one that Vera had heard and enjoyed before, but now it was a prelude towards sudden panic! No direction, no motions, nothing to even help Vera know which was what! The only thing they recognized was fifth position and fondu. The rest was a mystery and now they had to perform it!

"And five, six, seven, eight—" Fin Ississ demanded.

Already Vera was sweating, a quick glance at Thora and she too was at a loss for what to do. So Vera looked around for someone close by to mimic and latched onto a student who was just a barre away.

They bent their knees in plié, then drew their leg up and extended it in front of them in a développé but by the time that they were confident that they managed it mostly correct, they had skipped the retiré all together and had to re-position to attempt the attitude devon, which was rushed as their leg needed to be bent in a 90 degree angle inwards and raised in front of them. Despite its brief two count debut, Vera had to hasten to the tombé.

Already their heart was racing, embarrassment and fear caused them to feel flush , and their mind swirled with terrifying thoughts, echoing up through them as if spawned from the darkest pit, *"You're going to fail just like you failed your family."*

Vera pushed the thought down as best as they could. What they needed most was to focus and a body that could keep up with the counts. Sadly, today was not going to yield that to them, not even by an inch.

Gander lifted his head from its resting place on the floor, already sensing that awful tinge of desperation from Vera. That same sensation that existed back home in those awful moments where all he could do was protect them and snuggle close. He believed that it was one of those moments, as it had not been long before when he was called upon to be there for his truest friend. He got up from his place and quickly ran to them.

Past the fondu devon and into the rattata towards the barre, which seemed more like a quick spin, Vera was giving it their best shot until their leg connected with something unknown, and lost their balance completely. One hand gripped tightly on the barre, while another grasped at whatever they could, which just so happened to be a handful of feathers on the kornig's back, but it wasn't enough to stop them from spilling down onto the floor with a shriek.

And to the untrained eye, it may once have seemed like a single inexperienced dancer had attempted something far outside their expertise and simply tumbled over themself, but the sudden jerk on Gander's feathers caused him to back away and having such a long body was enough to back into the wooden barre, pushing it towards the front of the room before toppling over itself. A couple of students leapt out of the way, startled by a suddenly animated barre which cared very little for their perfected arabesque and instead drove towards them with seemingly malicious intent.

In all this calamity, Thora was able to escape unphased after having released her grip on the barre as soon as it shifted from its prescribed location. Her hands covered her mouth to conceal any noise that wanted to escape as everything unfolded.

From across the room Lyro's eyes widened and a smirk crossed their face. It was a smile of sheer satisfaction from the chaos that had disrupted the order in an otherwise painful routine. Meanwhile, Saffie worried terribly from their heightened view and hoped that no one had gotten hurt.

The music halted, all eyes were on Vera, and Fin Ississ descended upon them like a bird of prey, with sharpened talons set into the reflection of her eyes. "What is the meaning—" and no sooner did the words escape her lips when her legs bumped into something entirely invisible and her hands brushed against a collection of feathers that she understood the reason for it all.

"You!" She pointed at Vera who had not yet picked themself off the floor. "Undo your pantomime, this instant!"

Vera raised to standing, their face red with a variety of emotions all pushing themselves into their head. There was a tingling in their chest, one spurred by anxiety and worry. But they complied, having to begin with the correct motions with their fingers, yet to start over at least twice due to having difficulties with concentration. Yet, in a flash the pantomime released and Gander's invisibility fell off him like a mud onto the floor – revealing the beast, who released a brief whine into the classroom.

"Let me make something perfectly clear to you." Fin Ississ bore into Vera with her fury. "Each distraction, every disruption, every second you steal from these students could lead to one less chevalières upon graduation. One less dancer between us and the jaws of narghoulim. Do you have any idea how many lives you are putting into jeopardy for upsetting my class? Do you? Hundreds! Thousands! Do you see the significance? Do you see what is at stake! Come, now, answer me."

Vera stared at the floor. *Tandermundt.* The word that flashed in their brain that now felt etched in a headstone. "Yes…"

"Good! Because when I tell you to do something, you do it! That's how we save lives! That's how *you* save lives! This isn't a game. Your childhood ended the moment you walked through those doors. Now, I am certain that Fin Benopal advised you to house your pet. So don't come back here, until you do!"

Vera felt like crying but did everything they could not to. So much was clouding up inside them, but they did not – could not, let it out. "Yes, Fin Ississ." Vera muttered.

"Lyro, presuming you're rooming with our new students, take them to Silva's. And if you don't breach the Glass when your time comes, we know who to blame." She turned away from Vera. "Everyone else, we're going to do the motions *again.*"

Thora hastily picked up the wooden barre and set it back into place, then joined Vera as they ran out of the ballroom with Gander in tow. Lyro was soon to follow.

Chapter 21
Lessons in War & Dance

"The strength of the chevalières allows them to wield the mighty geist weapons as forged by the Ashwyn. Named after the accursed Tintergeist, these weapons are too bulky for a regular soldier to manage. Rivaled only by the heaviest of siege weapons, a geist weapon is weighted, so it could pierce through the hardened armor of a narghoulim in order to ensure their destruction. However, a chevalière cannot simply strike where they please and must aim for vulnerable spots in order to wound the creature. Once the abomination has been sufficiently injured, it leaves it open for a final strike – one accompanied by the release of one's resonance."

- Coppelia, Professor of Dance, The Regal Ballet Academy, Adalace.

Lyro shut the doors behind them, placed their hands behind their back, and motioned with their head. "This way."

Thora gave Lyro a suspicious glare, one filled with a condemnation and ire. "You knew something like this would happen, didn't you?"

Vera clenched their fists, in and out, fingers digging into their palm out of a desperate desire to fight back the pain inside them. *You're losing family all over again,* came the voice from inside of them. *Stupid finni.*

Gander ran up alongside Vera and nuzzled slightly into them, as he had so many times in the past, to let Vera know that he was present and here for them.

With a shrug and a smile, Lyro replied calmly, "It's hard keeping a pet inside the Academy, even an invisible one. It was only a matter of time before he was discovered."

As they descended the staircase, Vera whispered to the world, "I made Fin Ississ so mad."

Whether due to keen hearing, or the excellent acoustics provided by the hall, Lyro offered a reprieve from Vera's guilt. "Don't worry about Fin Ississ. We've all heard the speech on more than one occasion. It's always, 'Every moment is a theft', 'the world depends upon you', 'if you tamper with the barres one more time, Lyro, so help me'. Though that last one may be more specific to myself." They chuckled, and continued on until they all reached the front doors. Lyro stopped to remove their ballet shoes.

"You'll want to remove your shoes, too. If they get dirty from being outside, you'll make Fyr Drussel cry. You don't want to see Fyr Drussel cry. That finnyr has an unlimited amount of tears and you'll be forced to watch every single one of them fall. It's not a pretty sight."

Lyro untied their bun while Vera and Thora removed their shoes and shook out their curls. Sadly, Lyro's attempts at lightening the mood seemed to have been wasted, as Vera was very much still inside their own head worried about never being able to see Gander again.

"This way," they motioned, "just a ways across the yard and down the road is where Silva's place is."

They all walked in silence, and all around them they could hear the sounds of the city bustling, chatting, and going about their lives without fear of the narghoulim. Above, Thora was able to hear the cry of a few ayreena birds, whose red heads and yellow wings were distinct, as well as their long golden tail feathers which were deemed to be good luck if happened upon.

They reached a two-story building made of stone and lumber, with a barn accompanying the bottom floor, and a series of different outdoor cages containing birds, and a couple of nyris. A fence lined the perimeter, which stretched back into a wide-open space where a few peppenachs strolled about.

"Well, this is it," Lyro pointed out. "I'm sure Silva is in the barn tending to the animals."

"I'm sorry…" Vera offered to Lyro as they ran their hand through Gander's feathers.

"Sorry for what?" Lyro's eyebrows dropped over their eyes in confusion.

"For interrupting your training… If I'm responsible for you not becoming a chevalière…"

"You don't have to be sorry. I'm fated to be a chevalière, a seeress told me so. Just my lot. The worse you did was get me out of Fin Ississ' class, and I've been dying for a break. So, I should thank you. Despite being caught, what happened back in class was the most fun I've had in a while. I'm sure other students enjoyed it as well. Broke up the routine, shook things up. We all need little surprises."

Vera nodded, relieved in a sense, but there was still that overwhelming sensation of dread boiling up inside of them as they looked at the building where they would have to leave Gander.

With a deep breath, Vera said, "I'd like to go by myself, okay, Thora? Just wait right here and I'll be back."

"Are you sure?" After everything that Vera has been through, Thora wasn't confident on how well Vera would be on their own.

Vera solemnly nodded, anxiety pains dancing across their skin. "Come on Gander."

The two of them trudged up to the barn. Knocked on the exterior doors, then after hearing a noise, before proceeded inside.

It wasn't long, perhaps ten minutes or so, before Vera reemerged. Vera's face was rife with consternation yet their hands were open and no longer clenched.

"She said I can come visit anytime I have a free moment and that, despite my doubled up schedule, there should be at least one hour a day. Which is something…" Vera looked directly at Lyro with a flash of anger. "You said I'd never get to see Gander again!"

Thora crossed her arms over her chest and leaned back into her hip with disdain.

Lyro tilted their head, "To be fair, I said there would be little time due to dancing, studying and training. Not that you'd never see him again."

Thora jumped in with a touch of venom, "But you made it sound that way!"

Lyro nodded, "Yes, I did do that. Yet, if I hadn't you never would have tried to keep him, and where's the fun in that?"

"Unbelievable." Vera turned back towards the Academy. "Come on, Thora."

"Vera, come on—" Lyro protested, yet still reserved a smirk on their face.

"Don't talk to me!" Vera angrily shouted back.

Thora shook her head in damnation of Lyro's actions, but said nothing. She silently followed after her friend, leaving Lyro behind.

"Today, we'll be talking about the Thruom." Came the words from the porcelain construct.

She wore a high collared jacket, one with rope shoulders, military cut with twelve buttons which were the size of coins, and wide sleeves which appeared big enough to fit three arms inside. Her hands were covered in leather gloves and her leggings were made of nyri silk. Her boots were journey pointe shoes, for which she remained en pointe for the entirety of the lecture – granting her considerable height, and some would say, authority. Everything was black, from her shoes to her raven colored hair - with the exception of her purely white face which captured the light as she moved about the floor. Her eyes were larger, like a dolls – except not *like* a doll, for that is *exactly* what she was; Professor Coppelia.

It was a smaller class, composed of her, Thora, and a handful of younger students who were perhaps seven or eight years old, many of whom continued to steal glances at Thora's antlers.

Before them was a table, about three feet off the ground, with fifteen swan handled rapiers with the point of the blades flared out like a fan, and the handles pointed towards them.

However, the most domineering portion of the room was reserved for the twenty-foot canvas, where drawn upon it in charcoal was the image of a gigantic narghoulim, as well as two ten-foot structures which were mysteriously hidden beneath red sheets.

"Don't be fooled by the proportion of the drawing, it is actually quite larger and terrifying. As you can see, it has thirteen octopus like tentacles that are approximately 2,500 to 3,000 feet long and it exudes the stench of rot. It uses these tentacles to drag itself across the landscape, and to climb the sides of mountains with ease. Atop it sets a Finni-like torso which is covered in near impenetrable bone carapace, and as depicted in the rendition behind me has extended structures coming off the back and shoulders. The neck and head are exposed points. You may also notice a resemblance to Finni by its four horns which protrude 600 of feet above it. It has four arms, with two pairs of hands set with eyes in its palms and the other two have vicious circular mouths with multiple rings of teeth." She paused before continuing. "Can anyone tell me another feature of the thruom?"

A finnae with one horn curved up and the other curved down raised his hand and was called upon by the doll. "The

167

spike above its head!"

"That's right." Coppelia raised her leg in a very mechanical and precise manner, using her toes as a means to point at a location on the drawing. "The spike is suspended one-hundred feet above the thruom's head and is made entirely out of iron. It is two-hundred and fifty feet long and is fifty feet at its widest base. It is completely under the control of the thruom which it uses it to destroy large targets." She turned back towards the class. "While vertical, the thruom can move at twenty miles per hour, but if it dropped to a horizontal position and uses its arms, it can effectively double its speed."

Vera raised their hand.

"Yes." Coppelia's eyes fell upon Vera and she stood perfectly still in anticipation of their question.

"How tall is the thruom?" They remembered their encounter with the skullwalker, who appeared to be a one-hundred feet in height, but from her descriptions with the tentacles alone, it seemed more.

"A good question. The torso is approximately one-thousand feet, and adding the length of the tentacles and the horns, you can expect it to be about four-thousand-five-hundred feet. However, while vertical, most sit at around three-thousand-five-hundred feet." The doll's response lacked emotion and was very matter-of-fact.

The velocitrix seemed just as high, but fighting something that large seemed impossible. Thora raised her hand. "How do chevalières even reach that high?"

Coppelia turned her gaze to the young students. "Can anyone answer that question?"

A finni Nadin whose horns were massive and swept back past her head and curled behind her raised her hand. She was immediately called upon. "At their peak, a chevalières has a vertical leap of eight-hundred feet, and through a series of planned leaps, can position themselves to perform strategic assaults."

Thora nudged Vera with an echo of concern, "Eight-hundred feet?"

"Let's move on." Coppelia selected a rapier from off the table and flourished it, cutting through the air with a whoosh. "A chevalières can perform a succession of rapid attacks with a weapon such as this, allowing them to pierce areas that otherwise are exposed." She demonstrated a quick attack as her blade zinged through the air. "The thruom is most vulnerable in the eyes and the mouths." Coppelia pointed to the palm of her hand and tapped it. "Today we'll focus on the eyes."

She strode towards the covered object on the left-hand side of the room. "Now, steel yourselves, as this model was created based upon the input of first-hand accounts. Keep in mind that the real thing will be much larger."

Vera watched as eagerness spread across the faces of all the other students. An excitement built in the room. A few Finni bounced on their toes, while a finnyr clenched their fists in front of them as if about to cheer on the unveiling. Perhaps for some, this was the first time they would see something akin to a narghoulim, that or for their entire lives they have been taught to fight a distant enemy and their eagerness to engage one has been pooling inside them for years, now ready to burst!

To Vera, there was a sensation of imminent dread. A drawing is one thing, but seeing it close up even without the threat of danger trudged up memories of them being back inside that cave with the winds licking the entrance like some ravenously hungry tongue.

Coppelia pulled off the sheet, and it dripped off the object like the spilling of blood. What it revealed struck Vera's brain like an arrow, which caused their stomach to churn so quickly that they had to immediately slam their hand against their mouth. Their stomach offered no mercy, and they did everything they could to prevent themself from retching right there on the floor. So, Vera fled, as far out of the room as physically was possible until they could no longer fight it.

Thora ran after, hoping to save their friend from the terror they were now suffering through, leaving behind them a ten-foot severed hand, stained with the color of rot. From its palm stared an accursed yellow eye which bore into their souls with true horror.

Vera wasn't sick, at least not in the way that Ruby believed. It was funny, as there were pantomimes for healing a wound, and pantomimes for mending a broken bone, but there weren't any pantomimes for curing sickness. If there were, Vera could be subjected to it, and the worry would be gone and they'd be back dancing, or learning how to stab a gigantic hand with a rapier. Instead, they were here, stuck laying in bed for throwing up in the hallway.

Thora eased into the room with a tray which featured a bowl of warm soup, a bit of bread, and some milk to help calm Vera's nausea. She passed Lyro's bed, who too seemed to have taken ill, and was staring at the wall opposite of where Thora and Vera presently occupied, with the covers drawn up over their head. Thora paid them no mind as she was still mad from before.

"I got this from the kitchen. Special. They made it just for you so you could feel better." Thora sat on the side of the bed next to Vera, who had shifted to sitting up with their back against the headboard.

"I'm feeling fine now. Everyone didn't need to go through all this trouble. I'll have to thank the kitchen staff once they let me out of bed."

Thora moved the tray into Vera's lap so that they could start eating. She shifted the spoon so that it was closer to Vera's dominant hand.

"Listen, Vera, you've been through a lot this season. Longlyn has already had six days and nights pass, it'll be halfmorn soon. You haven't really had a chance to rest, not since…" Thora trailed off, fearful of sticking her fingers in a wound that hadn't even started to heal yet. "Do you think the reason you got sick was because of what happened, back at the cave?"

"Thora, please. I don't want to talk about it. I don't want to talk about what happened at the cave, or about Tandermundt—I just want to dance, to break the Glass, and become a chevalière." They stirred their soup. "And see Gander…"

Her antlers swished through the air as Thora nodded. "No matter what you decide, I'll be here every step of the way."

"Thank you, Thora… really. I couldn't have asked for a better friend." They sat their tray to the side. "Would it be too much to ask for a hug?"

A smile raised across her lips. "Never."

They embraced, and Vera squeezed as tightly as they could, as the thought of wind brushed across their mind, a wind that could not whisk the two of them over the mountain.

Chapter 22
Pas de Deux &
Pantomimes

"Many would claim that the chevalière's most powerful weapon is their resonance, and when it comes to defeating the narghoulim that is mostly true, there is one often overlooked strength – known as sync. Becoming in-tune with other chevalières, learning their movements, their minds, and their hearts allows a chevalière a closer tie with their fellows. From this comes a sense of knowing, an ability to anticipate each other's motions which add to the performance and emboldens the vivitah for which they harness. In essence, the stronger the relationship between chevalières, the better the dance, the higher the leaps, and the stronger the strikes."

\- Metalli Faunis, Corps de Ballet

Halfmorn came and the students received a single day to get out of the Academy and see their families. Thora and Vera used their time to visit Gander, and practice. Despite being the hottest period of the season, the studio they found was built farther inside the mountain, allowing for cooler temperatures to prevail. The space was empty, and it was a touch relieving to work on their techniques by themselves without the pressure of the professors or other students consistently judging them. Though enough could not be said about the gleasne who would watch them from mirrors.

There was a pair, one took on Vera's horns upon their brow, while another who mimiced Thora, and drifted between the two of their reflections. They would make faces, or try to distract, but Vera was set to their task and ignored them. When they realized Vera's determination, they joined them at the barre and would offer slight corrections to their motions, while also offering silent reminders.

Thora and Vera both felt that they were getting a better

grasp on the elementary positions and foot placement, yet were still struggling with arm placement. Unfortunately, it was not long before the holiday was over, the students returned, and they resumed their regular classes.

"The pas de deux is a chevalières saving grace. Reaching to the point of resonance is otherwise difficult, oftentimes impossible, without a partner to help elevate you. While the corps de ballet is tasked with infusing a chevalière with enough vivitah to engage a narghoulim, that power drains quickly while moving about the battlefield and conducting strikes on vulnerable locations." A finnae, with drabby brown hair, and horns that extended straight out from his brow a good eight inches then turned upwards at a ninety-degree angle for a good foot, paced about the room.

Vera recognized him as a Fendurdan, if they recalled correctly, his tribe originated from the Fel Lands just east of Adalace; a swamp filled area, with dangerous creatures who dwell there. Fens, as the Fendurdan are nicknamed, were excellent at hiding themselves and remaining perfectly quiet. Even as he shifted from one place to the other, Vera struggled to hear any sort of noise.

Professor Fendurdan Golvorah Fane, or as he preferred – Fan Golvorah – walked down the aisle of students; finni on one side, finnae on the other and finnyr sprinkled between the two sides in order to keep things even. "It is the duty of the finnae to be available to support their finni partner. For finnis, they have the priority of carrying strikes against the narghoulim. Finnyr, have the traditional duty of being both support and assault, as your troupe requires."

He stopped in front of Vera and turned his back on them in order to address the line of finnae. "As with every class, I am obligated to remind each of you that a finnae's job is to support and protect finni, as well as the designated finnyr, even at the cost of the finnae's life. Finnaes do not, and will not, put their life ahead of finni or designated finnyr. Do you understand?"

"Yes, Fan Golvorah!" The finnae replied, all except for one who raised his hand.

"Fan Golvorah, can you help me understand? Why is it important for finnae to sacrifice themselves for finni?"

"Because, Yori, finni have a better chance at conceiving children when they are alive, than dead. Not to say that children are a requirement, but the narghoulim devour us by the hundreds despite our best efforts. The recent census shows that we are just inching over a surplus population, but all that can change in the blink of an eye. Every day, we face extinction! So to answer your question Yori, it's to give finni's and some finnyr's chevalières. the opportunity to produce a family."

"But aren't finnae's lives—"

Yori was immediately cut off by the professor. "No more questions, Yori. This isn't a debate hall. If a finnae or designated finnyr fails to lay down their life... you'll *wish* you had." He spun back around to face the line of finni and finnyr. His eyes settled on Thora, who also happened to be standing in the finni line. "Now, partner together. As we'll learn how to perform a pas de deux in arabesque, and later we'll move into pirouettes."

Vera was across from a dark skinned finnae who had short black hair and deep auburn eyes. His horns shot straight out of his head, about a foot and a half, and they curled tightly from base to tip. He was Niecen, a tribe who hailed from the island south of Arcadia. Vera had encountered merchants whose ships had docked in Ishorn on their way northward to Cornelis, some of which took wagons to Tantermudt, offering strange and unusual trinkets from the Lost People. Vera always found Niecen's to be smart, capable, and very exotic. Vera would be lying to themself if they weren't looking forward to dancing with him, let alone learning his name.

Thora was set to dance with a Caetin, the same tribe as Vera, which certainly made the prospect of dancing with a complete stranger more enticing to her. Vera didn't know him, as he was likely one of many other Caetin who was born here in Adalace.

After a quick assessment of him, Vera returned their eyes to their future partner and was immediately taken back. In the Niecen's place now stood Lyro, who despite having their hair tied into a bun, had a few curls hanging down in front of their face. Vera desperately looked to see where the beautiful Niecen had wandered off to, and after finally finding him already with his hands around another finni's waist, Vera sighed heavily and rolled their eyes.

"I know I'm probably the last person that you want to partner with right now." Lyro offered, as they pushed a curl away from their eye.

Vera vehemently crossed their arms over their chest. "That's the truth."

"I just wanted to apologize to you." Lyro kept eye contact, despite having an overwhelming desire to stare at the floor. "While I know I made it sound like you'd never get to see Gander again, and at the time I knew how important he was to you. I admit I had some ulterior motives, but I realize now that what I did was terrible. You didn't deserve that, and neither did your friend. I was selfish. So, I'm sorry." Lyro fidgeted with their hands, picking at the spaces beneath their nails. "Is there anything I can do to make it up to you?"

Vera stole a glance back at the Niecen, before returning their thoughts to Lyro. "Well… Thora and I will need practice. Tons of practice, and it would help to have someone who knew what they were doing to instruct us."

Lyro tilted their head to their side heavily, as if giving into a lifelong commitment. "Of course, I'll help. What are friends and roommates for?"

With an extended hand, Vera said, "I forgive you then. Friends?"

Lyro smirked, extended their own hand, grasped Vera's firmly, pulled them towards themself and hugged them tightly. With their cheeks pressed together, Vera could not help but get a whiff of their scent which consisted of oranges and marigolds. They were also quite warm, far warmer than Vera had been.

"Assault team," came the boom of Fan Golvorah's voice, "In position."

Lyro and Vera stepped away from one another momentarily as Vera swept their leg backwards and held it up as high as they could without hiking their hip, while also their supporting foot remained flat on the floor. Vera's arms extended out into forth position in front of them, yet one of their arms was extended too far back in arabesque. Lyro placed their palm against Vera's limb and gently pushed it forward so that it fell in the correct positioning.

"Support team," Fan Golvorah called out once more, "In position."

Lyro placed one hand slightly above Vera's hip, and another beneath their extended leg's thigh. Which to Vera, seemed like the perfect opportunity to rest, but as some of their weight transferred into Lyro's hand, they whispered, "Don't relax, keep your leg strong." And Vera recovered their weight so that they were holding it once again.

"Now relevé." The instructor demanded.

One of the few words in a rapidly expanding vocabulary of ballet terms that Vera recognized meant to raise on their toes, which Vera was easily able to comply with. Lyro was able to provide a sense of stability, to help Vera not pull forward or backward, by guiding them to exactly where they needed to be. In a sense, Vera felt like they were back at the barre, with one hand keeping them from toppling over.

"Excellent. Nice form." Fan Golvorah paced past each couple. "Ursalin, raise your chest, please." He stopped at Lyro and Vera. "Well done." Then continued on. "Let's move into a lift. Assault team keep it solid."

"Keep strong, okay, don't let up for a second." Lyro whispered, then bent their legs and lifted with both arms together.

Vera was hoisted into the air, at least two feet or more. They struggled to keep their muscles tight. They could feel everything shaking, the pain building in the muscles from over straining and the fatigue starting to set in. Vera wasn't used to holding an arabesque for this long, let alone being hoisted in the air. Yet, they needed to push through it. They *had* to push through it!

With a quick glance to their side, Vera was able to catch a glimpse at Thora who too seemed to be having issues holding things together. There was a sense of desperation sweeping across her face, a touch of panic – perhaps in a fear that she will be stuck up there forever until her ultimate, and inevitable, collapse.

"And down."

Lyro brought Vera gently back to the floor, almost effortlessly as if Vera was nothing but a feather. Then there was a brief pause, as Vera remained in their arabesque waiting for the professor to allow them to drop out of their position, where they realized just how strong Lyro was – and how long they had been doing this to make it seem so effortless.

"Thank you everyone. Assault team, you may come out of your arabesque."

Vera knew that they were going to be sore, probably sore for the rest of their life.

"You were great." Lyro offered with sincerity. "Almost like a fifth year, which is a compliment for someone who just started."

"That was awful." Thora mentioned beneath their breath. She turned to her partner and placed a hand briefly on his chest and patted him. "But you were fantastic. Thank you."

"Remember." The professor offered as he assessed the class. "It's important now to build confidence and trust with your partners and classmates. No one knows who will break the Glass when the time comes, and your relationships with one another may be the very thing that saves your life, and the lives of countless others. So, rotate partners, and we'll continue with pirouettes."

When it came to the pantomimes class, Vera was at odds. Since Thora was Fauni, she was excused from attending. Having Thora with them in every class so far had really spurred their motivation and had given them the support that they had been so desperately needing. It wasn't until this particular class that Vera truly realized how much that they had relied on her. Already Vera felt the jitters. At least Lyro was with them and even the softhearted Saffie.

Professor Nadin Frenwyn Tilly, whose horns had at least a three-inch diameter, and curled back three and a half feet and with ends pointing towards her back. She stood at the front of the class in a white corset and skirt, with the sleeves pleated halfway down her arm, and a white skirt which matched in style and came down mid-thigh. There were golden vine-like designs embroidered up along the corset with some of it stretching out into the sleeves and skirt. She wore flats, and kept swylnn plumes of white and gold in their red hair which spilled down the entire length of her back. Her ears were faun blessed, like Vera's and had quasils down her nose.

Unlike the rest of the professors who specialized in dance, Fin Frenwyn was from Riloshek, a school separate from the Regal Ballet Academy otherwise known as the Pantodieses whose primary subject was pantomimes.

"Can anyone tell me…" the professor asked everyone who was presently seated, which currently scored over fifty students, "what are the five most important pantomimes that are taught to chevalières?"

Saffie immediately fell to fret. She brought a finger up to her mouth and started to chew on it. "Oh jeez, I know this one. I just can't put my finger on it. Think Saffie, think."

They were sitting just far enough away that it would have been impossible for Fin Frenwyn to hear. A couple times Saffie tried to raise her hand but doubt swarmed over her, and her hand was buried back into her lap.

A Leekyn, one modeled in perfection with straightened bleached white hair and marblesque features raised her hand.

"Yes, Opeena?"

Vera straightened their spine, as if the gong of memory had just been rung. "Why does that name sound familiar?"

The finni recited the answer with a clear and precise voice, "Amplify, heal, revive, shrink and throw."

"Excellent. And why is that, Opeena?" Came the instructor's retort, as if trying to probe how far the Leekyn's knowledge could be tested.

"*Amplify* in order for chevalières to be heard over great distances. *Heal* in case someone born beneath the Chevalière constellation forgets the motions to heal the injured, *Revive* in case someone born beneath the Glisene constellation forgets the motions to awaken the unconscious…"

Vera's ears twitched. "Wait, I can revive people?"

Lyro whispered with a grin at how cute Vera's ears were when they heard something surprising. "Born under the Gleisne constellation, huh?"

179

Vera just nodded with their jaw partially hanging open.

"*Shrink* in order to better manage one's equipment, and *throw* in order to pass equipment between chevalières over great distances."

"Ugh… Saffie, you knew this one." Saffie grumbled to herself. "Don't worry, you'll get the next one, okay? You can do it!" She clenched her fists on her lap as if preparing to race to the next question.

The professor thanked Opeena and continued on with her lecture.

"You sure will, Saffie. I believe in you." Lyro quietly cheered. They pressed their shoulder against Vera's and replied to their prior question. "Opeena is the top dancer. Her mother is a chevalière, making Opeena a legacy. Everyone believes she'll be the first to break the Glass."

"Oh yeah and she's just absolutely perfect in everything." Saffie added from the sidelines while she kept her eyes fixated on the professor. "Perfect hair, perfect fashion, perfect dancing – even her manners are perfect. She's just so intimidating. I bumped into her the other day and she apologized to me before I could even say I was sorry. I didn't know what to say after that and I've been too scared to tell her that I didn't mean to bump her."

"And who else can tell me another reason chevalières need pantomimes?"

Saffie raised her hand and shouted, "MALFINAE!"

Everyone turned to look at her, and Saffie's cheeks blossomed into multiple shades of red. She stuttered, "Mal-Malfinae, r-right?"

"What a perfect display of the *amplify* pantomime." The professor chuckled at Saffie's enthusiasm. "But yes, quite right, Malfinae. Aside from the narghoulim, chevalières also engage more domestic threats such as kaedra, and sorcerers where it may be necessary to use pantomimes to undo the damage they sow."

Vera swallowed hard. They weren't aware they would have to deal with malfinae, let alone kaedra. Malfinae were all the subject of fairy tales and ghost stories told to them by their parents and people in the village. It was used to scare children into behaving, but what made them so real was that they did exist – supposedly, in far hidden corners of the world. But chevalières fought them, and provided that Vera broke the Glass and survived their battles with narghoulim, they would one day have to fight a being who had found a means to break several rules of pantomimes which governed them all.

The whole thought of it made Vera's heart pound heavily in their chest. Becoming a chevalière just became more terrifying.

Chapter 23
The Aness

"Kaedra live within us. They are the claws in our veins and the terror in our dreams. They begin as whispers, echoing our fears, guilt and blame. When misfortune strikes, the Glass within us cracks, and they scratch at those shards that have yet to come loose. After experiencing years of torment, should a Finni die in front of a mirror, the kaedra will break free, where all they'll bring is cruelty, pain and torment. As if not nightmarish enough, should an experienced pantodess take a kaedra within them, they become a malfinae; an evil sorceress with the power to affect all, both Finni and Fauni alike, with their magic – including killing with a single flick of their hand."

– Caraboose, *Journal of a Malfinae*

Practice accompanied most cycles, and just as Lyro had promised, they taught what they knew. Sometimes, when classes were over and they were settling into their rooms to rest, Vera would continue through the motions they had learned that day, using the back of a chair as a barre. Lyro would comment from their bed, or would come up alongside to make various adjustments. Thora would practice too, if anything to provide Vera the motivation that they needed in order to keep going.

However, as their moon-world often did, tillmet arrived. Temperatures dropped down into the lower 60s, trees started to lose their leaves, and already the nocturnalis started to bloom, and within a few days would show its blue and purple petals once again. As the sun descended in the western sky, it cast purples, blue, reds and orange against the clouds like a painters' brush and the brightly lit Longlyn cast it's glow. For many, it was the time for romance, arm-in-arm strolls through gardens of night flowers, and a time for hand fastings. To Vera, it was the transitioning of the world. Nillveness was on its way, which would begin the fourteen days of darkness while the planet above them would see its surreal passing of day and night fourteen times before gillmet.

It was during this time when Vera, Thora and Lyro were in the middle of practice in their room, when a knock came at the door.

"Come in." Vera replied as they checked themself in the small mirror that had been particularly arranged so that they could see their placement.

A plump finni walked in the door, her faun-blessed ears twitched with excitement and her cheeks were puffed out and red from a smile. She wore a green dress this time, with a few brown feathers drooping off one shoulder like browning leaves about to fall from a tree. She did not come very far inside, no more than the edge of Lyro's bedpost and crossed her hands in front of her stomach.

Mattie leaned in as she spoke. "I have some very special news for you Vera. There is someone here to see you." She noted their dance attire and gazed at their wardrobes. "You'll certainly want to get dressed for this. You'll want to look your very best."

"Who is it?" Vera asked, rather perplexed that someone would be asking to see them, and as it seemed, someone outside of the Academy.

The Alshep giggled with glee. "It's a surprise! But you need to hurry, we can't keep her waiting."

Vera raised their eyebrow and looked to Thora with confusion. "Her?"

Outside of the studios and classrooms, there was a place set aside for the students to unwind just outside the west wing, where after climbing a set of really steep stairs that were hidden inside the mountain, they came to a garden terrace.

Here there were benches, a wading pool - surrounded by a

183

neat stone path - with delicately tended bushes, trees and a variety of flowers. At the farthest end, nearest the balcony, there stood a dancer's tree, where the trunk appeared like it was a finni and faune in a pas de deux, with their arms and legs extending out into beautiful white wood branches. The tree was still lush with its blue leaves, but many were already starting to fade. The gardeners could only do so much to stave off the changing seasons. The white star-shaped flowers occasionally drifted off the tree and they spun towards the ground, settling on the stone pathways with dozens of others who have not yet been swept up by the staff or carried away by the winds.

Sitting there, watching the setting of the sun was a finni adult, straight backed with beautifully braided hair that extended down past the seat of the bench for which she sat. Her horns denoted her a Leekyn. She wore a satin white dress, and a small coat which was composed of a white fur and feathers. It was difficult to discern who she was from behind, but there was a calming air about her that mixed with the sweet smells of the garden.

"Go on, honey." Mattie encouraged. She looked at Thora and Lyro, "But you two will need to keep with me, okay?"

They nodded silently, eager to know who it was and what she wanted, especially if it was important enough for all of them to look their best and how Vera had to go it alone.

There was a touch of nervousness brewing inside Vera's stomach. *"Who is it? Who could it be?"* They thought as they took careful steps toward the individual at the far end. *"I don't know anyone…"*

However, as they stepped nearer, their mind began putting the pieces together, and by the time they were a stone's throw away, it all came ahead and they started to shake.

The individual must have heard them approaching, and she slowly eased into standing and turned to greet them. Despite the distance, Lyro covered their mouth to quell a gasp, while Thora's eyes widened with disbelief.

Vera too was in a sense of shock, as the person before them was someone they saw every day in passing – from portraits and statues. She had striking young features, deep brown eyes, and smooth chestnut skin. Atop her brow sat a golden headpiece which extended out to the side of her head like fins, and displayed several exotic feathers, two of which they knew to be firebird pinions. She was poised, graceful, and kept her shoulders pressed downwards and her chest slightly forward.

"Hello, young Kom. It's so lovely to finally meet you. I've heard so much about you." Her voice filled Vera with an untold amount of reverence and warmth. She smiled as Vera wrestled with a reply. "I take it you recognize me."

"You're—" Vera took a pause, then swallowed what felt like a pile of petals lodged in their throat. "You're the Aness."

"I am." She closed her eyes in acknowledgment and with it came the rising of her chest, as if the very action made her taller. "And you've been through quite the ordeal." She motioned to the bench with an open palm. "Would you care to sit with me for a moment?"

The Aness, the spiritual head of the Rushinay – one who walks with Queens and the head of the Sisaness – waited patiently as Vera made their way past the nightblooms. They sat down on the bench and upon a small blanket aimed at shielding them from the chill which occupies seating this time of the year.

With charm, the Aness eased alongside Vera, who for a moment paused and looked out across the darkening sky. "It's beautiful, is it not?"

Vera could only nod their head, as they were still afflicted by their nerves.

"You've been through so much." The Aness said as she

continued to look wistfully off into the horizon. "More than anyone should, and yet your story happens all too often." She placed her hand lightly, so as not to add any weight, upon Vera's shoulder. "Yet unlike many unfortunate others, you've pushed yourself into becoming a chevalière. And I find that very admirable."

"You—" Vera struggled with the words as bewilderment settled into their being. "You admire me?"

"I do." The Aness placed her hand back into her lap gently. "Is it so hard to believe?"

"It's just that… you're the Aness. Everyone looks up to you." Vera felt that their words were all jumbled up. They knew that becoming the Aness required the majority of the Sisaness' vote, that there were rigorous trials, and afterwards a lifetime of tending to the needs of Finni.

"People don't stop admiring others when placed into positions of admiration. Strip away the traditions and ceremony, you and I aren't that different. And like me, you're working towards being the change that you hope for in this world."

"I suppose I am." There was a sense of confidence building inside of them, something they didn't know was missing.

The Aness slowly raised her shoulders and closed her eyes in recognition before returning to her posture.

"If you'd be so willing..." She stood up and extended her hand. "There are some people who are eager to meet you."

Vera was filled with questions, but they also did not want to disappoint her. Vera placed their hand inside hers, and stood carefully so as not to cause any imbalance with the Aness.

"Can my friends come with us?" Vera asked as they strolled together through the garden, and back towards where Mattie, Thora and Lyro were waiting.

"Of course." She offered with a soothing voice. "I think it would be best if they all came along."

When the Aness meant "all" it also included Gander, who was sitting happily between two guards in thick armor, decorative swords and helmets, with a white and purple plume. Vera recognized them as being part of the Sestipheu, elite guards dedicated to the protection of the Rushinay, as well as the three schools of discipline which included the Regal Ballet Academy.

As soon as Gander saw Vera, he rushed across the cobblestone road, clacking his claws as he went, and nearly knocked them to the ground. He jumped up onto his hind legs and licked their face before settling back down on all fours. Vera gave him a big hug; pressing their face deep into his feathers.

"I missed you!" Vera squeezed as tightly and Gander licked his own face in response.

Thora came alongside and ruffled a few of Gander's feathers before they all continued along the path that the Aness directed. The guards followed as well, but kept their distance so that the Aness could keep alongside Vera, Thora and Lyro.

Vera could tell that Thora was ancy, maybe even more so than they were, yet Lyro kept a surreal level of calm. Despite not knowing where they were going, Lyro was enjoying the whole mystery of it.

The walk was not as long as Vera had expected. They turned down a few cobblestone streets, many of which were empty and there were more sestipheu positioned through their route, as if they had planned this outing in advance. Considering who was walking alongside them, it was understandable. The houses were two-story structures, built with stone walls and ceramic tiled roofs. There were street lamps which were lit by pantomimes in anticipation of nillveness, and as the lights danced inside their glass compartments, the scent of spices and roasting meats hung in the air. It was enough to make the three dancers hungry. Gander sniffed the street, and it led him from house to house as he followed some invisible trail.

Finally, the Aness stopped at a house with a red door. There was a sign hanging off a metal frame just slightly above it which read, "Eastern Spinsters" with a painted spinning wheel. The lights on both levels of the building were on, and there were people inside going about their life.

Vera looked suspiciously at the shop, then peeled their gaze from what seemed to them as a very arbitrary spot in the city, to the lavishly dressed Aness and her escort. They broke the silence that had been following them this whole journey, "I don't…" Vera looked again at the shop, hoping to see something that perhaps they had initially missed. "Why are we here?"

The Aness chuckled, it was light and mischievous, and yet filled with a joy that the rest of them couldn't even fathom as to why. And without so much as offering a hint, the Aness opened the door and led the parade of confused dancers inside.

Within there were wooden stalls displaying a variety of yarns, each dyed a different color. Towards the back, there was a giant spinning wheel which nearly reached the ceiling, alongside two smaller ones. There was also a counter which displayed a till box.

The Finni who tended the shop were Caetins. There was a finni who was in her thirties, a finnae of roughly the same age, and two children – one just shy of Vera in height, with horns the same length, and a finnae who looked to be about ten years of age.

"Oh, Maevis! They're here. Oh, thank the NIИ, thank the Aness." She hurried through the labyrinth of the shop, and wrapped her arms so tightly around Vera that they struggled for air.

For a brief moment, Vera was pushed back so the finni could get a better look at them. She had freckles spilled across her nose and beneath her eyes, with many others reaching up towards her horns. Her hair was a mousy brown and her maple eyes sparkled with fresh tears. "I can't believe it—I just can't believe this is true. When we heard the news, we were all just devastated." Vera again was pulled into an embrace, one for which they had no idea why it was all happening to begin with.

With their face smooshed against the finni's chest Vera managed to squeak out, "Who are you?"

"Who am I?" The finni released their grip to wipe their eyes. "I'm Dinaira. Kom Dinera. Sweetheart, I'm your mother's first cousin, your first cousin once removed. We're family, honey. We're your family."

"You're my…" Vera's eyes swelled and a pain flew inside their chest to roost. Their skin tingled and for a brief moment they felt nauseous, like they were about to throw up. And yet one look at the beaming Aness, and the tear struck eyes of Thora whose hands were clasped tightly over her mouth, Vera fell into sobbing.

Vera threw themself into Dinaira, grabbing tightly for fear that if they didn't the wind would sweep her away. "I have a family!"

The two Caetin children fell into the embrace, wanting so desperately to wrap their arms around their lost family member, and Dinaira's husband came as well to help usher Vera back into what they had believed was fully lost – a family, and now a home.

The youngest was Jiro, and the oldest who was Vera's age, was Seena. Dinaira's husband was Maevis. They were all Vera's cousins, to whom Vera recognized by name when their mother used to read from their family book.

After all the tears had finally dried, and introductions were given, Vera, their friends and the Aness were invited for dinner in their home above the shop. It was a stew that Maevis had been preparing since they had been advised of the meeting, and it was rich with potatoes, carrots, spices and chunks of meat from roasted ruffleloven. There was a special place set for the Aness at the head of the table, and Lyro, Thora and Vera sat on one side, and Seena, Jiro and Maevis on another. Dinaira sat at the other end, while Gander had a special place near Vera where he was offered a ruffleloven bone which was already soften by boiling it.

"Aness, would you lead us in a blessing?" Dinaira asked, not certain if it was appropriate or not. "If it wouldn't be too much trouble."

She smiled and with a nod, extended her hand to Lyro and her other one to Jiro, and everyone around the table joined hands with those closest to one another. "Bless this family, our children and all relations. Allow them to flourish, to grow and to find the strength in one another as we head into the long night. Protect them from harm from those who would trespass against us, and let them know harmony and peace. By the sacred role in which I inhabit, let it be so."

"Thank you, so very much, for everything you have done for us." Dinaira offered with rosy cheeks and eyes that were once again filling with mist. She wiped her eyes and offered a quick means to distract from her emotional state, "Shall we then?"

Dinner was accompanied with questions, some directed at Thora about her people and what life is like traveling from place to place, while others at Vera and Lyro wanting to know what it is like training to become a chevalières. A few questions were asked to the Aness, such as how life at court was, and who was her favorite queen. Yet as all things do, the time together came to an end, and the Aness and the three dancers needed to return to their respective places.

After saying their goodbyes, with the offer that Vera visit whenever they wished, Vera, Lyro, Thora and Gander found themselves back on the street with the Aness.

"Many apologies for not escorting you back home, but there are some matters I'll need to tend to right away." She folded her hands in front of her. "Lariel here," she gestured to one of the sestipheu who stood nearby, "Will take you home. I've had Fin Benopal place a parting gift in your room for you Vera. I am sure that you will find a good use for it. I wish you all the best and am looking forward to hearing about your progress. Remember, do your best. That is all anyone can ever expect from you, including yourself. Thank you all for such a lovely time."

"Thank you, Aness — for everything." Vera offered, while the other two extended their own thanks for a lovely evening.

They all departed.

Gander was returned safely to is housing, received an enormous hug from each of them. They returned to their room at the Academy, still talking about the events and how exciting it was for Vera to have met their family. They all were extremely curious to see what the Aness had left for Vera.

Resting on Vera's side table, was a rectangular object no larger than a foot in length, wrapped in a brown paper and tied with a blue ribbon. Vera untied it carefully, then drew their hair up and tied it back with the ribbon. They removed the brown paper carefully, worried that ripping it would somehow ruin whatever was hidden inside.

Thora and Lyro had gathered around them and were just bouncing with anticipation. Once the paper was removed, it revealed a brown leather book, with the word "Kom" stamped on the front. The first page revealed their name, Caetin Kom Vera and then their parents above them. And with each turning of the pages, it revealed more of Vera's family just like the family book that their mother had read from.

Vera, both elated and overwhelmed with sorrow, just buried their face into their hands and sobbed. Thora was quick to wrap their arms around them, and just held them as tightly as they could.

It was at that moment, putting everything together that Lyro had witnessed in the last hours, they realized that Vera's family had been taken over the mountain. Lyro hugged Vera too, shedding their own tears for the pain which Vera had carried all this time, and for the people they never knew.

Chapter 24
En Pointe

"Logic would dictate that engaging a five-hundred foot or more narghoulim in battle, while balancing on the tips of one's toes, would spell nothing but disaster for the dancer. However, logic in this case has been overruled by the laws of magic and the otherworldly powers hidden behind the Glass. For it is that very thing, the pointe shoe of the chevalières, which aids them in gathering presence to fuel their resonance. Without it, less chevalières would return home. While some can equate pointe shoes to torture, it seems those dedicated to art have not only managed the pain, but welcome it as the means justify the ends."

- Ishaya Von Rothbart Oldie, *Musings of the Black Swan*

Vera laid on the padded examination table as Ruby pressed on their foot, then rotated it from left to right, then back again. He then pressed their foot to point and checked a few places on their ankle to see how their muscles were developing.

"Well," he said as he set their foot back on the table, "From what I can tell you seem ready for pointe shoes." He picked up his book and scribbled a few things down with his quill. "Normally, it takes many years of training before you have the correct muscle strength to maintain being en pointe, but it seems that your practice of… what did you call it?"

"Kick feet." Vera offered again while sitting up. "It's a game where you score points by kicking players' feet. The higher it is, the more points you get."

He blinked a few times. "The things you Arcadian kids do for entertainment is bizarre. But—" He took a second look at their feet. "I can't argue with the results. I'll send a recommendation to Fyr Drussel to start having shoes sent to you on a regular basis. With your advanced classes, make sure you keep it to no more than thirty minutes at a time for half a season, then feel out the rest. Too much at once could lead to toe fractures and don't want to have to visit you straight away."

"Yes!" Vera tried to contain their enthusiasm by providing a calm response, but it squelched out as a cheer. "I mean, of course."

"Oh, and congratulations. I know this is a big step for you. Do us all proud, Vera." He gave an encouraging smile then pointed at the door. "Now get on out of here," he joked, "I have things to do."

Vera rushed out of the room, and back out into the hallway of the Academy. Outside both Thora, Lyro and Saffie were waiting for them.

"So what did he say?" Thora asked as the anticipation was already getting to her.

Saffie took one glance at Vera's glee-filled-face and immediately sunk in spirits. "He didn't pass you did he? Ah – geez, and you worked so very hard for this."

"He passed me!" Vera squealed as softly as they could for fear of her voice carrying back into the examination room. "I get to go en pointe! I'm so excited!"

Saffie let out a huge breath of air. "Oh, that's much better news." She straightened her back and placed her hands on her hips. "Have more faith, Saffie."

"I can't believe it, myself." Lyro offered with a grin. "Guess all those times we practiced outside of class really paid off. Now you can have ugly beat-up feet like me." They chuckled at the thought of Vera's ill-fated toes.

"Lyro, what a thing to say." Saffie truly looked hurt, and her eyes misted a little. She swept her arms around the shorter finnyr and pulled them into a strong embrace. "You have beautiful feet, okay?"

"Okay — okay!" Lyro tapped on Saffie's arm like a criminal trying to tap out of a choke hold.

"What about you, Thora?" Vera asked. "Do you want to be examined for point shoes?"

"Actually…" Thora looked down at her feet with a tinge of nervousness, then back at Vera, "You know…" She cast a look towards Saffie and Lyro who seemed very invested now in her answer. "I think I could wait a little bit longer you know… I'm not in any hurry to have my toenails fall off you know."

"Don't worry, Thora." Saffie jumped in. "That only happens if you don't clip your toenails, have an ill-fitting shoe – pfft, like that'll happen because Fyr Drussel is so good at their job – or if the box of your shoe is worn. I'll come over after class and I can show you how to wrap your toes and proper foot care. It'll be great, almost like a sleepover. Wait, can we do a sleep over? I don't know if I'm ready for that. What would I wear?"

"That sounds lovely, Saffie. Thank you." Thora nodded with sincerity.

"We need to celebrate!" Vera exclaimed, this time loud enough for several rooms over to hear. "But quietly," they giggled, "Come on everyone, we have a few moments before classes start again."

And they all followed Vera's lead as they rushed down the hallway towards some unknown destination.

Vera took out the pair of pointe shoes they had received on their first day, well before their last class before their resting period began. They were gorgeous, copper in color to match their skin, and despite how pristine they were, Lyro helped Vera break them in.

They banged the box of the shoe on the floor repeatedly. They squeezed the box, as well as the front of the pointe shoe causing all sorts of crunching noises. Finally, Vera placed the shoes on their feet, but the shoe was loose and so they had to pull the draw strings tight so that it enclosed and gave their foot a good wrap. Lyro helped with the ribbons, showing Vera exactly how to wrap them around their foot and tie them off. Then came small exercises in demi-pointe, just rolling up through the shoe until both feet were en pointe, then returning back down to the ground. The arch seemed a bit stiff, and so Vera went en pointe with one foot and pressed their heel of their other foot into the arch to help stretch it. This was followed by a few échappés, where the feet extended outwards into second position then crossed in front of one another into fifth position.

And while Vera was wanting to prance about the room, wearing socks over their pointe shoes in order to prevent them from getting dirty, they were all due for the advanced class with Fin Ississ.

Class proceeded as usual, with everyone starting off with their ballet slippers. And as normal, Vera and Thora struggled to keep up with everyone – however, they had noticed that their memories were getting better and while their technique required a higher degree of talent, they knew what was coming next and how to prepare for it. This left them both in a position where they weren't scrambling to get to the next motion and falling behind on counts.

Yet, when it came to switching to pointe shoes, where normally Thora and Vera would follow along in slippers, keeping to relevé instead of being en pointe, Vera enthusiastically began putting on their pointe shoes.

From across the room, Fin Ississ called out. "Vera, what do you think you are doing!?" Her voice was shrewd, venomous, and chastising.

Vera took their shoes off and stood up to address their

easily-agitated instructor. "Ruby cleared me for pointe shoes, so I'm putting on pointe shoes." While a touch confused, deep down Vera knew something like this would possibly arise, some objection, or ridicule from the professor who has had it out of them since day one.

Fin Ississ made her way through the other students and stood before her like some looming giant. "I don't care what Ruby has said, it takes years of ballet training before you can start en pointe. You haven't the core, the strength or the means to begin these now."

A heat raised inside of Vera, one that not only felt long overdue but one backed by the support of both the Aponae and the Aness, reinforced by friends, and all the hardship and loss that Vera had suffered. "I don't have years to wait!" Vera shouted. "I have less than two years before I'm 16, and you know as well as I do that my biggest chance to break the Glass is being en pointe!"

"You are not breaking the Glass. You just started." She waved to the rest of the class. "All these students have worked hard since they were seven-years-old. Day after day, they put in the work. They didn't have the Aponae waltzing them in here at five till the hour. You'll be lucky if you make the corps de ballet." Fin Ississ' eyes were narrow and sharp, like an assassin sizing up its mark.

"I've been putting in the work!" Vera screamed. "I didn't walk all the way from Arcadia with a velocitrix chasing at my heels just to be told I'd be lucky to make corp. I lost my neighbors, my friends, my betrothed and my entire family – taken over the mountain! Gone forever!" Their eyes dripped with tears, but not from sorrow. Vera was beyond the point of begging for other people's pity. They were fuming on all accounts, a rage that swelled inside them that made everything shake. "I am here to be a chevalière! And whether you like it or not, I'm going to break the Glass and I'm going to kill that thrice-cursed narghoulim even if it kills me along with it! And no,

197

BITTER old finni is going to stop me!"

Lyro's jaw dropped, Saffie covered their mouth, and Thora, who was standing nearby through the whole affair, was smiling widely with pride.

Fin Ississ' eyes looked Vera over with a sneer. Straightened her back to its fullest extent. "You're coming with me right now!" She turned away from Vera, and quickly strolled towards the door and out into the hall.

Vera scoffed, kicked their pointe shoes out of the way of the barre, and followed after in huff.

With no directions given to the class. Saffie rubbed the back of her neck and said, "Opeena, I guess you're taking over class again."

Vera was expecting another round of yelling as soon as they entered the hallway, however Fin Ississ had something else in mind. "Keep up." Was the only thing the finni expressed to them, as she fumed through the hallway, then led them down the grand staircase and out of the Academy. As soon as she went across the courtyard and towards a familiar staircase, Vera knew precisely where they were going – directly to the Aponae.

The anger that Vera had moments ago was soon replaced with fear and anxiety. *Did I go too far? Will the Aponae side with Fin Ississ on the recommendation that I'm not chevalière material? Would word reach the Aness, and all those kinds words would be retracted?* And as they kept getting closer, the questions kept coming and their fears kept growing.

The doors to the great hall were wide open, and the sestipheu guards didn't even change their positions as they saw Fin Ississ coming. They knew her, and that her coming here was more than routine.

Gorvo was standing in the center of the room, wearing an

open white shirt and his hair looked as perfect as it had the day Vera had first met him. He was lording over a scroll which was being held by a shorter finni, whose clothes seemed more poised towards courtly intrigue than the casual wear of the Aponae.

"You!" Fin Ississ' voice boomed through the hallway with disdain. She hastened her steps, so that she could meet the six-foot-six finnae face-to-face.

He sighed. "Yes, Belle. What can I do for you?" However, he did not lift his eyes from the matter before him.

"You brought me this student and failed to tell me that their entire family had been taken by a narghoulim! A velocitrix no less!" Her anger had not subsided since they had left the classroom.

"It wasn't quite my information to share, was it? Besides, isn't it the responsibility of the staff to get to know their students in order to better meet their needs?" His voice was calm, and yet reeked of dismissal.

"It is your information to share, you're the Aponae for Anessa's sake! We could have given them counseling, special sessions, instead you dropped them on our doorstep like a naked babe and expected us to unquestionably train them like a seventh-year student who's been with us since day one."

Gorvo wrapped up the scroll and handed it back to the finni. "Thank you very much, I have what I need. You may go."

The finni nodded, turned and quickly stepped out of the room as fast as they could whether it be on important business or trying to escape the storm that always brewed between Fin Ississ and the Aponae was uncertain.

He finally addressed her. "So what's the problem? Have you not been training them?" He looked down at Vera, who was now severely overwhelmed and uncertain as to what was taking place. "Hello, Vera. Nice to see you again."

199

"Don't shower them with platitudes, you know very well what you did. You placed this child into our care, into MY class, without any information and you expected us to just follow your orders without so much as a question about the reasons why? You're reckless! I've always seen you as reckless! And I know it brings you great pleasure to torment me, but how dare you use this child as a pawn in your twisted little games."

Gorvo cocked his head to one side. "This child came to me requesting to join the Academy in hopes of becoming a chevalière. They auditioned, and I granted their request. Are you saying that I shouldn't have agreed to it? Are you stating you are not willing to teach them?"

Fin Isisis grinded their teeth. "That is not what I am saying at all!

"Then why are you here, Belle? Why are you here and not teaching?"

"You're infuriating! Know that if this child breaks the Glass, it won't be because of what you did that day, but because of their own hard work and dedication. Do you understand me?"

"As you wish." The Aponae wore a devilous grin. "Anything else?"

Fin Ississ turned away in disgust. "Come along, Vera."

Baffled by what just happened, and still uncertain as to their future, Vera cast their eyes between the two feuding individuals. However, when their eyes landed on Gorvo, he simply gave them a short bow and a wink to send them off.

Following as quickly as Vera could, they overheard Fin Ississ muttering angrily to herself as she continued back through the path they had just taken to get there. And it wasn't until they reached the courtyard when Vera had the nerve to ask, "So... I'm not going to be expelled?"

Fin Ississ stopped, clenched her fists, took a huge breath of air, then released her fists so that her hands hung slack. She turned around, this time with a calmer face. "No child, you're not expelled. I'm sorry, I misjudged you. Gorvo and I have bad history, but that's not what matters. I know what it is like to lose everyone you ever loved to the narghoulim. More than I want to discuss." She kneeled down and looked up at Vera. "You have a place here. You will always have a place here. You understand?"

Vera just nodded, uncertain as to what to feel or what to say.

Fin Ississ stood up. Starting today, after dinner you will meet me for an hour where we usually have class. Additionally, you'll be up before breakfast and meet me there again for another hour. We can't give you the same training we have given everyone else. But I can at least give you your best shot."

"Meeting for what?" Vera asked suspiciously.

"Training, you silly finni. I'll be training you personally, one-on-one. And with a lot of work, and a ton of luck, maybe you'll have a chance at killing that abomination that took your family away from you."

Vera could not believe it. "Are you serious?"

Fin Ississ nodded with conviction.

With tears building in their eyes, Vera rushed Fin Ississ and wrapped their arms around her. "Thank you so very much! I'll work awfully hard, you won't regret this."

Surprised by the sudden intrusion, Fin Ississ wasn't certain how to respond. However, she did the only thing she could, which was to return the child's hug. "I hope, in time, you'll forgive me."

Chapter 25
Ḣail the Awakened

"No one knows why some individuals are able to break the Glass while others aren't. While talent and passion are simply a must, there have been more students with just as much talent and passion than those who have broken the Glass and become chevalières. At their highest peak, one out of ten students will become a chevalières or three out of a class of thirty. Those who fail to break the Glass up to the very hour of their 16th birthday are faced with a difficult decision, to continue as a member of the corps de ballet or return home. Either way, it's heartbreaking."

– Professor of Pantomimes, Nadin Frenwyn Tilly of Riloshek.

Fin Ississ was true to her word. After dinner, Vera would meet her in the ballroom for private lessons. A single barre would be set out, and the movements would be fully explained and demonstrated. When it was Vera's turn to perform the motions, Ivicti the pianist would play. Then, after resting and prior to breakfast, Vera would return to find Ed at the piano. Thora would accompany them, and she too was allowed a side of the barre, but the instruction was always meant for Vera. Though, there would be times when Fin Ississ found Thora's presence to be useful when trying to show Vera exactly what was needed of them, rather than looking into a mirror.

Vera wasn't used to the number of corrections that Fin Ississ was offering. "Mind your turn out, deepen your pliés, rotate your thighs, tilt your head more, extend your arms, your arms are too far back…" it was endless. On tendu devant, Fin Ississ would push Vera's feet so that they were back into correct alignment, then tap their tummy so that Vera would pull it up. Yet as Lorilyn's days turned, the corrections came less and less and a new sense of confidence rose in their dancing.

Before long it was halfwen, the halfway period of nillveness before the sun would start to rise in gillmet, breaking the long period of night before morilyn would return. It was the time when the veil between the physical world and the bond between the dead and the living were at their strongest. Throughout the city, people hosted balls. The streets were filled with individuals wearing elegant masks, conducting business in the shadows while others giving into all manner of gaiety. Vera took their holiday to visit with their new family. However, when the festivities had ended, Vera found themself back in their room next to the window.

The usual smells of incense had wafted away, as there was cantankerous wind that had suddenly given rise, and it carried with it the faint scent of upturned soil and grass. The skies were fortunately clear of clouds. Yet it seemed like there was something, just beyond the horizon, that was watching them.

The cycles continued, and so did Vera's training. Nearly twenty-four had come and gone, and Vera was now fifteen years of age, on the cusp of their sixteenth birthday and their technique was flawless. No longer did Thora and Vera struggle to keep up in the advanced class, as their movements were perfectly synced, and when it came time to do floor work, their grand jetés, soubresauts and cabrioles were one of the most elegant, and for brief moments it seemed as they effortlessly flew through the air.

Yet, there was a nervousness that descended upon the entirety of the dancers as it came time for them to focus on the final steps to becoming a chevalières. Rounded into an auditorium, where all their instructors sat upon a stage, Fin Ississ took to the podium to address the gathering of over two-hundred students.

"Each of you will be given an entire rotation of the seasons to work on breaking the Glass." Fin Ississ declared while keeping a stone face and trying to remain as matter of fact as possible. "We have assigned each of you a room, set with a

203

waterclock which will begin its countdown a season prior to your birthday. In these rooms, you'll dance from your heart." She gestured to her chest, and for a moment Vera could see her hand trembling. "But you won't be alone, as you'll have a second. A member of the corps de ballet will be there to keep you company." She paused and moved her eyes from faces which were filled with determination and those who were anxious.

"Now, they are not there to distract you. Every moment you are in that room, you need to focus on your dancing. By the NIИ, if you happen to break through the Glass, you will enter into what we call the apotheosis. Your bodies will be flooded with vivitah. It is imperative that you continue to dance until the vivitah has waned, as you could risk being completely consumed by it." She closed her eyes as if in remembrance of past disasters.

"The member of the corps de ballet will open a shutter in order for you to exit the Academy so you have the room to expel this energy. Please keep clear of densely populated streets, and refrain from coming into contact with anyone while you are dancing. Your second will be additionally tasked for ringing the bells, which will alert the Academy as well as anyone on the street that you've broken through the Glass. It will also signal members of the Regal Music Academy to sing, 'Hail the Awakened' which can be heard from every corner of Adalace."

She stopped for a moment to catch her breath and to give them all a reassuring smile. "You've all worked so very hard for this moment. Rest assured, that no matter what happens in that room, whether you breach the Glass or not, we are all so—" her voice quivered as tears welled in her eyes, "—so very proud of you, and everything that you've sacrificed to get here." She wiped her eyes. "A roster will be posted in the grand hall as to what time, and what room you are assigned." She inhaled deeply through her nose. "I speak on behalf of all your professors and I can say with confidence that it has been a pleasure teaching you."

All of the professors erupted in applause, and provided the students with a standing ovation for all of their achievements and hard work.

Vera was not first on the list, but they weren't last either. They recognized many names, but the first ones which stood out the most were Saffie and Opeena. Neither of them would be attending class any longer, they would take their meals in their rooms, and would vanish for thirty passes of light on the surface of Longlyn – all of which were counted on the waterclocks outside their assigned room.

As the drips continued to fill the float tanks, a few additional students were pulled from classes, causing each lesson to shrink in attendance which left Vera with a surreal sensation, as if they would never see those familiar faces again.

Then, during pas de deux class, the bells resounded! They were so numerous, so powerful, that it drowned out the music of the piano. Fan Golvorah dismissed everyone, and Vera, Thora and Lyro, among several others, rushed outside to one of the balconies in order to see who it was that had first broken the Glass.

It was morilyn, yet a soft breeze fell upon the mountain school. They searched the cloudless sky, and the rooftops eager to catch a glimpse of a newly awakened chevalière. And as Fin Ississ had claimed, music rose from the Regal Music Academy – which was loud and resounding, having been empowered by amplify pantomimes. There were deep cellos, violins, drums, and each stroke across their instruments was electric and it pulsed within each of them. Then came a voice which screamed in a melodious harmony that sent shivers down Vera's arms:

"Hail to the Awakened, the boundary is shattered.
Through the skies you tear, wings now are beating.
Here to slay the cursed ones, the NIMs work be done.
Saving us from despair!

Then, from a rooftop, in a brilliant grand assemblé en tournant, where she leapt hundreds of feet into the air, arms above her head and fingers from both hands pointing towards one another, she spun in rapid succession. In the classroom, they would perform the same motions in a circle, one student following after the other, and when they leapt, they would clear two to three feet. In mid-air, they would turn twice, rotating their heads in order to spot something to keep their focus on so they wouldn't get dizzy as easily. However, the dancer was doing twelve of them in a row, so quickly that Vera would not have been able to tell were it not for her spotting.

She was swirling with a ribbon-like energy, similar to how some pantomimes would glow. It was a yellow-ish light, similar to the color of the sun, and it burned with ferocity. As she danced towards them, Vera was finally able to make out who it was that ruptured the Glass.

The individual held broad shoulders, with a towering height, bulging muscles, blonde hair and large insect-like horns that placed her as part of the Erdo tribe. Immediately, before Vera could say a word, Lyro grabbed hold of them and shook them with violent excitement. "IT'S SAFFIE!" Lyro screamed! "IT'S SAFFIE! DO YOU SEE HER! IT'S FREAKING SAFFIE!" Lyro flung themself against the balcony, and with hands planted screamed, "WAY TO GO SAFFIE!" And as Saffie performed a scissor leap while bounding off another rooftop, Vera swore that she gave a wink.

Thora called out, "GREAT JOB SAFFIE!" while cupping her hands against her mouth. And Vera, now brimming with excitement and joy, joined Lyro at the balcony and screamed, "SAFFIE! YOU DID IT! WHOOOOOOOO!"

And now that all the other students recognized who it was that was the first among them to breach the Glass, they too joined in with jubilant cheers.

Yet for many the waterclocks dripped their last drop, and for those students their time had run out. It became a familiar sight for Vera and Thora to pass by other dorm rooms and be assaulted by the muffled cries of dancers who had failed to breach the Glass.

As Nillveness was upon them, having returned from playing with Gander, Thora and Vera had entered the great hall which was normally empty at that time as most students were inside their rooms resting. Yet sitting there, face buried into their arms while they squeezed their legs together, they recognized Leekyn horns and bleached white hair.

"Opeena?" Vera asked as they approached. "Are you okay?"

The finni raised her head, tears streaming down her face, and sniffled. "I didn't make it. I was…" She pinched her fingers together. "So close and it all just faded away. Just slammed shut. Shut forever." She covered her eyes with one hand and her heart with the other. "I let everyone down. I let my teachers down. I let the academy down. I let my mom down."

Vera sat down on one side of her and Thora on the other and they both wrapped their arms tightly around her and all she could do was cry.

And when she pulled herself up from her tears just long enough to breathe, Vera asked, "Why are you here? Why didn't you go back to your room?"

Opeena struggled out, "I felt like I didn't deserve to be here anymore. After I—I just started walking out the door. The biggest disappointment. And I was going to leave, and I made it," she pointed behind her, "just down the stairs until I realized that there was no where for me to go. Who would want a failure at home?"

Thora grabbed her hand and squeezed it tightly. "You're not a failure. You didn't do anything wrong. Since we got here, everyone has been saying how much they admire you and

207

think the world of you. Your dancing has been perfect." Thora tossed a quick glance at Vera for confirmation and Vera nodded.

"That's right, even Saffie was saying just how perfect you are and how highly she thinks of you."

Opeena wiped her eyes. "Saffie said that?"

"Yeah," Vera thought a bit in hopes of recalling that initial conversation. "I think she said, 'perfect hair, perfect fashion, perfect dancing' and maybe even something about perfect manners."

"I do try really hard to be my best for everyone." She flashed a brief smile.

"Opeena." Vera took her other hand and looked her straight in the eye. "Sometimes things happen, and we have no control over it, even when we do our best. And...", *it's my fault.* Vera swallowed the intrusive thought away. "It's *not* our fault. The world is filled with tragedies. And you not becoming a chevalière is a tragedy because you would have made the BEST chevalière. But you didn't let anyone down. You're not a disappointment and everyone still looks up to you."

She sniffled. "Do you really think so?"

Thora nodded her head. "I know so."

"Same." Vera smiled while biting back their own tears for the pain that Opeena was presently feeling. "I promise."

"Do you think, that Fin Ississ will be mad at me?" Opeena asked as a few stray tears fell down her cheek.

Vera shook their head slowly. "No... I don't think she'd be mad at all. I think she'd do exactly as we're doing right now."

"I don't know if I could see her by myself." Opeena paused to take a breath. "To-to tell her. Will you both come with me, so I don't have to do it alone?"

"Of course, we will. We can go right now if you'd like, okay? I think she'd be in her office."

Opeena nodded. "Thank you." She wrapped her arms around Thora and gave her a kiss on the cheek. Flashed a brief smile, then did the same with Vera. She took a deep breath in, wiped her eyes, and took up both of their hands.

Together they walked up the grand staircase, leaving behind them the tall statues of long past chevalières. They continued beyond the hallway which led to the now empty classrooms, past the barres and the mirrors, until they reached the wooden door to Fin Ississ' office. Opeena raised her chest, pressed down her shoulders, and after taking another breath, she rapped on the door. And once she heard the welcoming voice of Fin Ississ, she sullenly turned the knob and stepped inside with Thora and Vera courageously behind her - to help her say goodbye to a dream.

Chapter 26
The Waterclock

"Waterclocks were set to measure the days and nights of the planet Longlyn. Before them, time was determined by the position of our sister moons Tshir and Illune. Some waterclocks measure the passing of a Longlyn day, while others will measure the time between half seasons and full seasons. For smaller periods of time, hourglasses blown by the Alshep tribe have always been in high demand. Since its creation, the finni have been ruled by its measurements. Resting periods were once dictated to when the Finni grew tired. Now, we all toil beneath the thrall of the water clock's drips. One wonders if we are better off without it."

– Observations of Orabelle, Doctor Niecen Coppelius.

One-by-one, the schedules were removed from the great hall and the names of dancers who have not yet had their run at breaking the Glass. Then came the moment that Vera both anticipated and dreaded. Prior to breakfast, Fin Ississ took Vera and Thora to the eastern wing of the Academy, where iron doors secured the entrance into a twenty-foot high, by thirty-feet wide, and twenty-feet long room of pure stone. There were no mirrors, there was no barre, and there was no piano. As Fin Ississ had previously described, there were shutter doors which were tight shut. However, there was plenty of light provided by pantomimes that were suspended high above the ceiling.

Outside the room, nestled in a nook in the wall alongside the entrance was the water basin. Already drops of water were slowly leaking into it. The outside of the glass basin had marks that measured the passage of time. Each drip Vera observed felt like a weight dropping upon their face.

Fin Ississ placed her hands together and gave a heavy sigh. "This room is yours. You may come and go as you please. You may shut the doors if you require privacy or you may leave them open. You'll have neighbors, but try not to distract each other."

Vera nodded as dutifully as they could.

"Since Thora is bound to the corps de ballet, I thought it would be fitting that she serve as your second. In the event, and blessed moment, you break the Glass, she will open the shutter for you and be tasked with ringing the bells which are at the end of that corridor." She pointed further down the hall.

Thora flashed Vera a smile, happy to be here to help.

"Food and drink will be provided, here, in your room. You are invited to use your own dorm to rest, or you may make use of the adjacent apartment behind us." She pointed to the wooden door straight across from the iron ones. She then placed her hands on Vera's shoulders. "This is your moment. Find the music within you, and dance to the melody that you feel in your heart. You may not find it right away, and some never find it at all. It's time to be in tune with all that you are and gain strength from it. Passion is the power in which we are made. Do you understand?"

"I think so." Vera offered in return, not fully clear on what she meant but confident that they would soon discover that for themself.

Fin Ississ nodded with a smile. She briefly touch Vera on the cheek with her hand. "I'm so very proud of you. What happens in that room, no matter what the outcome, my esteem for you will not change. May the NIИ guide you."

Then, as she had done for every other student, Fin Ississ turned and walked away – leaving the outcome of their fate in their own hands.

The room felt cold, as they often did prior to dancing. Yet, once they started moving the chill would be welcomed. Thora, however, had prepared and wore heavier clothes. It was the early hours of nillveness and already the temperatures had dropped. Over two years ago, Thora was putting the finishing touches on the birthday gift they were making for Vera, surrounded by family, the gorm and the familiar sight of her people's caravans.

Vera was already in the center of the room, stretching as best they could. They planted themself on the cold floor and began to tie up their pointe shoes, being ever more diligent to ensure that the ribbon was properly wrapped and tied, with the drawstrings tightened.

As soon as they were finished, they started with a few échappés, then in sauté and changement. Each time they switched their feet, beat at the thighs and rolled through their shoe, nothing seemed different and Vera wasn't certain if they even *could* break the Glass, let alone the *how* to break the Glass. Were it not for Saffie and several other dancers who they had seen, Vera would almost go so far as to say it wasn't even real in the first place.

Fin Ississ said to dance from their heart, and so Vera placed their hand over their chest and listened. All that they could feel was a thumping sound, one that would travel up their arm, behind their neck and into their ears. *Thump, thump, thump, thump.* And suddenly, they were back in Tandermundt and the wind was swirling about them and the howling pierced through their ear and imagined the screams sucked into the void.

Vera pulled their hand away and cast the unwanted feeling to the ground like a detested shawl and took a few moments to breathe. They fell into a tombe; traveled across the floor in a pas de bourrée; leapt into a sissonne where their back foot pressed them out of a fifth position, shot out behind them and returned to fifth; then raised en-pointe in attitude. Vera kept to the basics, but then shifted into more complex motions, from traveling steps such as pas de chevals to turns such as fouettés en tournant and they were all beautifully executed, but outside the feelings that Vera normally felt there was nothing new rising. Despite it all, Vera continued to dance.

Meals came and went, and so too did multiple resting

periods. The waterclock reached a quarter of the way full, and Vera was filled with frustrations and doubt, that they heard the bells ringing for other students. They were unsure as to who, or as to how long those students had been in their room, but it felt like a personal defeat. And each time they pressed their hand to their chest and struggled to listen to what their heart's song would be, it always came back as the same thumping as before.

On one occasion, Vera needed some air and not the type that the shutters would offer. They threw on a heavy coat and walked through the Academy, back to where they had met the Aness. The garden looked more beautiful than before as all the nocturnals and moon flowers were in bloom. They sat on the same cold bench and imagined what kind of advice the Aness would give to them during this difficult time.

Behind them, they could hear the sounds of boots clomping on the pathway and they imagined that it was either Thora or some other student, yet when the person came beyond the path and stood in front of them, it was someone Vera did not ever expect to see again.

While older than they had first seen him, he had the same sunken blue eyes, the same bushy eyebrows, and the same wide brimmed hat that hid several of his other features. His hair was longer, but well groomed and he was bundled in a long coat that reached his ankles. "Many apologies for disturbing you, Fin Kom."

Vera shot up from their bench and wrapped their arms around him as they shouted, "Tage! It's so wonderful to see you."

"And I you," he paused briefly and returned their embrace before Vera pulled away. "Though I was not expecting such a warm reception." His voice was still as smooth as nyri silk.

Vera returned to their seat and motioned for him to join them. "I'm surprised to see you, especially here at the Academy. What brings you here?"

He eased himself to sitting and looked at them with a sincere smile. "I've come multiple times to the Academy, yet each time I was politely turned away. I don't wish to take up much of your time, especially now, considering how precious it

213

is to you. So, I'll get right to it. Ever since that day I saw you in Cornelis, I felt the procession of spirits walking with you. They've chained themselves to you, waiting for your grief, waiting for you to tell them it's okay to depart this world. I'm here, if you'd like, to help you mourn them so that they may be released from this world."

Vera thought for a moment, knew he didn't mean any harm, but they shook their head. "I'm sorry. I just… I can't mourn them. I don't have time, and I don't have the means." Their heart pained them to think about those who were taken. "Not until the narghoulim responsible is slain. Maybe then, I can mourn them. It's just…"

"I understand." Tage nodded his head a few times. "You know, a lot of times people focus on the pain caused by those they have lost, which can make it hard for them to remember all the reasons why they miss them so. Our departed loved ones can invoke feelings of weakness and vulnerability, but they also can be a form of strength and security. Those you have lost, are still with you, Fin Kom. What kind of strength do they give you?"

Vera looked out into the darkness, casting their eyes to bathe in the star constellations that twinkled above them, to the glow of Orabelle's sisters, and back to a time where they sat on the hill overlooking their family's trip of goats. The feeling of the chill wind blowing across their cheeks, making them rosy by the time they returned home. "The will to survive… and the strength to kill the narghoulim who took everything away from me." They clenched their fist, then stood. "Thank you Tage for seeing me. I need to get back to my room and focus on breaking the Glass. After the narghoulim is dead, then I'll be ready to mourn."

Tage nodded once more. "Then I shall remain until that time. Not as a reminder, but as a friend, and someone who wants you to succeed in all of your endeavors."

Vera flashed a brief smile. "Thank you for all you've done for Thora and I. If it wasn't for you, I don't know if we would have made it here on our own."

Tage stood, his height still towering over them, and gave a short bow. "I live to serve."

Vera returned to their room with a new resolve. They dared to place their hand on their heart, to hear the thumping inside, and while it frightened them, they felt a new sense of determination – to look past the sound and to see it as proof that they were alive, that they had survived what some would see as the impossible. So they pushed through, and danced harder. With each continued drip of the waterclock, they danced, and they leaped, and they twirled, and it was all to the beat of their own heart.

During periods of rest, they would have dreams that they were standing in Tandermundt, and they could levitate off the ground, about a foot at most, and they wished to fly up into the sky where all their friends, family and neighbors were. Yet, it felt like there was something holding them back, like there was something in the way, some barrier that they could not find or push against. And when they would wake up, there would be that lingering sensation – that feeling of performing a grand jeté when at the very apex of the jump they glided through the air and for a brief moment felt like they were flying.

Then came gilmet, and with it, Arrivée. The waterclock's basin was nearly full and Vera felt the pressure stronger than ever before. And after several adagios and a few allegros, Vera was struggled with defeat, when they remembered their audition with the Aponae, and all those times they had watched Ayren, Nam and Felicity practice with the rest of the children for the Danse de L'arrivée. And they realized, it was their turn, and their time to take their place as an adult in their village just like they would have if the velocitrix hadn't stolen everyone away.

In their mind, they could hear the drums beating out their counts. Vera, called out to the sky, and leapt into the air with a scissor leap, then landed gracefully, turned and raised en pointe in attitude devant. Returning their foot to meet their other, Vera bourréed, with both feet keeping close together, then fell into fourth position and twirled gracefully in a quadruple pirouette, before ending with arms in fourth before quickly descending their arms in bowl shape below their hip in first. Tombé, glissade then tour jeté, throwing themself high into the air, floating, then retreating back to the ground.

Combré back, facing the sky.

There was a tingle in the air, a building of the invisible and Thora could feel it pulsing through her body. She stood up, as the change in the room caused her heart to quicken and shot goosebumps across her skin. Her eyes locked on her friend.

Vera could feel the world as it was lifting, the weight dissipating, a hidden strength pooling into their muscles, and so they ran, following the stream of energy as it carried them like a friendly wind, and they launched themself into a firebird leap, where their backfoot raised behind them, their arms outstretched above their head, and their spine curved like a sail to connect the top of their head with their pointe shoe.

Their leading foot warmed, and it spread through their body like a blast of morilyn heat, and their whole body connected against a thin invisible wall that gave way to their passing.

Then boom! the Glass shattered in a flash of intense light, and pieces flung in all directions, and from it a force like a hurricane gale which knocked Thora off her feet and to the floor. Her left eye burned, as if something had gotten lodged in it; like a speck of dust that just wouldn't go away. She blinked, to clear it away while picking herself back up only witness a sight that sent shivers across her entire being.

Ribbons of light fluttered around Vera, weaving in and through their body, like peddlewing birds diving for insects. Vera glowed, surrounded with the glimmering of light, and an aura which beamed with such intensity that Thora had to squint so not to be in additional pain.

Vera stood there in awe, examining their hand and the radiating beams which flowed around it, feeling the sensation of the world no longer pushing down upon them, feeling light, and euphoric, as the joy of the chains which shackled the common finni were lifted and they were now like the clouds drifting carelessly and free above.

"Dance!" Thora screamed as she covered her left eye. "You have to keep dancing! VERA! DANCE!"

Vera nodded, and stepped into an arabesque and the light pulsed from them and out into the room. They then pulled their leg behind them and drew it now in front in attitude enface. And the power which now flowed within them followed their motions, fueling their strength, and guiding them towards other motions. So Vera flew into foutettés turns, where they pivoted on one leg and shot their leg out, then in towards their knee, before extending their leg out again – like whipping the air to cause them to turn – doing so in rapid succession, ten, twenty, thirty, forty times and spinning at incredible speeds, their head spotting the entire time, before keeping their leg pulled inwards, releasing their arms from being cupped in front of them, to drawing them up over their head and spinning sixty, seventy, eighty times!

"Woooooooo!" Vera cheered with an overwhelming sensation as joy rushed through her body like a waterfall. "YOU DID IT!" Thora rushed to the chain next to the shutters, and yanked it as hard as they could to release the latch and counterweights, which flung the shutter doors wide open, sending cool air and the light of gilmet bursting into the room.

"THE BELLS! I HAVE TO RING THE BELLS!" Thora ran towards the other end of the room and out the doors, screaming behind, "GO! VERA! GO!"

Vera flung themself out of their turn, like a shooting star, burning brightly across the floor, towards the shutters, and leaping from the edge out into the waking horizon. One hundred, two hundred, three hundred feet, high into the sky, through the cooling breeze, and into the chill – where the forces of being no longer held control over them. They were free, capable of reaching the highest of heights, and when they fell it was because they allowed themselves to fall, and so they did – down towards the city below and onto a roof top en pointe, where they performed blancés, swaying back and forth on the ceramic tiles and falling into a waltz step before chasséd – chasing their forward foot with the back – and performing a stag leap, which took them off the top of the roof and back soaring high into the air.

Thora reached the bell tower and frantically pulled the ropes, and even though they rang, they didn't feel like they were ringing loudly enough, so Thora flung herself onto a high point of the rope and drew it down with their entire body so that it rang stronger, louder and more forceful than before.

217

The bells resounded through Adalace, and the people looked upwards, searching for the newly born chevalière. All cheering, all applauding, all sending their love and adoration into the sky. Vera could hear them, could see them from high above, and as they descended, they spun in the air, then landed with a single touch of their pointe shoe along the top of a home, before chaînés turns – where their feet were close together and they spun down the length of the building – then launched back into the sky in a calypso – their front leg rotated forward, extended, then the back leg drew up in attitude and continued with the spin.

Then the music exploded into the city, the very lyrics that Vera had heard time for the announcement of the other chevalières. The music inspired them, caused them to dance harder, bounding from roof to roof, and from parapet to balcony. Their heart filled with rapturous accomplishment, one celebrated by thousands, now causing tears to swell in their eyes while they soared across the city one leap at a time.

> *"Hail to the Awakened, the boundary is shattered.*
> *Through the skies you tear, wings now are beating.*
> *Here to slay the cursed ones, the NIΛs work be done.*
> *Saving us from despair!*

On the street there was a Caetin, no taller than Vera, who caught sight of the shimmering dancer, and waved frantically. "VERA! BY THE NIΛ! VERA!" It was Seena, who pointed at them between waves yelling, "THAT'S MY COUSIN!"

And while the music was loud, and they were in the middle of shifting from one movement to the other, Vera caught their cousin's motions and leapt towards an adjacent house, and gave her a hastened wink before performing a spin, then a leap, over and over again until they reached the end of the building before firing themself straight up into the air while extending a leg up towards their head.

From a high balcony of the Aradis'a Monti, seat of the Rushinay, the Aness strolled out in a long sheer dress, to where long red feathers with white tips extended from her collar. She smiled warmly to herself, as she recognized the new chevalière. She touched her lips with her fingers, then placed it delicately on the wind so that it would be carried dutifully to Vera as they danced by.

Gorvo exited from his hall and raised his hand in greetings, then knocked his fist against his chest and gave a slight bow to Vera as she danced briefly down the stairs before leaping away to the next portion of the city.

Everyone saw. Everyone knew. Vera was a chevalière! They had done the impossible, they survived and now they thrived! And somewhere in the distance, the wind roared.

Chapter 27
Geist Weapons

"Chevalières each have different resonances based upon the constellation they were born under. For those born under The Bard, they are capable of releasing the Songbird, which briefly bends the rules of magic, allowing one to extend the reach of their pantomimes beyond their wingspan. Those born beneath the Donkey manifest nine illusionary duplicates of themselves for which a chevalière might use as decoys while fighting narghoulim. There are even resonances, if timed correctly – such as The Phoenix – which allows a chevalière to return to life if slain while their resonance burns. However, there is one constellation which is avoided in conversation – The Fallen, which has the power of destroying any narghoulim instantly, but at the terrible cost of the dancer's life."

- Coppelia, Professor of Dance, The Regal Ballet Academy, Adalace.

Vera breaking the Glass spread through the school and the city like sweth vines from the underland of Niece. Everyone hugged them, from fellow classmates, to instructors who could not, and would not, stop telling them how absolutely proud they were of them. Vera now joined an exclusive roster of individuals such as Saffie, Yori, Ursalin, Rothe, and a few others.

However, while Vera was being provided a new schedule for classes, which now included Geist weapon training, they were more concerned for Thora who, having been inspected by Ruby, found nothing in their eye which could be causing the irritation. Luckily, the pain had subsided and was now more of itch than what they had experienced previously.

Excused from class until their eye was fully better, Thora was able to follow Vera around in order to help sort their new found status as a chevalière. Many of course were suited to dealing with their new found abilities, such as how to land from an eight-hundred foot drop, or which type of pointe shoe was best matched with each narghoulim. Vera especially enjoyed the classes on the different styles of tutus, such as defensive tutus which were lined with pieces of glass to reflect light into the eyes of opponents, flaming tutus which were designed to be lit on fire to either act as a lure or intimidate, floating tutus which softened a chevalières fall should they find their vivitah drained and unable to soften the blow of the landing, or perhaps Vera's favorite which was the bladed tutu. This one carried individual blades which were attached at the hip and while performing turns like a pirouette, the blades would rise up and slash at anything in striking distance like a saw blade.

Thora was busy taking notes, feeling that it was her job to ensure that Vera was properly equipped and not dancing into danger without the proper items available to them. Soon, Thora would be returning to her own classes which, as it were, involved her training as part of the corps de ballet.

When it came to geist weapon training, Vera and Thora stood alongside Saffie, who was raising on relevé on one foot, then rolled through the foot, back down, and switch to the other side before ending on relevé in order to alleviate some anxiety.

"What's the matter, Saffie?" Vera asked while they waited for the instructor. "You seem a bit tense."

The room was empty, no barres, no mirrors, just a large empty room with tall window that let in the light of morilyn and a ten-foot-tall leather disc-shaped case that rested along a wall.

"Oh, you noticed? I've been trying my best not to show it because I don't want to make anyone uncomfortable." She stopped shifting through her feet and instead brought her nails up to her mouth and started biting them, but realizing what she was doing she immediately dropped them down. "I'm just worried about Lyro, they've been in that room for so long and I don't know what I'll do if they don't break the Glass."

"I'm sure that they'll be okay." Thora offered. "It was hard going for us, but we made it through and Lyro is such an amazing dancer."

"Yeah, you're probably right." Saffie crossed their arms. "I just think of how upset they'll be if they don't make it, and it would be hard if we all made it but they didn't. I would feel really bad about the whole thing."

221

"Saffie…" Vera offered a calm and soft voice. "No one gets to choose who becomes a chevalière, and it certainly wouldn't be your fault if they didn't make it."

"Maybe I took too much vivitah when I broke the Glass, you know? Like maybe there is only so much available and I stole too much."

A familiar voice waltzed behind them, "What are we stealing?"

Saffie's eyes widened and she raced over to where it came from and gave the person a tight squeeze. "Lyro! You're here!"

Lyro didn't say a word, just allowed the hug to nearly crush them before being placed back on the ground. "Wait, but if you're here, does that mean you broke the Glass?" Saffie asked with dropped eyebrows and a sunken jaw. "I didn't hear any bells or announcements or anything."

"Oh, yeah, I broke it. Just didn't feel like going through the whole song and dance, so I stayed in the room and burned it all off. Now I'm here." Lyro's features were placid, and slightly sullen, their voice had even dropped down into a lazy draw as if they had just gotten out of bed and had zero motivation for the day.

"But Lyro," Thora encouraged with twinkling eyes, "It's such an accomplishment. You didn't want to celebrate it? Not even a little?"

Lyro's head rolled to the side to address Thora. "Not even a little, I'm afraid." Their head rolled back to its normal position. "So, are we going to learn about stabby things or what?"

A finni Leekyn, with bleached white hair that extended all the way to her knees, adorned in white leather armor with spacing around the joints to allow a free flow of movement, strolled into the room. She carried a fifteen-foot scythe across her shoulder, where the blade was at least three times the size of a normal scythe, and had jagged teeth.

"Oooo, that's pretty." Lyro said with sudden interest. Then whispered to Vera, "And the weapon looks exciting too."

"Wait… is that Opeena's mother?" Vera whispered back.

Lyro shrugged their shoulders. "I dunno, maybe. I hear bleached hair is in this season."

Thora felt her heart sink into her stomach as a cloak of

dread draped over them. There were cracks, like those in glass or across a mirror, sprawled across the finni's features and from them poured out a yellowish light which glowed and pulsed. It was the same kind of energy she saw when Vera had broken through the Glass. The cracks on her face, the very cracks Thora had seen extending across their best friend's face, back in the cave that was imparted to her by yellow-cast eyes.

"What's wrong with her face?" Thora quietly muttered, too aghast to say anything more for fear of learning the answer.

Saffie did hear, and gave the finni a good look about. "I can't say exactly, maybe it's a lack of moisturizing, or too much time out in the wilds."

"No, I mean the cracks on her face." Thora whispered again, this time catching the attention of both Vera and Lyro.

"You know, it's not nice to point out wrinkles, Thora. One can only do so much past the age of twenty-five, you know." Lyro added with a slight smile.

"You don't see the cracks? And the light?" Thora looked between them all, hoping to discover some form of joke amongst them, yet they all provide her a befuddled look.

And as Thora looked closer, they realized the cracks were there and were not there. They shifted between their eyes, closing one, then closing the other. The right eye saw nothing, just a standard face, while the left showed a broken visage assailed by light filtering up through it.

"All right, listen up!" The armor-adorned finni announced. "Let's get this out of the way, yes, I'm Opeena's mother."

"Called it." Vera noted with a creeping grin.

"My name is Ashunaday, most call me Ash or Ashun. Either works, especially when we're out in the field, the quicker you get my name out the better. We're going to be focusing on armor-breaking techniques. Weapons such as Tilly here," she spun the blade of the scythe effortlessly as if it were made of light wood, "As well as other weapons such as axes, sword breakers and slam hammers are designed to break through a narghoulim's thick armor."

Saffie nearly drooled. "Slaaaaaam haaaaammmmerrrsss." She was transfixed.

Ashunaday continued, "No mundane weapon will do it.

223

they simply aren't heavy enough to carry though a powerful enough swing. Geist weapons are forged specifically to get the job done."

She whipped the blade off her shoulder, leapt back away from the spectating dancers, and spun the blade in a dazzling display before drawing it overhead and having it land tip down no more than a foot in front of everyone. "The teeth on the blade are designed to rip through armor, making it easier to reach vulnerable areas. And in honor of our more recent chevalière, Fin Kom, you'll be learning the proper method on how to kill a velocitrix."

"Wait? In honor of me?" Vera asked with a bewildered expression.

"Yes, in honor of you." Ashunaday echoed. "Ever since you've reached apotheosis, a velocitrix has been sighted, bouncing between settlements and ravaging everything in its path. From my understanding, you've encountered this narghoulim before. So now it's time for some payback."

Thora chimed in. "What do you mean by payback?"

"Unlike most narghoulim, the velocitrix is difficult to kill on account that if it even catches of whiff of chevalières it leaves. The only way to keep it from destroying everything is to surround it with chevalières then close in." Ashunaday pulled the scythe back upon their shoulder. "But as we all know, once a velocitrix gets a taste for particular Finni, they have to have more. So we are going to train hard and fast, because Vera here is going to help us draw it out and kill it."

Lyro's eyes grew. Saffie clenched her fists together and held them close to her chest and whispered, "Yes!", and Thora placed her hand upon her quickened heart. Vera stood there, searching Ashunaday's eyes for some kind of a joke, but when they realized that she was being perfectly serious her face reflected the same.

"You're damn right I will." Vera expressed with firm resolve.

"What?!" Lyro nearly shouted. "We all just reached apotheosis, and suddenly we're going to fight a narghoulim?"

Vera nodded. "Not just fight – kill! We're going to kill it! This is what we've been training for, right? Geist weapons are just larger weapons, right? We know weapons! We've been practicing for years. I'm sure that Ashun is going to show us what we need to know, is that correct?"

Ashunaday nodded. "I'll teach you exactly what you need to know, what weapons to use and what equipment is important."

"I'm going to hold a slam hammer." Saffie daydreamed as sugar-coated slam hammers danced in their head.

Lyro looked between Vera, Saffie and Ashunaday, then a quick glance towards Thora who seemed troubled over the entire idea then shrugged their shoulders and calmly added, "Okay, why not? Vera deserves some payback."

"So how are we going to do this?" Vera asked with resolve.

"I like your spirit, Kom." Ashunaday leaned their scythe against the wall and picked up the leather disc-shaped case and dropped it to the floor. There were several brass latches which were undone before she was able to pull the lid off.

The disc was a wooden replica, segmented off into different circular rings, and in the center was a black outline and a red interior. The artists really went for detail, showing bits of housing, rocks, trees yet further towards the center of the rendition, Vera saw dark twisted shapes of Finni bodies.

"A peppenach can travel up to speeds of forty miles per hour. A velocitrex produces winds that can reach two-hundred miles per hour. They can be eight to twelve miles high, and up to two and a half miles wide. As you can see here," she pointed to outer ring, "where all the trees and rocks are, this is called the debris field. And here," she pointed to the black circle with the red interior, "Is the apex, which is its heart. The black outline resembles a hardened exo-skeleton which protects its main organ. In order to kill it, we have to smash a hole in its armor, then perform a rapid flurry attack against the heart enough where it stops it from beating – any bladed weapon will do. It's not about dealing the most damage, but shocking it enough strikes that it stops beating."

"What's that section?" Vera pointed to the ring prior to reaching the heart.

"Bodies. Victims. A velocitrix doesn't kill for food. It kills for fun and keeps their bodies as trophies. This particular velocitrix has been killing for awhile now, so expect there to be a lot of bodies. Despite how gruesome it is, that will be to our advantage."

"Advantage? How are corpses going to be used for your advantage?" Thora asked with lowered eyebrows and tightly crossed arms over her chest.

"Despite our ability to leap high into the air, the winds of the velocitrix are too powerful and we will be buffeted away like gnats. So we have to enter its funnel low, and use the debris field – moving from rock, tree, house, whatever we find in there, we jump piece by piece. Untwist pantomimes will help slow the winds, we can use platform spears, bladed pointe shoes, and rope tutus to get us into position. Short, controlled jumps, will get us past the debris field and to the bodies. The more corpses, the more places we can leap to."

"I think I'm going to be sick." Thora moved her arms to embrace their stomach.

"Fall, rise and lower pantomimes will also help when it comes to getting us strategically placed. Destroy and stop pantomimes will be important too, since the velocitrix will be throwing whatever it can at us. Remember, that the rule *Of Beast and Material* applies to bodies, wherein you can use your pantomimes on them. And one last thing… remembering can mean life or death… when you feel the vivitah draining from you, if you cannot get support to renew your energy, you must leave enough to fall. If you do not have enough vivitah, and you fall – even as a chevalières– you will die."

Chapter 28
The Hunt & Hunted

"For the sacrifice they have made, chevalières are rarely asked to pay for anything. While the Academy provides most of what they need, there are times when special lodging, and other forms of accommodations are needed. At which point, the proprietors of those establishments are more than welcome to let them stay or to give them whatever they request. A full endorsement from a chevalière has the potential of bringing in far more money than they were to lose. Heroes in every sense of the word, chevalières never fall into short supply of receiving kindness or generosity. It is a rare soul indeed who would dare refuse them."

– The Musings of Von Rothbart Viktesh

The velocitrix was spotted towards the northwest, having moved away from the Anesian Coast and into Serishone just east of the village of Belaine which rested upon the banks of Lake Ester. It was also not far from Ribblesloche where a Lost People tower stood. For the longest time it sat vacant until the chevalières turned it into an outpost and hospital. From there, chevalières could be launched from catapulting springboards which send leaping dancers an additional five-hundred feet, and with the assistance of a gliding kit could help them reach farther distances if a narghoulim attack was imminent.

They rode upon peppenachs, with a team of six pulling a wagon which contained twelve members of the corps de ballet, Thora being one of them. And at Vera's behest, Gander was allowed to ride along with them. His front paws were placed on the bench and his head stuck out into the wind, which caused his jowls to turn up into a smile.

Ashunaday rode in front, followed by Lyro, Vera, Saffie, Yori, Ursalin and Rothe. However, when it came to actually entering the vortex, only Ashunaday, Lyro, Saffie and Vera

227

would go, as the others were required to surround it from farther away to keep it from escaping. Not that Vera believed it was necessary… it wanted them and only them. Wherever Vera would go, it would follow.

At the tail end of the procession was a finnae in a long coat, wide brimmed hat, and bushy eyebrows. Across his back was a long bundle wrapped in black cloth, that was eight feet in height. The whole trip he was silent, observed and kept his distance.

When they stopped to allow the peppanachs time to rest, Vera, Lyro and Saffie would be grilled by Thora, asking them questions about their equipment and ensuring that they had a firm grasp of technique. It wasn't that Thora didn't believe in their ability or knowledge, but more so devoted to the task of drilling the information into their heads enough that their equipments' use was a reflex rather than relying on thought.

In two Lorilyn days, Vera found themself on the top of the tower. It was a square building, seven floors in height with long rectangular windows of glass which ran the length of the building, but were thin so much as one could almost fit a head through. Vera watched the horizon, out across the plains, looking for signs of the velocitrix, and remembering those few years ago.

It had come so quickly. Clear skies one moment, then dark and overcast the next. Green lightning, and the rumbling of the ground. The high-pitched howl, and the thumping which resonated deep into their chest. It was terrifying to them then, and now? It was just as frightening. However, as a chevalière, Vera had a new strength in confidence, a power which even without the corps de ballet, flowed through them. It felt as natural to them as the breeze, as warming as the sun, and as lifting as water. It was as if the weight of the moon-world had been set aside.

Thora had just climbed the final stair, followed by Tage, who hung back while Thora strolled casually up beside her best friend. She took in a large breath of air, a distant scent of upturned soil and vegetation in the air, and she knocked her hip into Vera's playfully.

"How are you doing?" She asked with resolved steadiness. It was one that was practiced, as this entire journey she has been filled with dread.

"Scared, yet determined." Vera replied as they bonked Thora back. "It's out there, Thora. Not only can I smell it, but I can feel it. Like a pounding in my chest, foreign and resounding. As if it's calling out to me, demanding that I let it take my life." Vera continued to watch the horizon. "But, I'm not going to let it." Vera placed their hand on their belt and ran their fingers over the antler handle of their obsidian dagger; a birthday present. "I'm going to kill it."

"Vera… we should talk about what you might see in there." Inside Thora quivered, the very thought of what was floating around the heart of the narghoulim. "You may see more than… strangers…"

Vera was quick in their response. "I know. And I don't think any amount of preparation or conversations are going to make it any easier to see."

"If it is of any consideration…" Tage allowed his voice to step between them, "Those who you remember have been with you since their ghoshas were taken over the mountain. "What you'll see up there are simply the shells they once wore." He stepped up towards the two of them, and when Vera turned around to face him, he placed his hand calmly and reassuring upon their heart. "They've been rotating around here, your heart; not some heart of an abomination." He offered a brief yet sincere smile. "They've been there since this all began, and you'll bring them up with you when you put it all to an end."

Lyro and Saffie emerged from the lower level to join them. Saffie was the first to speak, "All the others are now in place."

As the wind brushed through Lyro's dark hair, they thumbed to where they had just climbed. "Ashunaday says it's time for us to armor up.

Vera nodded to Tage as he removed his hand. "Thank you, for everything."

"I'll be here when you return." He promised.

With one last look at the horizon, Vera straightened their spine and joined their friends with Thora close behind.

They covered themself with leather armor, shoulders, chest, arms, knees and legs. It was an off-white, set with the etching of several different birds and images of feathers painted across its surface. They were given a helmet, one that allowed room for goggles to help keep the grit blown from the tornado out of their eyes. Adorn on each side of the helmet were metal wings, which unfurled like a swan about to take flight. Vera took hold of a breaker sword, it was seven feet in length, with a single sharpened edge and a heavy block on the other end to give it that extra weight to shatter armor. They used the shrink pantomime to reduce platform spears down to only six inches in size from their usual twelve feet in length.

With the assistance from the corps de ballet, and Thora to double check its fitting, Vera was helped into a rope tutu which was bell shaped and contained two-hundred feet of nyri silk rope capable of holding up to two-thousand pounds in weight; hooks gleamed at each end. Finally, when everything was in place, the corps de ballet added the last touch - bladed pointe shoes. There were blades attached via the heel, and a quick release on the inside; causing the blade to spring into place at the block of the shoe. Lyro took on a winged axe, while Saffie - with eyes all aglow - gripped her majestic slam hammer.

Once they were completely outfitted, Ashunaday - with their fanged scythe, inspected each of them. "Saffie and Lyro, you are support. Lyro, your primary is Vera, and Saffie, you're with me. Vera, I will do everything to position you for the kill, however, should that not be feasible, I will make the final strike. Today, it's as much about vengeance as it is about ending the threat."

"I feel like I should be taking more with me, and a couple extra shrunken weapons in case I lose this one?" Lyro suggested while turning their geist weapon over in their hands.

"While shrink pantomimes make things easier to carry, it does not make them weigh any less. Trust me, you're not wanting to be weighted down when you get struck by those winds. Fighting against your equipment and two-hundred mile per hour gusts is not going to go in your favor. So, whatever you do, don't lose your weapon." Ashunday slapped her hand against Lyro's armored shoulder. "Now, huddle up."

Vera, Saffie, Lyro and Ashunaday were closest to the center, and all other members of the corps de ballet including Thora met with the outside. The corps placed their hands on the shoulders, backs and heads of the chevalières, while Ashunaday joined hands with Vera and Lyro, and they with Saffie.

Ashunaday bowed her head and recited, "Today we ask the NIИ to guide us, to allow our weapons to strike true, to protect us as we face evil. We fight for our ancestors, we sacrifice for our people, we vanquish for our future. Let their darkness not consume us, let the vivitah flow, and grant us the power to drive our enemies into the earth. Bless us, in these moments as we face oblivion and empower us to look into the face of horror and proceed unwavered. Let not our people perish from this world, and if we are to die in the coming moments, let it be in safeguarding their existence."

The room, Lyro, Saffie, Thora and Vera echoed, "Praise the NIИ and our blessed Aness."

Outside, Vera gave a strong hug to Gander, ruffling his feathers and pressing their cheek strongly against his. "You be good, boy, okay?" Vera held a tinge in their chest, as they worried that this could be the last time they ever see him. "I love you so much. And I will always love you." Gander gave a brief whine, but licked their face in response.

With a quick wipe to alleviate the wetness, Vera turned to Thora. As dew grew in their eyes, Vera wrapped their arms tightly around their friend, who returned one of their own.

"It'll be okay." Vera whispered, as much to reassure themself as well as Thora, before kissing her on the cheek.

Thora returned the kiss but whispered back, "Don't make promises that you have no control over. Stab that narghoulim a couple times for me, okay? And do your best to come home in one piece."

"That I can promise!" Vera offered.

Ashunaday called out. "Chevalières in position!"

Vera, Lyro and Saffie came alongside Ashunaday. Vera raised en pointe, stretching out the leather in the pointe shoe before returning back down to the ground in fifth position.

Ashunaday then motioned with her hand, "Corps de ballet, begin."

Thora joined ranks with the corps, where each staggered behind the four ballet-knights. They drew their legs together and shifted their feet into fifth position. Their hands lowered below their waist, elbows bent and fingers readied so that their index finger and thumb formed a U, and the middle and ring finger bent inwards.

"And FIVE!" Ashunaday shouted.

On the horizon, the sky began to darken and the low rumble of thunder jittered across the plains.

The corps raised their arms, keeping a tight bowl shape in front of their chests.

"SIX!" Ashunaday bellowed.

The dancers behind them parted their hands out towards the side.

"SEVEN!"

The wind pressed against them, a sudden shift from the calm breeze that had existed before. It forced the high grass against the ground as it battered them.

It's here. Vera thought. *It's been here the whole time, waiting for me.*

The corps pulled their hands back together in the previous position.

"EIGHT!"

Their right hand rose above their head, their eyes following their fingers upwards, while the left hand extended outwards. They fell into a tombè on their right foot, extended their back leg high into the air behind them into an arabesque. They threw themselves into the adagio, a pas de bourrée and pas de chat. And from their motions, it channeled the vivitah - the energy of the divine - out and into the chevalières. Thora could see it, one eye closed, as the glowing ribbons burst from the hidden cracks all over their bodies. Even with her injured eye shut, Thora could see them shimmer, glowing as they once did when they had breached the Glass. It sparkled and pulsed with power, enveloping every aspect of their being.

Vera felt the rush they had when they had first breached the Glass. As if their body was no longer constrained by the laws which held them afloat. Existing in a perpetual state in the apex of a leap, that very moment when it seemed as if they were flying, now made manifest in every breath they took. It filled them, and took all fear from their being and replaced it

233

with an unabated strength and determination.

A crack of green lightning tore across the sky as Ashunday screamed, "NOW FOLLOW ME!" She leapt high into the air, escaping the bonds of the moon-world and launched as high as they could go, hundreds of feet into the air, forward into the emptiness of the plains and towards the hungry clouds ahead.

Vera leapt after, gripping their geist weapon with unparalleled power and skill. They felt the wind parting as they sped through the air, sailing across the sky alongside both Lyro and Saffie. And when they descended, having given the tower and the corp de ballet a wide enough berth, they found themselves surrounded knee high in what would have been waist high grass, which now bowed and trembled before the might of the wind. They kept their eyes transfixed upward, as a sinister cloud drew itself across the once sunlit sky.

A great shadow descended upon them, lit by the occasional baring of horrendous emerald claws. There came a blast of air, one which tossed dirt up from the ground to shower them with tiny pellets. From above, the clouds swirled, pulling the very atmosphere into a weapon to bear against them. It was slow at first, but quickened as it swirled to form a rotating vortex. The sky continued to crack, as the funnel dropped heavily to the ground like a gigantic spear. The ground rumbled and quaked, and the winds howled as if it were a chorus of a thousand screams. It was upon them! A twisting terrifying force that glided across the ground, ripping up weeds and rock to join its miles-wide carousel of destruction.

Inside it, the lightning flashed again, revealing a ghoulish face composed of wind and debris. Its eyes transfixed, its mouth agape as if it released a maddening wail.

Vera clutched their sword with both hands, drawing it close to their body. Before them was the very being who took their neighbors, friends and family away. This was the being who hunted them as they tried to escape to Adalace. This was the monster who sundered their mother's hand and left it to haunt them. Hate spread through their body like a venom and anger rose into their teeth causing their lips to sink into a sneer.

"STEADY!" Ashunaday warned as they twirled their scythe in their hands, causing the blade to whip across the top of the prostrating grass.

A pounding hammered across the landscape, one that resounded inside their body like a drum. *Thump! Thump! Thump!* It grew in loudness and intensity, bearing into them as if they were the teeth of the creature itself.

It took everything for Vera to be patient, the desire to slash at the very wind that beat against them to unleash years of pain and fury onto the creature was overwhelming but they knew it would do no good. The true monster was not in range, it was much higher. The winds were only at its command.

"STEADY…" Ashunaday crouched low as the winds pulled at them, trying desperately to sweep them all off their feet and draw it inside like some gigantic maw.

Vera crouched, followed by Lyro and Saffie, each who dug their feet, tightened their muscles, and twisted their thighs inwards - ready to spring as soon as the word was given.

The velocitrix was set to swallow them, the thumping was so loud Vera could feel it in their teeth, and their feet were pulled against the earth as their entire body was drawn towards the narghoulim.

Then, moments before the wall of wind slammed into them, Ashunday screamed, "NOW!" She leaped into the vortex with weapon in hand.

Vera released their fury and followed in after!

Chapter 29
Enemy of the Wind

"To kill a narghoulim, a ballet-knight must raise their presence. Through dance, passion and desire, the power builds within. While drawing the vivitah into a chevalière grants them the strength and ability to perform powerful strikes, in order to truly kill a narghoulim one must be able to have enough presence to release their resonance. The vivitah must be coaxed, channeled, and directed - preferring a delicate choreography. Without it, all is lost. Adding more complication to the measure, one must continuously expend vivitah. Every leap, every strike, every motion - chevalières are consistently siphoning their power and if they lose too much in the midst of engagement, they become vulnerable. A time when their enemies are best to strike."

- Caraboose, *Journal of a Malfinae*

Vera was struck by the full force of the gale, like being slammed by a gigantic rock which continued to press against them with the might of a god. Yet, their body resisted, as the vivitah inside of them pushed back. The airy, weightless, feeling that they had encountered before had been replaced by the oppressive grip of the velocitrix, who continued to howl so loudly that even an amplified shout would be stolen as soon as it left their lips. The thumping noise was deafening.

They had lost sight of Ashunaday, as they tumbled and twisted through the vortex. Yet, Vera was not ready to give in so easily to a fate where they'd be battered to death. They yanked some of the rope from their tutu, tied it with the hook and launched it ahead of them to what seemed to be a piece of debris. The hook snagged, and Vera pulled themself towards it as quickly as they could, all the while spinning in circles which was enough to make them sick.

The moment they reached the debris they were able to identify it as what appeared to be boulder. They climbed atop it, then pulled the rope and leaned to one side to steer it so it wouldn't tip them over. Ahead, upon a uprooted tree which was a short leap away, Vera was able to locate Saffie who struggled to maintain her footing.

Vera pirouetted, using the momentum to unhook from the boulder then launched into a stag leap to vault across. The wind threw dirt into their face and stung their exposed skin. The tree was at least four feet in width and twenty or so feet long - having been stripped of most of its smaller branches it was now but a log floating in the wind. Vera landed with an attitude devant before they dug deep into their plié to keep them rooted. Saffie felt the shift in the tree and raised their slam hammer just briefly before recognizing who it was.

A lightning bolt streaked by them, and the hairs across their entire body stood on end. It was followed by a startling clap of thunder which roared through their entire body. Saffie dropped into a grand pliè herself in order to avoid being struck by a stray bolt.

Saffie slapped the side of Vera's shoulder then pointed up, to where Vera could barely make out what appeared to be the remnants of a house. Segments of walls, doors, and flooring spun about in an almost staircase fashion. Squinting, Vera was able to locate both Ashunday and Lyro who seemed to be looking for them. Saffie slapped the trunk of the tree then gave a thumbs up then pointed to Vera, and mouthed the words "Up".

Vera nodded with understanding. Crouched, they drew their sword close to them and dug the blade into the tree to serve as a brace before opening their fingers just a little bit. Their left hand flattened parallel to the tree, twisted at the wrist to place their palm up, then curled their fingers inward starting at the pinkie, then straightened them once again. Their pointer and middle finger extended tightly together on their other hand, while they drew in their pinkie and ring finger in towards their palm. Their thumb stuck straight out. With a quick jab, their right hand crossed over to their left and slammed into their

237

palm, then twisted so that their right was now beneath their left without breaking the connection. Then, they quickly touched their thumbs together, flayed out their fingers like wings of a bird and pointed them palms down towards the tree.

A burst of white light rippled from their hands and spread across the tree like a wildfire. The very thing propelled them up into the air, and closer to the remnants of the house. As soon as it reached the right height, Saffie and Vera performed a grande jetè to reach their intended spot. The tree continued upwards and disappeared into the winds.

Lyro noticed them first, quickly waved their free hand and motioned for the two to join them. Ashunday was just completing an untwist pantomime that summoned a burst of sparkles which fluttered all around them and latched onto the winds. Sadly, it only slowed the velocity a smidge and it seemed to be isolated to a small pocket of the vortex. Already Vera could tell the difference, and the house they stood upon felt like it had dropped slightly.

Ashunday turned to face the rest of them, and pointed upwards. Vera shot their gaze to the top and saw the eye of the vortex. Miles above them was the velocitrix's heart, a single black mass that expelled winds from long curved tubes. It pulsed with a red light which partnered with the loud thumping that reverberated through every nerve in Vera's body. There were also small black masses, bodies, floating around the heart like a swarm of angry wasps.

Vera and Saffie leapt again, and this time landed en pointe. A boulder slammed into the wall where they previously stood, sending planks of wood and splinters all around them. A quick balancè and glisade helped them reach the rest of their team. Yet as Vera turned to see what had happened to their prior platform, they immediately spied a vicious rock speeding towards them.

A strong arm grabbed Vera and flung them towards Lyro and Ashunaday. Saffie threw their body up as a shield, and squared off with the menace. With several quick jabs with their hands, a rounding of their palms, then circling of her arm, she closed a fist pointing to the sky - Saffie pushed their hand forward, sending a shockwave to roll over the stone. It exploded into dust, spraying them with a shower of grit.

Ashunaday gave Saffie a strong nod, while Lyro helped Vera to their feet. Then, with a motion forward, Ashunday fell into a tombè, traveled with their feet in a pas de bourreè, soared across the house with a glissade, then leapt with an assemblè where their feet closed together and fell into a deep pliè the moment they reached a higher piece of debris that was large enough to stand on. Each followed in turn, with Ashunday followed by Saffie, then Vera and finally Lyro.

They leapt from piece to piece, slowly reaching higher and higher through the howling tornado. Each movement, every dance, helped them build each of their presence. As they fell upon higher debris, the velocitrix roared with hatred. Trees, stones, bricks, and all other sorts of things were flung at them. Each time, Vera and the others would have to divert their course, leapt to higher fields of debris, and burned vivitah with every dodge, in order to avoid the narghouim's ghastly attacks.

Vera shrunk their weapon, and pulled out their platform spears. With quick hand motions, they used pantomimes to return them to their original size. They were twelve feet long, with a razor sharp triangular head and about two-and-a-half feet out there was a notch where a piece of wood - two feet long and one foot across - lent them a place to stand upon. They hurled them at rocks whose surfaces were too jagged, or at stumps that were otherwise too broken to assist them. Each spear struck true, granting the chevalières a place to land on. Lyro, Saffie and Ashunday aided as well, flinging as many as they could to give them the space they needed, building a staircase to the top. However, soon they were out. Vera managed to save one, one they intended to use against the heart.

239

With great effort they were nearly there, a few leaps away from a cloud of corpses who floated around the heart. There was a final rooftop, one that was angled like those they remembered from Tandermundt, which they all landed upon. It was there that Ashunaday released her resonance. Green ribbons of light fluttered, swirled and danced around her as tiny motes of white light scintillated about her like an aura. From her heart, a bubble of similar energy enveloped them all, creating a field around the roof that was at least three times her size. The winds calmed around them, the howl turned to a whisper and the thumping felt like it was some distant drumming.

"We haven't much time!" Ashunaday called out. "The velocitrix is more tenacious than I thought. My resonance will protect us from attacks, but not for long. Vera, partner with Lyro, build up your vivitah and take their presence. Then together, we'll strike at its armor. Once the armor is gone, unlease a flurry at it as fast as you can!"

Vera nodded, took one look at the blackened husk that was their target, then reached out to Lyro.

Together, they ran to one another. Anticipating each other's motions, sensing their next steps. Vera hurled themself into a swan dive, and Lyro caught them, with Vera's face not far from the ground. With a quick motion, Lyro threw them into the air far enough to raise them into a lift. Vera released their tension, and fell as Lyro dropped them to hip height. Vera then wrapped a single leg behind Lyro and another in front, both in attitude. Lyro repositioned their hands on their hips as Vera leaned backwards and raised their hands above their head. Together, their passions merged into a single feeling, allowing the vivitah from Lyro to pull into Vera, bolstering them to renew their strength. Their bodies illuminated with the energies from the Glass.

Effortlessly, Vera drew their legs back together and landed their feet en pointe. A memory flooded their mind, reminding them of being back on the rooftops with Ayren, kicking at his feet and doing their best to beat him. And with it, they raised their leg in a develope which reached high above their head. Vera crossed their left arm over their chest and Lyro grabbed hold of it. Vera fell, one leg still in contact with the wood while the other stayed high. Lyro wrapped their arm around their waist and lowered them towards the floor, appearing like a Vera was a bow and Lyro a seasoned archer.

They continued in their pas de deux. Lyro felt the power inside them draining. With each breath, Vera pulled more and more until finally, Lyro was near their end, and Vera stepped away renewed and resilient.

"Now it's time for you to leave, Lyro. There's nothing more you can do here." Ashun ordered.

Lyro nodded, gave Vera and Saffie a remorseful look but offered, "Best of luck to you all." Before they ran off the rooftop and leapt out into the winds and escaped power of the vortex.

"Weapons ready, team!" Ashunaday called as she prepared her scythe.

Saffie pulled out her slam hammer and swung it a few times in front of her to get a feel for it and Vera re-enlarged their breaker sword and pulled it behind them, ready to strike!

The green ribbons which surrounded Ashunaday dissipated, and the howl returned in full force.

Together they left the rooftop for the higher points in the tornado. Then, as they reached the layer of corpses, in a single jump, they all clicked their pointe shoes together at the heels, releasing the blades in their feet, and plunged them deep into a a carcass with a squelch to help them stand.

Finni of all kinds, finnae, finnyr, the old and the young all floated together. Many were maimed, some were rotting, while others were as fresh as the scent of grass which permeated the air. All of their faces were twisted and haunting, as if screaming out their last moments of existence as their life was strangled out of them.

Vera did their best not to look. Instead, focused entirely on the heart which thumped maliciously ahead. Green lightning flashed all around them, and a stray bolt flung close by.

Saffie and Ashunaday leapt ahead, moving between the remains as if they were stepping stones. And as they reached the heart's exo-skeleton, Ashunaday swung their fanged scythe against it, causing it to crack. With the momentum from their swing, they jumped to the next body and began circling around for their next strike. Saffie followed after, jabbing their pointe shoes into a large finnae before bringing their slam hammer overhead and jamming it square onto its surface, creating a small rupture.

Vera then came upon their own pass, drew their sword back and with all the might that they could manage, with a cry that no one could hear, the blade connected against the exoskeleton and with it came a loud - CRACK!

Their vision was filled with a painful emerald brilliance, their body jolting and convulsed, while it felt as if their insides were baking. Their body was tossed to the winds and they felt themselves falling. Vera's hand flashed to the hook in their tutu, and tossed it to where they thought they had previously stood. To their luck, it snagged on something, which caused their body to lurch, and be dragged along with it.

Their legs flailed and their hand dug into the nyri silk tether for fear of it slipping. As soon as their vision cleared, they followed the rope upwards and into the mummified face of their father!

His eyes were empty sockets, his skin was shriveled up and taught against his skull, and his mouth was slack. Yet, despite his horrific state, he still carried the features that Vera kept so vividly in their memories. Their hook was now embedded into his shoulder, causing his arm to descend towards them as if reaching out to pull them up.

Vera's heart pounded in their chest, as they took the nightmarish vision in. Despite it all, they took a deep breath, grabbed hold of the rope, and drew themself up as quickly as they could. With a deep sense of guilt, Vera stabbed their pointe shoes into her father's back and raised to standing.

Ashunaday and Saffie were nowhere to be found. And Vera no longer possessed their sword. When the lightning struck, they must have dropped it. Presumably, Ashunaday and Saffie were hit as well. They could have survived, they might be dead. But whatever the case, there was nothing they could do about it.

The vivitah that once coursed through their body from the pas de dex had dwindled, having been drained to protect them from the lightning. They had not come this far, gotten this close, just to give up. Vera could not allow another village like Tandermundt vanish from the world. Vera was done hiding, done with being afraid, and done with all the lives the winds continued to reap.

Speedily, Vera drew the last remaining platform spear from their pack and used a grow pantomime to bring it to bear. As streaks of emerald clashed inside the vortex, they examined the exo-skeleton, looking for any breach that was wide enough for them to get through. Then, as another flash illuminated the sky behind them, they saw exactly what they were looking for. There was a hole, no bigger than a fist, and very apparently caused by the swing of a slam hammer.

Vera raised the spear, waited for the right moment as the heart spun, doing their best to ignore the thumping which echoed in their brain, and threw it. The spear struck and embedded up to the notch, creating a small platform for Vera to stand upon just below the hole.

Then, with one final leap, they used their remaining vivitah to bring them atop the platform. They raised en pointe, drew out the knife made of obsidian and plunged it through the glowing recess; directly into the heart of the narghoulim itself!

They called upon their resonance. It was like being filled by a warm jelly which flowed to all of their extremities. Their body was enveloped in a ghostly pale light. Their mind was suddenly possessed with the memories of those who came before them, of Ayren, Nam and Felicity; of Finnyr Gilshen and Gorn; of their mother and their father; grandparents and distant cousins. They all manifested around Vera, like a ring of orbiting phantoms, each in appearance as they had remembered them, spectres of the past.

Then, the spirits shot into Vera! With each one possessing their body, they felt the bubbling of vivitah. Their muscles tensed, their arm raised, and from it they plunged the knife once more into the narghouim's heart.

Each corpse produced a spirit, strangers and those familiar who all fell victim to the winds. Each flew into Vera, each throwing their being into Vera's arm, spurring their attacks. In rapid succession Vera withdrew the dagger, then stabbed the heart again, five, ten, thirty strikes, each one more faster than before!

Vera cried with each strike, for they could sense the spirits' warmth, smell their scents, feel their presence. With their mother they felt a kiss upon their forehead, and their father's hand upon their cheek. They could hear Gorn chuckling as he did when the goats were playful, and Finnyr Gilshen praising them for being such a strong influence. They heard stranger's whispers, shared in past joys, and the loving pressure they once bestowed in each of their embraces.

As they pulled back for the last stab, as a dark sanguinous fluid now coated their armor and flung freely from their blade, they heard the familiar voices of their parents whisper, *"We love you, Vera. Never forget."* They then plunged the dagger as deep as they could reach!

The thumping ceased, the winds dispersed, and all the corpses, the lone chevalierè and the stilled titanic heart of the narghoulim, plummeted to the ground below.

Vera was spent. Not a single strand of vivitah remained inside of them, and despite the harrowing realization that they would die upon striking the ground, Vera was prepared for the release. They felt like they were finally home, that they were on the cusp of passing through the veil and into the Faydren - the realm of spirits and the dead. It was as if all who they once knew waited for them, welcoming them to the beyond. They closed their eyes, and allowed the wind to flow over them. No longer afraid.

Yet something miraculous occurred at that moment. Among all the falling bodies now free of the cursed velocitrix, a transformative light enveloped the dagger for which was still stained by the blood of the velocitrix in Vera's hand. The handle to Vera's knife extended, their blade grew longer, and from it expelled the wind that they had just extinguished moments ago. Instead of a vile twisting tornado, it summoned a pocket of air to slow their descent, and when Vera connected with the ground it was not a violent end, but instead like tumbling onto a soft bed.

Chapter 30
Triumph

"Vivitah can influence the world around it. It can cause animals to become monsters, or turn monsters into trees. It can reshape mountains, or bring rain to a droughted river. And at times, when passion is at its height, it can bring magic into the very objects we hold most dear. These artifacts can display the most wondrous of properties. Some can bring the recently deceased back to life, while others can purify water. And for others, they can provide the very saving grace for which they are presently in need. One can almost find magic in everything, and in everyone.

- Wanderings, Viliph Drosselmeyer

Vera stared up at the sky and watched the clouds drift on by. The wind was calm, softly brushing through the grass, causing the green to wave at them from above. No longer where they bending to the power of some inescapable being. They were free. Free from the wind. And so too, was Vera. The only thumping that they could hear was the one that beat in their chest. So they laid there, for what seemed to be an hour, just watching the clouds and hearing the chirps of birds and the trilling of insects.

Then something shifted through the brush, sniffing along the ground and occasionally raising his nose in order to follow a scent in the air. He fell upon them, moved his snout from the stalks and directly into their face. His tongue lapped against them, causing Vera to stir and who in turn wrapped their arms around him. He drowned their face in several more licks before Vera couldn't take any more. They sat up, wiped their face, then took the moment to look about them.

Moving through the field was Ashunaday, Lyro, Saffie and the entire corps de ballet, using sticks and blades to help push back the grass, all looking for signs of them. Gander barked, and Thora was the first to spot them.

"VERA!" Thora yelled both out of relief and joy. She ran as fast as she could then she tackled Vera back to the ground with her arms squeezing tightly around them. "Thank the NIИ you're alive! I was so worried! I thought I had lost you." Thora's eyes beaded with tears as she touched the back of Vera's head, then pressed their forehead against theirs.

"I thought I was lost too. I was ready to die, I didn't have any vivitah left. It took everything to stop its heart. But when I fell…" Vera pointed to a place in the grass next to them, where Vera's once dagger laid firmly in the grass, was now nearly four times in length than it had been before.

"Is that…" Thora stared at it in disbelief, uncertain of what to make of it. She scrunched her eyebrows and ran her eyes over the antler handle - her antler. "Is that the dagger I made for you?"

Vera nodded. "I lost my sword, and so I had to use your dagger. And as I was falling it grew and it saved me… somehow." Vera too wasn't sure what to make of it.

Thora laughed. "Looks like it's all grown up."

"Grew up? Dagger's don't grow up into swords!" Vera playfully pushed Thora off of them.

"I hate to be the bearer of unusual news, but yours did! So that means all daggers do!" Her laughter followed her as she leaned back on her hands, now sitting with one leg curled in front of her and one in back.

"Or maybe just the daggers you make." Vera teased.

Saffie and Lyro soon arrived, having jogged to them after hearing Thora's proclamation that Vera was alive.

"Ah geez, Vera, I'm really sorry. I saw you get struck by lightning, then I got struck by lightning. Well, Ashunaday got struck by lightning too, and we were thrown from the velocitrix. We certainly didn't mean to leave you all alone up there. Are you okay? Are you hurt? I really hope you're not hurt."

Vera softened their voice, and tried their best to reassure her. "Saffie, it's okay, really. And I'm okay. Things got pretty intense up there."

"Wait…" Thora lowered her eyebrows in anger. "You got struck by lightning?"

"Hey, Vera?" Lyro nodded their head to the still sitting Caetin and matter-of-factly proclaimed, "You killed a narghoulim."

"I did!" Vera quickly replied, eyes widening at the idea of it. "I DID!" They shot up to their feet and en pointe. "I KILLED THE NARGHOULIM! WOOOOOOOOOO!" They threw their hands into the air in celebration. Then the blades which were attached to their feet caused them to sink in the ground. "Oh, no…" Vera frantically looked at both feet. "I might need some help getting these off of me."

Ashunaday watched from afar, standing alongside Tag who kept his head beneath his hat. She eyed the velocitrix's silent heart which now stuck out of the ground, nearly twenty feet in height, then cast her gaze across the plains, noting the several dark blotches on the green grass where the fallen corpses now dwelled.

"There's an awful lot of them." She said with a flutter in her heart.

"The narghoulim took far more than its fill." Tage replied as he squatted down to the ground and laid out the black cloth wrapped item which had previously occupied his back. "It may take me some time to sort through them." He untied the rope which bound it all together, then rolled out the object that had been hidden beneath.

He took up his long staff, one carved with prayers to the dead and tipped with a spike of a foggy white selenite crystal.

He pulled it close to his chest and rested his forehead lightly on the crystal allowing the coolness to seep into his skull. He whispered, "To all the spirits who dwell here in this hour, know me as Kyph Ravoysn Tage. I walk with you, speak to me your heart, of your loved ones and of home. I shall mourn you so you shall find peace. I will carry your earthly body to where you wish to rest. Let me know of you."

Tage lowered his staff so that the crystal reached but a foot off the ground and he swung it like a pendulum. Into the grass he moved, swinging the crystal back and forth, listening to the breeze and the whispers that called out to him.

A missive was sent back to the Aness and the Regal Ballet Academy to inform them of their victory. It was a victory that would be celebrated, but not before making a stop in Arcadia - to a place where there was only overgrown dirt streets, stone foundations and walls that once marked where Tandermundt had stood.

The mourner had drawn back the soil using a pantomime, providing a grave for each of the neighbors Vera once knew. Several were still unaccounted for, but it was more than what they ever expected to find. Among the missing was their beloved Aryan, and their friends Nam and Felicity. But that was the way of things. When one is taken over the mountain, it usually means that they are never coming back.

Vera and their friends helped plant them in the ground. Each body wrapped in linen and buried with handful of wild flowers. For those they couldn't bury, Vera wrote their names on a piece of paper, placed it in a glass container, and buried it near the rest.

Their father and mother were laid alongside their friends and good neighbors, including a piece being reunited with their mother, which until now had resided in the ground by the mouth of a cave along the Anesian coast.

249

Tage sang the old Caetin songs, ones of remembrance and comfort. And standing there, among friends and family, Vera let their feelings escape them. They cried for everything they had lost, everyone they had loved, and everything that might have been. They grieved, and they mourned, and with it they honored their ancestors spirits and encouraged them to move on.

While the funerary rites took place, far atop a hill where laid an abandoned campsite beneath an old statue of a lost one, stood a figure shrouded in a dark cloak. Their face was obscured by a white Adalacian mask, painted with blue, green and brown decorations across its surface in the form of peppanach feathers. Behind it, grinned another mask - this one painted with whites, gold, reds and silver which belonged to another being, one who had been here many years before. It was adorned in crimson robes, which were embroidered with golden flowers and vines. On one shoulder was a metallic epaulet and a full plate guard on the other. There was eagerness between the two of them, a cold heartless eagerness. For now, they waited, they watched, and they plotted.

Having returned to Adalace, there were four golden chariots drawn by beautifully adorned peppenachs, waiting for the slayers of the velocitrix. The finni drivers wore shiny ceremonial plate armor, with helmets that covered their face, giving them a short curved beak with brown and gold feathers that reached three feet behind them. The massive stone doors to the city remained shut, at least for the moment.

"What is this?" Vera asked with bewilderment as they stepped down from their peppenach.

A group of soldiers bowed, and took the reigns of their mount. The beasts were led off to the side, where soon a warm stable, and feed awaited them.

"Is this for us?" Saffie asked with diamonds twinkling in her eyes.

Ashunaday motioned to the chariots. "They await you."

Thora raised an eyebrow, "Who awaits us?"

She laughed. "Everyone. It's time for your triumph. They wish to see their valiant knights."

Thora looked to the rest of the corps de ballet who were already making their way to the back chariots and thumbed towards them. "I'll be with the rest of the corps de ballet if you need me."

Before anyone could say a word Vera raised their voice in protest, "Absolutely not!" Vera grabbed both of her hands. "You were there with me when no one else was. You helped me every step of the way and gave up so many years with your own family, just to make sure that I was okay. If anyone deserves to be at the head of those chariots… it's you." Vera gifted her with a wide smile, their eyes shrinking from the rise in their cheeks. "I want all of Adalace to see that my best friend, a Fauni, and an amazing member of the corps de ballet, was at the heart of it all."

Saffie wiped her eye and wrapped her large arms around the two of them. Sobbing she said, "You too are such an inspiration to me. When I was in that room, dancing my heart out, every time I wanted to give up, I said to myself: Saffie, if Vera and Thora made it this far, you can make it too! I love you both so much!"

"I don't know about you three…" Lyro made their way to the leading chariot. "I've been dreaming of riding in one of these since I was seven. So maybe we should get to it, huh?" Lyro gave them a wink, pulled the ribbon out of their hair, shook it out, and let their curls fall freely.

Saffie released the two of them, gave both Vera and Thora a pat on the shoulder, then joined up with Lyro.

"Thank you, Saffie." Thora beamed with appreciation.

251

"You're an inspiration too, you know!" Vera pulled Thora towards the chariot, and together they stepped onto it and all placed their hands on the railing that rounded the vehicle. Gander barked his excitement and jump into the back so he could be alongside Vera.

"Hey Ashunaday!" Lyro called out. "Are you coming?"

Ashunaday shook her head. "Naw. This one is all for you."

Thora looked at Ashunday with just their injured eye. The cracks along her face were deeper than before and the light of the Glass shone brightly through it, threatening to swallow her whole. She seemed slower, pained and yet she continued as if all was normal. Still uncertain what to make of it, Thora focused on the chariot and the ride ahead.

Ashun signaled the gatehouse high above. The clanking of metal from the mechanisms within caused the doors to opened, revealing clear streets, with sidewalks lined with armored soldiers in well polished armor and crowds packed tightly together behind them who roared with cheers and applause. Horns sounded, music erupted, drums and horns all playing together; welcoming them home.

The charioteer spurred the peppenachs forward, keeping at a steady pace as they moved beneath the gate and onto the thoroughfare. Homes and businesses alike had their shutters flung open, and the people within tossed flower petals out onto the street. Children sat on the shoulders of their parents, the elderly sat on stools, while others watched from balconies.

Vera tried to look at every face, absorbing the joy and adoration they had for all of them. The ballet knights waved to all those who loved them, with the entirety of the crowd shouting back their names.

To the people of Adalace, it wasn't just a story of fearless warriors riding off to slay the beast who terrorized the countryside. This was a celebration of life. It was more time upon this world, more time with their relatives and loved ones; of having everything that they have built, strove for and survived for to continue just a little longer. It was a reminder that not everything would be taken away, that there were those who would fight for them - even if it came at tremendous personal sacrifice.

And like they had several years ago, Vera and Thora were taken to where ten chevalières stood tall, where a proud staircase carved into the rock of the hill, drew up towards the entrance hall of the Rushinay. Where upon, after the first fifty steps and on the landing, stood all their professors, members of their family, along with the Aponae and the Aness.

A grin crossed the Apoane's face as he stood, draped in a long white robe that revealed his chest, and was tied around his waist. His clothing matched that of the Aness, who looked ethereal in nyri silk, gold embroidery and a several pieces of glittering jewels which dangled between her horns.

The Aponae leaned down and whispered to the old dance professor who had been conveniently placed at his left. "It looks like these late enrollments did well for themselves, wouldn't you agree?"

Fin Ississ scoffed as quietly as she could muster. "No one likes a wise ass."

He chuckled to himself and continued smiling.

Vera, Thora and the rest climbed the stairs together, side-by-side, followed by the rest of the corps de ballet. And upon reaching the top landing, the Aness opened their arms for each of them. One by one, the chevalières, Thora and the corps de ballet were granted a hug. Gander was given a deserving pat on the head. And when it came to Vera, the Aness hung on just a little longer and whispered softly in their ear, "I'm so very proud of you."

Over her shoulder, Vera could see their cousins. Dinaira had their hands clasped together over their mouth as her eyes were flush with joyous tears. Her husband smiled widely with admiration while Seena and little Jiro waved feverishly.

Then, as everyone was greeted, they turned to the crowd who had poured onto the street. They gazed across all of Adalace, and all who continued to sing their praise and shout their names.

The Aness stepped forward, with Vera's hand in hers and a hush fell over the city. She raised both of their hands in the air. Connected together in reverence. With resounding declaration, the Aness announced to all:

"People of Adalace, I give you Chevalière Caetin Kom Vera - Slayer of the Velocitrix."

And the crowd erupted once more in powerful effervescent cheers.

www.ingramcontent.com/pod-product-compliance
Lightning Source LLC
Chambersburg PA
CBHW051126300726

48981CB00024B/564/J